I0641464

THE STRANGER

By

Sylvia Massara

This novel is entirely a work of fiction. The names, characters and incidents portrayed in it are the work of the author's imagination. Any resemblance to actual persons, living or dead, events or localities is entirely coincidental.

Published by Tudor Ent
Australia
(61) 419 492 623

This edition 2024
First published in 2016

This book is sold subject to the condition that it shall not, by

OTHER TITLES BY SYLVIA MASSARA

<u>Romantic comedies</u>:

Like Casablanca
The Other Boyfriend

<u>General fiction/drama</u>:

The Soul Bearers

<u>Mia Ferrari mystery trilogy</u>:

Playing With The Bad Boys
The Gay Mardi Gras Murders
The South Pacific Murders

<u>Sci-fi action/romance</u>:

The Stranger
(2024 edition)

<u>Historical/contemporary fiction
action/romance</u>:

Heroes
(Due for release by end of 2024)

ABOUT THE AUTHOR

Sylvia Massara is a multi-genre author based in Sydney, Australia. She loves to dabble in wacky love affairs, drama, murder, sci-fi (and anything else that takes her fancy) over good coffee.

Born in Argentina from Italian descent and with a fusion of Spanish, Swiss and Scandinavian lineage, plus transplanted to Australia at age ten, Sylvia describes herself as a bit of a moggie cat by way of mixed pedigree. She is also a citizen of the world as she has travelled widely throughout most of her life and she's the proud owner of three passports.

As with most authors, Sylvia draws on her varied experience from the often puzzling tapestry of life. She loves nature and communing with the animal kingdom (as her pampered kitty, Mia, will attest) and vicariously through the many characters inside her head. Occasionally, however, Sylvia ventures into the world of humans, albeit for a limited time as she prefers the unconditional and genuine company that animals bring to our planet.

Currently, Sylvia is working on her next novel plus she has a number of other projects on the go which have been approved by her eternal muse—the great David Bowie.

DEDICATION

In loving memory of David Bowie
8.1.1947—10.1.2016

You will always live in the
hearts, minds and souls of
those who love you.

I'm loving "the alien"— now and forever.

PROLOGUE

The flames raged through the Jamison Valley as they made their way around the entire Blue Mountains National Park, flanking the township of Katoomba in an arc of fire that engulfed most of the forest. It was almost impossible to breathe out of doors and Carla looked out through the study window to see ash raining down from the sky as if it were snow and settle silently on houses, gardens and streets.

"This can't be happening. It can't be!" Carla uttered aloud, ran to the back of the house and hugged her dog, who was pawing at the back door. She saw the fear in Tom's eyes. "Don't worry, boy. We're safer inside." She tried to comfort him in a soft voice while they crouched together on the kitchen floor of the cottage. She thought of the sandstone embankment that lay behind her back garden and prayed the rock walls would provide a safeguard against the advancing bushfire as they had done for the past 110 years of the weatherboard cottage's existence.

Outside, the only things that could be heard were the deafening sounds of the advancing inferno drowned by the sirens of fire engines as they sped past on the way to meet the monster fire. Overhead, the rumble of helicopters and helitankers kept getting louder as a number of them amassed in the airspace above the township in case they had to release water in order to save the town; others flew past on their way to the raging fire to dump thousands of litres of water in the hope of containing the killer flames. It didn't help that wind gusts blew in from the Megalong Valley at around 100km per hour and creating more force for the fire to keep on burning.

Carla switched on the radio sitting next to her on the floor just in time to catch the tail end of the latest news update. "... and the battle is proving to be a tough one. This is an unprecedented disaster never before recorded in the history of Australia. It seems the prediction of the worst El Niño event to date, due to global warming, is now a reality. Record lows of rain plus dry winds created this tinderbox scenario; one that even the most hardened of firefighters has ever experienced. Weather patterns around the world have been unpredictable in the last couple of decades with mammoth superstorms, superfires and other catastrophes that..."

Carla switched off the radio. She didn't want to hear any more. This was the end. It was what humanity had brought upon itself due to its arrogance, greed and the exploitation of planet Earth. There was no respect for Mother Nature and no respect for the planet—and now mankind was paying the price.

Carla buried her face in Tom's silky neck and held onto the dog, hoping for a miracle. It seemed nothing could save them and this was how they would perish. Carla coughed while Tom whimpered at the burning smell drifting inside and penetrating the entire cottage. Carla tightened her arms around the dog and closed her eyes.

1

Carla looked up and down the expanse of open ocean beach from her perch on the rocky headland which backed onto dense bushland in the Kioloa State Forest. She sighed with an air of melancholy at the beauty before her.

Tom, an Irish setter, seemed to sense her mood and without any prompting from his mistress he inched his way closer, sat down and insinuated his presence by nuzzling the side of Carla's face with his red, silky head.

"Hey, Tom." Carla softly ruffled the dog's ears, which he enjoyed enormously and which made him respond with more nuzzling, this time with his cold, wet nose. Carla smiled and wiped her damp cheek with the sleeve of her sheepskin jacket. "I haven't forgotten you, boy," she assured the dog. "I was just musing, that's all."

Tom looked back at her with butterscotch eyes and remained seated next to Carla on the rocky ledge they had made their own since they arrived at Merry Beach over two weeks ago.

The sun was high in the sky, but despite its warmth the early winter breeze made Carla snuggle deeper into her jacket and cross her arms over her chest for extra protection. Sitting at her favourite spot with legs dangling down over the ledge and with the Pacific Ocean in front, while behind her the cliff gave way to the bush, Carla thought she could have been on another planet.

There was absolutely no one around except she and Tom plus a few seagulls circling high above in the sky, hoping to hone in on scraps of food that were sometimes left behind by rock fishermen. The fishing usually took place at either dawn or dusk and by now, almost noon, whatever bits of food may have been lying about had been consumed by any one of the many bird species inhabiting the area or any of the hundreds of kangaroos and wallabies that usually came out of the bush and down to the beach to enjoy whatever warmth they could get.

At this time of year it was quiet in the popular beach resort with its many log cabins and permanent caravans, some of which were owned by regular holidaymakers while others were reserved as casual rentals for tourists.

Carla gazed out to sea at the perfect line on the horizon which seemed to go into infinity and unblemished by any passing vessels. She felt truly alone and tried not to think of Michael. Right now, all she needed was peace and quiet before she could make any decisions about her life.

"Okay." She turned to Tom, standing to her feet. The dog mimicked her, already wagging his tail in anticipation of the magic word that escaped his mistress's lips. "Lunchtime."

Carla began to make her way carefully along the rocky ledge that stood at least fifty metres high from the rock base below, where waves crashed unendingly. Tom followed close behind as she accessed the narrow dirt path leading down the cliff and onto the beach.

She kept a slow, cautious pace lest she trip over the rocky outcrops flanking the path, and Tom stuck by her instead of rushing ahead as he usually did. Carla realised the dog had sensed her mood and wanted to comfort her with his company. Animals were usually much better than people at showing empathy, she mused.

It took them over half an hour to reach the highest point of the cliff face before the downward descent began. When they reached it, Carla stopped and as was her usual habit she paused for a moment to take in the majesty of the ocean and open beach below her. Today it felt as if she owned the whole thing. The place was desolate, not even a kangaroo in sight. The landscape seemed pristine, as if this was how the world must have looked before mankind evolved, and the feeling of being the only person about surrounded by nature—the cliffs, the bushland beyond, and the open expanse of ocean without an end in sight—was exhilarating. Carla felt her spirits soar for a moment. She was powerful. She was free. She was immortal and a part of all around her. The world, as it were, was hers for the taking.

Tom barked, bringing her focus back from the wonderful feeling that had taken over her seconds earlier. "What is it, boy?" Carla followed the line of his vision, but didn't see anything except the empty beach and the whitewash of waves as they made their way to shore. She shook her head at a sudden feeling of fancy, like she was being watched, and made to move on. Tom barked again, his eyes still fixed in the distance.

"Stop it, Tom!" Carla chided him, starting to feel somewhat nervous. "There's no one out there. Now, come along and let's go and get something to eat."

The dog still would not move. He stood as if transfixed, his gaze following something Carla could not see. She watched Tom's stance for a few seconds and once again turned her eyes towards whatever it was he was looking at; and it was then she spotted it.

Far in the distance, a lone figure strolled along the beach moving in their general direction. Carla laughed in relief. For a moment she'd thought Tom had sensed some sort of danger. Nevertheless, she could not explain why the dog had barked at someone who was walking such a long distance away from them. His behaviour was rather peculiar, but she put it down to the fact that her own behaviour would have felt strange to Tom. She hadn't exactly been her usual happy self of late, but rather subdued and given to attacks of sadness.

"Let's go, Tom," she prompted the dog with a pat on his head. "It's only someone on the beach."

Tom decided to take her at her word and suddenly raced down the cliff path towards the beach and waited for her at the bottom while watching her every step with his ever-wagging tail until she reached him a few minutes later.

"I don't know what's bugging you today," she told the dog

when she reached him and he greeted her effusively. "I think you need feeding, my boy."

The dog's tail wagged more excitedly in response and Carla smiled as they made their way together to a grassy area by the foreshore that forked into two paths, the left leading to the cabins and the right down to the beach. They walked quietly for a few moments and then, without warning, Tom was off again over the grass and onto the sand where the figure he had espied earlier was now standing by the shore observing them.

Carla stopped in her tracks and stood gazing at the male form across the way. She couldn't quite make out his features as he stood on the wet sand with the whitewash around his bare feet. He seemed to be having a chat with Tom, however, who stood silently by him wagging his tail. Carla shrugged and decided the man was not a threat; Tom's senses were never wrong, and right now he seemed to be enjoying the man's company.

She walked on towards her cabin, feeling rather hungry and looking forward to some lunch. Tom would catch up with her when he had enough of the intruder. For a reason she could not comprehend, Carla felt annoyed at the man for having the nerve to walk along *her* beach, dispersing her earlier illusion of being the only person around. Thankfully, her mobile phone rang at that moment and though it made her jump in surprise it distracted her from her whimsical thoughts. She took the phone out of her jeans pocket and checked the caller ID. It was Jana, her work colleague and friend.

"Aren't you supposed to be working?" Carla greeted her with mock admonishment.

Jana laughed. "I'm on my lunch break, thank you very much."

"So what's up?"

"Well, I know you probably don't want to hear this, but Michael called me." Jana was always direct and to the point. She obviously did not stop to think the kind of impact this would have on her friend.

"And?" Carla prompted quickly, like any scrap of information about her ex was better than none.

"And he's wondering why you didn't take any of his calls," Jana replied. "He told me he's been ringing you constantly, but the calls go to voicemail."

Carla rolled her eyes and remarked with bitterness, "Well, he's lying as usual. I've only had two missed calls from him in as many weeks, plus he didn't leave any messages." Carla became aware of the tension starting to build up in her shoulder and neck muscles.

Michael had turned out to be a pathological liar and much to her derision—mainly aimed at herself—it had taken her five years to catch onto his ways. Anger burned inside her stomach when she thought what a fool she had been and how despite all this she still hankered for information about him. She sighed in order to give her emotions time to settle and then realised Jana was still talking and she hadn't heard a word.

".... and looking for you all around." This was the only fragment of the conversation Carla managed to catch because her strong emotions suddenly ebbed for some strange reason and to her surprise Carla found she no longer cared about Michael's movements or what he had been up to of late. She sighed again, thinking she must be going insane with her contradictory feelings about the ex, and she glanced towards the shoreline where Tom was still playing with his new friend. They had gotten slightly closer to where she was standing and she could now make out the man's slim build and the startling appearance he made with hair of flaming orange interspersed with both brown and white blond streaks. He wore his hair quite short towards the back and long at the front with a fringe falling over what looked like an attractive face.

"Carla, are you still there?" Jana's voice brought her back to the conversation.

"I'm sorry. I didn't get most of what you said. The signal down here tends to be rather weak." Carla heard Jana sigh with frustration and although the signal did tend to be weak, unless one stood at the top of the cliff, Carla wasn't sure whether in this case it had been the signal or herself, simply tuning out of anything to do with Michael.

"I don't know how much you heard," Jana explained in a louder tone of voice as if this would overcome the weak signal. "Look, I'll email you, okay? And then, I can tell..."

Carla kept her gaze trained on the man. Why was Tom so friendly with this guy? "Yes, okay." She heard her own voice reply to Jana in a rather disembodied manner before she pressed the off button on her phone. She had absolutely no idea what Jana had been trying to say before she ended the call abruptly.

The man with Tom began strolling in her direction and for some unexplained reason Carla stood rooted to the spot, her eyes staring at him. Under normal circumstances, she would have ignored him and walked off, but there was a certain air to him that she could not quite put her finger on, and she was suddenly curious to check out Tom's friend. She waited and as she did so she took in the rest of his appearance while he and Tom approached at a leisurely pace.

He was tall, possibly around six feet, and seemed to be around her age, early thirties or thereabouts. His slim build was like that of a long distance runner and he possessed a fluid grace to his movements that was lithe and magnetic. It felt almost a pleasure to watch him move. He wasn't clumsy, nor did he have the gait of a macho type. As he came closer, Carla noted a refined looking face set with high cheekbones flowing onto a well-defined jaw. What struck Carla most of all, however, were his eyes. He was gazing at her with large almond-shaped eyes, like a cat's, and of a most unusual colour of sky blue mixed with purple. They were mesmerising eyes and their intensity made her feel self-conscious and somewhat vulnerable.

It was an inexplicable feeling that Carla experienced, but this guy was quite unusual—unlike anyone she had ever met before. At the same time, in contradiction to her vulnerability in his presence, she felt a sense of peace and a deep knowledge that everything was as it should be. She must be going insane after all, she thought.

The man was almost upon her when she noticed his easy smile, which revealed even white teeth with slightly longer canines. Instead of looking odd, though, his mouth looked as it should for his kind of looks—just right. How she knew this, Carla had no idea, but Mother Nature had made him in such an extraordinary manner that he was simply perfect in a curious sort of way.

She stood speechless when he finally reached her, but she noted Tom still stayed by him instead of coming over to her side as he normally did when they met new people. The man exchanged a quick glance with Tom before he turned his gaze back on her.

"Your dog, I presume." His baritone voice matched the silkiness of his appearance.

Carla made every attempt to snap out of her trancelike state while she stared at this strange man. It didn't help that although unusual his looks were devastatingly gorgeous, and to add insult to injury the lightest of tans on his fair skin made a wonderful contrast to his bone, cable-knit fisherman's pullover and khaki cargo pants rolled up just below the knee.

"Tom!" Carla snapped at the dog more firmly than she meant to. "Time for your lunch." She wasn't angry at Tom for having made friends with the guy, but she had to cover her annoyance at her own reaction to the man's appearance by doing something mundane like chiding her animal companion.

Tom looked rather contrite and joined her at once sitting down by her side, but his eyes never left his new friend.

"Is that his name?" The man turned to Tom and patted his silky head. "He's a beautiful dog."

Why was it that Carla had the feeling the man already knew her dog's name? Perhaps, he had super hearing powers and he heard her calling after Tom earlier. But then why not say so? Why pretend he didn't know Tom's name?

"Who are you?" Carla decided to take a page from Jana's book and be direct. She knew she sounded ill-mannered, but right now she simply wanted to get away from the man's disturbing gaze.

"I'm Rhys," he replied, but made no motion to shake her hand nor did he smile. The look on his face was neutral.

Carla sighed. She was not the kind of person who greeted new acquaintances with rudeness. "I'm sorry, Rhys, I didn't mean to be abrupt. I guess I wasn't expecting to come across anyone today. I'm Carla." She extended her hand towards him and he took it for the briefest of seconds before he let go.

The feel of his cool skin when he touched her hand unsettled her somewhat, but not in a sexual way. It was something strange; something not quite real. Again, she could not explain what her feelings and sensations meant and her tired mind threw her the most absurd suggestion that he was a vampire who could handle being outside in the daylight. She almost laughed aloud at this fanciful notion and the whole nonsense of the situation. *For god's sake, get a grip!* She berated herself silently. As she did so, she noticed the man smile briefly, like he understood what she was feeling. Maybe, he was psychic. This seemed a more plausible explanation than the one about the vampire.

"Well, it's nice to meet you, Rhys," Carla stated in what she thought to be a normal tone, and added, "I guess you're on a break away from it all, like me."

He nodded. "Yes. It's quiet this time of year."

Carla decided to go one step further with her questioning. "Are you staying at Merry Beach?"

Rhys gestured with his eyes towards the cabins a few metres down the path. "You mean the cabins? No. I'm in a campervan farther down the road at Kioloa."

He offered no other information and Carla was not about to go on a fishing expedition, no matter how interesting he looked. "Well," she said, "I'm off to feed Tom now."

Rhys nodded and turned his disturbing gaze on the dog as he leaned down towards him. "I'm sure we'll meet again, Tom."

To Carla's astonishment, Tom did something she had

never seen him do before—he actually placed one of his front paws into Rhys's extended hand.

2

Rhys stood on the beach following Carla's movements while she headed back to her cabin with Tom. When he met her just now, the shock he experienced as he laid eyes on her struck him like a twisted bolt of fate, mocking him; he managed to hide his feelings in front of her, however, and make casual conversation instead.

Nothing could have prepared him for this meeting. The last thing he had expected to find was that he would once again be brought face to face with his dead wife. Of course, Carla was not his wife come to life but rather an identical twin. Even so, this was something he could never have imagined happening to him.

He had heard of people who had doubles; the term used to describe this phenomenon was known as doppelgängers. Rhys always believed these people were simply uncanny lookalikes rather than absolute identical twins. So when he saw Carla standing in front of him—slim, olive-skinned, attractive with shoulder-length brown hair and dark brown eyes—he could have sworn he was looking straight at his wife as she had been prior to her death and a jolt of pure happiness exploded in his heart before he realised he was deceiving himself. Death was final—no matter how much people wanted their loved ones to return or make contact in some way. Death, as far as he was concerned, was the end.

Rhys shook his head, still in disbelief at what he had seen in Carla, and then he began to walk back down the beach towards Kioloa Caravan Park. He was in need of strong coffee to help him get over the shock. Whatever were Carla's thoughts about him, he had decided to block out of his mind. He did not want to know her thoughts, although he possessed the ability to read people's minds. With Carla, however, he would have somehow felt like a stalker if he'd allowed himself to read her innermost thoughts. The little he knew about her, which he had learned from Tom, the dog, was enough to build a picture of her life during the past few years.

Carla suffered from the agonising pain of betrayal by the one she thought had loved her. Rhys could not possibly imagine how this must have felt as he had never been betrayed, so short of scanning her mind to feel her pain he merely likened the emotion to what he had felt when he lost Xaye, his wife, during a mass eruption of a volcano near the town where they lived.

A cold breeze coming in from the ocean ruffled his hair and made him shiver. He hurried to his caravan and put on a pot of coffee as soon as he arrived while he changed into a fleecy tracksuit and a woollen pair of socks. He heard the first drops of rain falling on the tin roof of his van and was surprised he hadn't noticed the gathering clouds earlier nor had he sensed the brewing storm. He had been too engrossed in thoughts of Carla and her identical looks to Xaye.

The coffee was ready and he poured himself a cup. Black and strong, as he enjoyed this beverage to which he'd taken a liking when he had first arrived. The rain began to fall steadily and Rhys sat at the small dinette nook in the van and looked out the window at the gathering force of the wind outside. He shivered again, not from the cold, but rather from the shock of what had happened. He pictured Carla sitting in her cabin and thinking of the pain she had been dealing with since her breakup. Rhys focused on peace enveloping her and dissolving the intensity of her emotional turmoil.

Tom had told him quite a lot about his mistress and Rhys was grateful for the insight. He knew that even from afar he would be able to lift her burden, if only a little. On Tyerra, they had taught him as a child not to open up entirely to his mental powers. He was what they termed an SSE (super sensitive empathic). This meant if his mind remained open to all around him, he would not be able to cope with the tremendous burden of everyone's feelings and energy pouring into him.

The thoughts and emotions of all living things, irrespective of whether they were plants, animals or people, intruded into his mind to the extent that they could drive him over the edge if he allowed it. As a result, Rhys had been trained to focus on the important information and shut off from the mental noise and thoughts of others. He was to use his mental ability when needed, and only for good. If he allowed himself to sense all thoughts and emotions he would feel what others felt and their pain would become his pain; their misery his misery; their dreams his dreams, and so on.

Everyone on Tyerra possessed this ability to a certain level, but Rhys was one of the truly gifted ones. Oftentimes, though, he wished he had not been born with this gift. It was a huge weight to have to bear and more often than not it proved to be an extremely heavy burden.

***

Carla loved the energy storms generated and she felt like going for a walk on the beach, but knew better than to go wandering around in the darkness with a violent thunderstorm producing huge bolts of lightning that split open tree trunks. The last thing she wanted was to make Tom an orphan so early in life. After all, he was only two years old and still like a pup in many ways.

That evening, she dined on a few slices of pizza she had kept as leftovers from the previous day and she finished off her meal with coffee, which she took out to the veranda where she sat cocooned in a fleecy blanket while she watched the storm rage around her.

Normally, Carla found storms projected her anger whenever things went wrong in her life, and she welcomed the release of her inner emotions to the point where they echoed the rage of the storm. Therefore, this evening was just right to let off steam about Michael.

She felt this was the perfect opportunity to go over her feelings about the breakup with her partner of five years—the person she had trusted the most in life aside from her parents, who were unfortunately deceased. Michael had lied to her from the very beginning, coming across as a decent and sincere human being whose aim in life was to settle down with the right person.

He had been charming and unassuming, and Carla found herself trusting for the first time after two failed relationships in the past. Michael had been so very different from the others, and Carla thought she had at last hit the jackpot. Michael had proved to be diligent and responsible; he was an excellent stockbroker and saving for their future through shares; he visited his elderly parents regularly and helped them out with odd jobs around their home; and he treated Carla like the only woman for him, forever expressing his feelings so she felt cherished, cared for and loved.

Over time, he had managed what no one else had been able to do—dissolve Carla's mistrust of men and encourage her to open her heart to love once more without the fear of being hurt all over again. Therefore, after a year of dating exclusively, they moved in together. Carla owned an apartment in the city and a cosy cottage in the Blue Mountains, and she shared both her homes with Michael. After all, this was her contribution to their future together. She helped financially by not asking for any rent from Michael so he could utilise the savings for their retirement.

Carla was over the moon when Michael finally asked her to marry him. She had accepted with delight and felt the warmth of real love envelop her in her new life with him.

"Of course, we'll have to get a bigger place in Sydney," Michael had said once they set a date for their wedding, which would have been last Christmas, Carla mused as she remembered their discussion.

"Well," Carla had replied thoughtfully, "I can sell my

apartment and then we could buy something bigger together."

They had agreed on the plan and once Carla's apartment was sold, they based themselves in the mountains cottage while they looked for the right place to buy in Sydney. In the meantime, the proceeds from the sale of Carla's apartment were invested in shares by Michael, and as both of them were telecommuters for work—Michael, with his stock broking business and Carla, freelancing in website design—they were able to save quite a sum of money by not living in the big city.

Almost overnight, however, things began to change. At first, Michael became moody. Carla thought it was because he missed living in Sydney and found the mountains too quiet for his taste. She consequently suggested he spend part of the week at his parents' place and go apartment hunting in his spare time, and she would then join him for an inspection if he found something suitable.

This worked well for a while, but as time went on she and Michael started to grow apart. Initially, it was the little things he did for her that disappeared, like the flirty notes he left for her in different parts of the house; the small tokens of affection, such as a chocolate heart on her pillow, a flower on the dining table, or a small stuffed toy on her desk; but most important of all, it was their lack of communication that really affected her. Gone were their long discussions about life, travel, culture, the arts, and everything that had drawn them together in the first place. Their verbal exchanges were suddenly reduced to day-to-day practicalities while trying to fit into a schedule that revolved around Michael's work and finding a suitable apartment.

This went on as Christmas approached and no more talk of marriage ensued. Carla tried to raise the issue on a few occasions, but Michael evaded this by becoming upset and giving her excuses about his stress levels with work and the fact that share prices were down and therefore it would be more prudent to wait before they cashed in. On and on this happened, until one day Carla decided to confront Michael.

One evening after dinner, Carla made coffee and they

sat out in the backyard of the cottage. Tom ran around them, showing off his antics and trying to get them to play with him, but Carla could not focus on anything else other than the conversation ahead. She had rehearsed for days what she would say to Michael. She had been afraid that a confrontation may not be the way to go about things, but living as they were these days, almost like two housemates sharing a place, and only communicating when needed, was not her idea of a relationship.

Michael sipped his coffee, looking serious and thoughtful, and perhaps he had an inkling that the showdown had arrived. Carla drew on her courage, however, and finally spoke. "Michael, you know this can't go on. Not like this."

Michael glanced at her and then drew his eyes to the coffee cup in his hand. "What can't go on?" His tone was almost casual, as if nothing was wrong.

Carla sighed. She would have to be more direct. "Surely, you've noticed? We don't talk anymore, we don't make love, and we hardly communicate, so please don't deny it."

He looked in her direction again, this time simply gazing at her as if he truly did not know what she was on about. The silence stretched for a few moments before Carla took the plunge.

"If we love each other, we can work through this—whatever the problem, but if there's no love between us, then it's best to call it quits." Carla looked to him for a response and felt alarm bells go off inside her head when he didn't react immediately. She had expected a huge denial that their love had fizzled out, and then Michael would draw her into his arms and tell her she was the one for him, but none of this happened.

Carla waited tensely and then felt her heart break when he finally spoke. "I think we should call it quits."

She had been too shocked to take this in, so she didn't go after him when he went inside the house and she heard him rustling about for a few moments in the bedroom. Then, the front door slammed shut and she heard him start the engine of his car and drive off. Just like that.

Worse was to come when the next day Carla received a call from Michael's friend and business colleague, Justin, who kept an office in Sydney from where Michael sometimes worked.

"What happened with Michael?" Justin's voice had been full of concern when Carla answered the call.

"What... do you mean?" She tried to swallow, but her throat felt dry. The only thing she became aware of was the foreboding knowledge that she was about to get an even bigger shock than that of Michael leaving the house.

"He's gone, Carla. He must've come into the office during the night because his computer's still on, but all his files and personal belongings are gone. And I hope you're sitting down for this one."

His tone made Carla's legs turn to jelly. She flopped down on a nearby sofa chair and waited for Justin to continue.

"I'm sorry to have to tell you this, but he's cleaned out his shares account and closed it."

"What does that mean?" Carla asked, dumbfounded.

"It means he sold all his shares."

"All?" Carla exclaimed. "But what about *our* shares?"

Justin paused for a few seconds before he replied gravely, "What do you mean by 'our shares'? Michael only had one account in his name; he told me he set it up this way to spare you from paying extra tax as a result of your property assets. Anyway, he cashed in all the shares and seems to have disappeared. I've been calling him all morning, but he's not answering."

It was at this point that Carla dropped the phone and ran to the bathroom, just in time to hang her head over the toilet bowl and vomit.

A particularly bright bolt of lightning, followed by the earth-trembling sound of thunder, brought Carla back to the present and she escaped inside the cabin where it was warm. She made another coffee while she let her tears fall. This time, however, she was surprised to find the tears were filled with pity for Michael. He must have been really sick in the head to do something like that—to string her along and pretend to love her only to con her out of a huge chunk of her money.

Carla had replayed this whole episode many times in her mind, always ending up with resentment, bitterness, and anger at the way she was used. During the past six months, since the breakup, she cried tears of torment, desperation, and disappointment. She suffered such disillusionment that eventually her heart hardened with a burning anger, which often turned to rage, and whenever she thought of Michael she felt the vomit come up to the back of her throat.

Jana insisted she go to counselling, but this had not really helped. The breakup of a relationship was bad enough when both parties knew the reason why—but to know nothing, to go on trying to figure out what happened, only to arrive at the conclusion that it had all been a major con, this was the most horrible of betrayals. Carla had fallen in love with a lie. One spun by a very experienced con man. As a result, Michael had not only robbed Carla of her money, but also of the ability to trust and love again. Carla would never be a whole person for as long as she lived because once a trusting person gave themselves totally and absolutely to another, when they thought they were of one mind and soul, and then to find it had all been a sham, what else was there?

After six months of struggling with her emotions and with counselling doing nothing for her, Carla decided to take a break from work and life in general. She had come to Merry Beach to be on her own, hoping to find a way to heal. This had been a haven for her when she used to holiday here with her childhood friend, Tracy, and her family, who used to own a caravan in these parts before they moved to live overseas.

Two weeks after her arrival, Carla was still very much up and down and she often sank into bouts of sadness and depression that eventually led to anger and rage. Now, as her tears fell freely, Carla waited for the sadness to turn into the usual anger, but it didn't. Her tears stopped and she became aware of a sense of peace instead. She tried to picture Michael's face, but the only thing that came to mind was a blurry vision of him and not the clear, sharp memory of the person she had once loved.

Taking her coffee to the sofa, Carla sat down and sipped the drink while waiting for she knew not what. It was like clarity had suddenly come into her mind. The victim of deceit was no more. She felt somehow lighter, more positive about the future —even stronger. She was a woman who had gone through a traumatic experience, but had come out of it in one piece.

3

Carla awoke feeling rested and refreshed. Tom, who had spent the whole night hiding under the bed, due to his fear of thunderstorms, now jumped on it to greet his mistress in the hope of a cuddle and a quick exit to the back of the cabin for a call of nature followed by breakfast; all in that order. This was how Carla woke up every morning and today was no different, except she felt lighter of mood and looked forward to the day ahead. She mused about this for a moment and put it down to the magic of Merry Beach.

Tom scurried outside as soon as she opened the back door for him and returned within moments for his breakfast, which Carla fed to him on the front veranda while she sat drinking coffee and eating a piece of toast, enjoying the clearness of the bright, shining morning after the night's storm.

Considering the strength of the storm, Carla did not notice any major damage except for leaves and twigs blown off trees and bushes, littering the grounds around the cabins. Branches and fronds from the Norfolk Island pines that lined the beachfront's pristine sands were also scattered all over the place.

There was no one about and Carla was glad to have the beach all to herself, despite the debris from the storm. Even so, a vivid image of Rhys's face popped into her mind and for a moment she wished he were here with her. The moment was of short duration, however, which suited Carla just fine and she did not want to think of Rhys at all. He had simply been one of the many walkers she often encountered on the beach, and they had exchanged a few pleasantries and then gone on their way.

As soon as she thought this, Tom looked up at her and

placed his head on her knee for a caress. Carla complied and was convinced the dog missed Rhys. She shook her head and spoke to herself aloud. "No way! There's no way a dog is going to miss a stranger he's only just met the day before."

Tom's eyes looked into hers and she shivered. She felt as though he understood exactly what was going on inside her mind.

"Come on, boy." She ruffled his ears and this got his tail wagging. "I'll go and get ready and take you for a real walk. Our usual place, okay?"

Tom responded with a bark of excitement and followed her into the house, thoughts of Rhys forgotten.

**

The sun shining on Rhys's face through the small window of the campervan awoke him to the glorious day. Rhys stretched in his bunk before sitting up and going straight to the small ring stove to put on a pot of coffee.

He glanced at the clock that hung on the wall by the door and noted it was barely seven. It was too cold outside to open the door, but while he waited for the coffee to be ready he peeked out the window and noticed the sun had just risen above the ocean line. It was not too high in the sky just yet, but the ball of fire dominating a large part of the horizon made him think of another sun, far away in another galaxy.

Then, another thought intruded in on his contemplation of the day and he picked up his thumb communicator and held it in the palm of his hand. The small screen on the device that was around the size of a USB stick was lit to a bright green colour. The communicator did not have a ring tone; it simply worked on mental process for people such as Rhys. The green screen meant the calling party was waiting for him to respond. Rhys communicated via thought. "Commander."

Commander also replied in thought form, so anyone watching Rhys would not have realized that he was having a conversation with whoever was at the other end of the device. Ironically, the device was not used to ring a person per se, it was simply used to minimise static on communication vibes across vast distances by cleaning any signal interference from space. The party being called instinctively knew via thought that they were being contacted. Rhys heard Commander's voice inside his head. "Make sure you don't burn your coffee," Commander said with humour.

Rhys took the espresso maker off the cooking ring and proceeded to pour coffee into a mug. Commander went on, "I see you've picked up yet another Earthly habit."

"You mean the coffee?" Rhys responded. "What's the other habit then?"

"Intense feelings for an Earthling."

As Commander's voice replied inside his head Rhys's hand shook slightly, but he knew it would be no good trying to shut off his thoughts from Commander. After all, it was this man, so much older and wiser than he, who had trained him to refine his thought process ability. "It was simply the shock of finding someone who looks identical to Xaye," Rhys defended himself.

Commander chuckled good-naturedly. "I'm not judging you, Rhys, but you must remember your mission. Nothing else matters right now."

Rhys did his best to shut out thoughts of Carla lest Commander pick up on them. "I haven't forgotten," he responded while he took a sip of his coffee and glanced out at the sun, still rising up above the horizon.

"I'm glad," Commander said. "I'd hate to think your judgement would be impaired by this. Whatever recommendations you submit to the League of Galaxies will be taken very seriously, and I don't need to remind you that you can't use your feelings for this woman as part of the equation."

Rhys sighed. There was nothing he could keep from Commander. "I need more time to compile the report," he said after another sip of coffee, ignoring the reference to Carla.

"There's no rush for now," Commander reassured him.

"But, Rhys, the more time you have with her, the more risk to your ability to judge neutrally and fairly."

Rhys held firm to the thoughts in his mind, once again ignoring Commander's comment regarding Carla. This time, he was sure his thoughts could not be sensed by Commander. "You know I'll do what's right."

Commander seemed to be satisfied with this. "We'll talk again soon. Be well," he said and the thumb communicator light went black. Commander had ended their exchange.

Rhys finished his coffee, dressed warmly, and stepped outside with a replenished cup of the hot drink. He walked away from the caravan and went to sit on the beach. He must be more careful with his thoughts in future.

Being near the thumb communicator, even if it was shut off, still made it possible for signals to get through; whereas if he was somewhere outside, his thoughts would be scrambled by all the noisy signals coming from Earth and the cosmic gibberish in outer space. In this way, not even someone as highly developed as Commander would be able to pick up on Rhys's feelings. The signal would be too hazy.

I'll be more cautious next time, Rhys thought again while enjoying the warmth of the rising sun as it started to heat up the sand under him.

He was well aware his mission came first. This was the entire reason why he had travelled so far from his home on Tyerra and why he'd been roaming the globe called Earth for over a year. His present beach holiday was to clear his head for a while. Culling through the millions of thoughts he was meant to focus on plus doing research through news and social media had worn him down and he felt exhausted. Empathy was considered a wonderful quality to possess, but in his case he was so very sensitive that there was always a fine line between coping with the feelings and emotions of a situation and allowing them to overtake him and send him mad.

He lay back on the sand allowing the warmth of the sun to seep into his being and for once he felt relaxed and content. The intense pain he usually felt at thoughts of Xaye had started to fade some time ago, partly because after her death he had become a workaholic and for many years had focused on nothing else. Then, he'd been sent on this mission to a planet so far from his own, where he lived among humans and this really helped take his mind off things. The other part, however, was due to his meeting with Carla.

Commander's warning flashed in his mind. He shouldn't allow his feelings for Carla to interfere with his mission and on a personal note he reminded himself that Carla was not Xaye. Carla was a different person from his wife, but her energy reminded him very much of Xaye's—kind, loving, vulnerable, and absolutely beautiful. This was why when Carla had offered her hand in greeting to him, when they had first met, he barely touched it. He knew if he had held on a second longer he would have drawn her into his arms, as humans tended to do, and held her there forever.

He sighed in frustration. No matter how pure her energy, Carla was an Earthling and she did not have his gift; therefore, she would not recognise him as a twin soul. This meant he would have to do things the Earthly way and win her trust, but with her state of mind after the breakup of her relationship this could take ages. To make matters even more complicated, he had chosen not to delve too much into her thoughts in case he found out she did not like him as a potential partner. Such a discovery would shatter his hopes, more so than the problems they would face if Carla did end up falling for him after all.

Too tired to think in this futile manner, Rhys relaxed on the warm sand and before he knew it he fell asleep.

***

Carla sat with Tom on their special rock ledge and closed her eyes while she basked in the morning sun. It was a magic day without the chilly wind and the warmth seeped into her, enveloping her in peace. Tom lay by her side with his head resting on her lap, fast asleep.

Carla stayed in this position for a while and was about to lie back for a nap when she was jolted out of the tranquil state she had sunk into by the buzzing of her mobile phone. She sat upright, eyes wide open, and drew the phone out of her jacket pocket. The caller ID told her it was Michael.

"Hello, Michael," she said in a neutral voice.

Michael sounded surprised when he replied, "I didn't expect to get you on the first go."

"Well, I'm on top of the cliff so the signal's strong. What can I do for you?" Her tone was calm, even pleasant, and Carla was grateful for this. On other occasions when Michael had finally made contact with her after the breakup, she had been tense and upset. Now, she had no idea what had brought about this change in her, though she was happy in the knowledge that she had the upper hand for once.

"Jana told me you'd gone away for a while. I take it you're at Merry Beach."

Carla thought he was buying time by making conversation. After all, during the six months since the breakup their communication had been full of anger, with Carla often telling him off for being such a bastard and Michael trying to lie to her repeatedly by assuring her he was in debt, but that he would pay back the money he'd borrowed. Carla knew better than this, and in the end any communication involving finances was turned over to their lawyers. Michael remained as evasive as ever and after a while Carla found herself paying hefty legal fees for something she knew she would never get back from him. Finally, she decided to cut her losses so she could have time to grieve for the death of the relationship itself instead of the loss of her money. There was silence for a while from Michael after this, but now, quite unexpectedly, he had started to ring her again. Carla hadn't returned any of his calls so he had turned to Jana.

Jana had not yet had time to email Carla about whatever it was she had been trying to tell her on the phone the previous day, but Carla no longer cared. "What can I do for you?" Carla repeated, totally ignoring Michael's chitchat.

"Carla, I meant it when I said I only borrowed the money," Michael tried to appeal to her. "It's just that things are tough and I lost so much on the shares we had. I wanted to let you know I'll pay you back, honest."

Carla rolled her eyes, not believing a single word, but this time she was not upset, only simply curious as to the real reason for his call. "So what do you want?"

There was silence at the other end of the phone for a moment and then Michael said, "I want you to give me a second chance. I was too stupid to realise what I was doing. I never stopped loving you, Carla."

Carla experienced a sudden desire to laugh—whether true or not, she no longer wished to be with someone like Michael. She had missed him terribly since the breakup, even though she believed she had been conned by him, but her feelings for him had been genuine. Then, after all the angry phone calls followed by dealings with their lawyers and finally total silence until about two weeks ago, Carla arrived at two conclusions: one, she didn't love him anymore; and two, somehow, after the previous night's storm, she felt free at last to get on with the rest of her life.

"Michael, whatever reason you have for your call, I no longer wish to know. You can keep the money. Just don't call me again." And with a calm she did not know she possessed, Carla ended the call by pushing the off button in a casual way. She felt indifferent about the whole thing and no longer relished thoughts of resentment towards the person who had turned her life upside down.

She switched off the phone altogether and lay on her back, looking up at the azure sky, a serene smile on her face. She must have dozed off in this way because when she came to, the sun was directly overhead and her tummy grumbled with hunger. She sat up and noticed Tom was no longer by her side.

"Tom!" she called out, wondering where he'd got to.

She stood up and dusted herself off while she looked towards the path that ran along the ledge. "Tom!" she called again, this time feeling concerned. Tom never left her side.

She waited for a few moments and then decided to make her way down the cliff and to the beach. Perhaps, Tom went looking for food scraps. It had been a long while since breakfast and he was probably hungry. Carla hurried her step despite the potential danger of tripping over the rocky outcrops and she called Tom several times to no avail.

When she reached the highest point of the cliff, where she could see the entire beach below her, she paused; down by the shoreline she espied Tom, playing on the sand with Rhys, his newfound friend.

At first, Carla felt upset with the dog for running off to be with a stranger, but she couldn't blame him. He was still a big pup, just wanting to play, and she had fallen asleep for a long time, leaving him to his own devices. Then, she became annoyed with Rhys for not knowing any better. Didn't the man realise Tom was wandering around without his mistress? He should have come looking for her.

Carla took a few steps towards the descent that led to the beach, but stopped again and turned to the two, playing like kids in the sand. What right had she to judge? Rhys had probably gone for a walk and bumped into Tom, who simply wanted to play. There was no reason why Rhys should be concerned about her. For all he knew, Carla could have been inside the cabin.

She took another moment to focus on them. Why was it she thought Rhys was talking to the dog while Tom replied back? From her vantage point she could not actually see Rhys speaking or Tom barking. All she could see was Rhys throwing a stick around and Tom retrieving it and getting a pat on the head whenever he deposited it into Rhys's hand. Besides, the whole thing was ludicrous. Dogs didn't talk.

At that moment, Rhys happened to look up at her and he waved. She blushed with embarrassment at having been caught spying so she decided to make her way down to the beach. Carla told herself she had every right to spy seeing as her dog had gone missing and she was concerned for him.

She took another peek at Rhys and noticed how the sun shining on his hair turned the colour into a rich, burnished orange with the golden streaks of white blond interspersed with dashes of brown. Something stirred in her—something she didn't understand. There was no doubt she found Rhys attractive despite his rather outlandish appearance, but this was not it. There was yet something else she couldn't figure out. Rhys seemed to possess an untouched kind of look, like a person who was not quite streetwise. There was in him a certain naïveté, and yet Carla was sure he was a man of the world.

When she got closer to the pair on the beach, Tom took off running in her direction while Rhys walked towards her at a slower pace. His purplish blue gaze unsettled her, but not in a bad way.

"Hello." Rhys smiled on approach. "I wasn't sure if you were in the cabin or not."

Carla felt kinder towards him now and was glad she didn't tell him where to go for stealing away Tom's attention from her. The man had been thinking just what she had concluded, that she was in the cabin and Tom had gone for a short jaunt to the beach.

When Rhys finally reached her, she returned his smile. "I actually fell asleep up on the cliff. It's a glorious day, don't you think?"

Rhys regarded her while at the same time he restrained himself from getting closer to her or even touching her to see if she was real. "Yes, perfect," he replied instead, his double meaning totally lost on Carla.

4

"I was about to make some sandwiches," Carla found herself explaining and before she could stop herself she said, "Are you hungry?"

Twenty minutes later, Carla set down on the table in her front veranda a platter of finger-cut sandwiches, a plate with a variety of cheeses and mixed nuts, and a bowl of fresh fruit containing large fragrant mangoes, kiwifruit, and plump purple grapes.

Rhys followed behind with a glass jug full of iced water in one hand and a four-cup size Bialetti espresso maker in the other; he set these down on the table. Tom ran around them with what looked like a big smile on his face as Carla and Rhys went back inside to get cups, glasses, plates, cutlery, and serviettes.

"Tom," Carla chided the dog gently, "please settle down!" She then turned to Rhys. "I have no idea what's going on with him. He never acts like this in front of visitors."

Rhys smiled at Tom and patted his head. "Tom and I are old friends by now," he explained.

Carla sat on one of the wicker chairs by the table and Rhys followed suit and took a seat across from her.

"Help yourself," Carla invited.

Rhys smiled in response and Carla held her breath for a second or two as if something of great magnitude was about to happen, but Rhys only uttered, "Thank you. This is a great lunch, Carla. I really appreciate you going to all this trouble."

Carla made herself busy by pouring coffee for both of

them. "Well, we all have to eat." Then, she noticed Tom's eyes on her and added, "Oh, I didn't forget you, boy. Your lunch is in your bowl already."

As if the dog understood, he raced inside the cabin and soon the other two heard him munching away.

"He's a great dog," Rhys commented, sipping his coffee. He noticed Carla had made vegetarian sandwiches and he helped himself to one with avocado, roasted vegetables and Feta cheese.

Carla followed suit and placed a couple of sandwiches on her plate. "He's excellent company, I must say, but I've never seen him so excitable before. He must really like you."

They ate in silence for a few moments and Carla watched Rhys enjoy his food and coffee. He ate in an elegant manner, just as he moved, with fluid movements. Perhaps, he had been a classical dancer or a gymnast at a young age, she thought.

Rhys's gaze found hers and Carla realised she'd been staring. How could she not, though? Anyone with his looks was bound to attract attention irrespective of whether people found him likable or not. He exuded a kind of magnetism that was difficult to ignore. "So what brings you to these parts?" Carla forced herself to make conversation while she picked at a bunch of grapes.

Even though he had made every effort to shut off his focus on her thoughts, Rhys had inadvertently picked up on most of them, which meant her vibes were quite strong. He was fully aware of her reaction to him, not unlike the reaction he got from other people he had met in his travels. They couldn't quite figure him out so they looked at him with curiosity. He didn't think he was so very different from any of the trendy types one saw in the streets these days, but there was obviously something about him that made people stare at times. In the case of Carla, however, Rhys didn't want to kid himself that she felt more than most others he'd met in the past.

"I'm a photographer," he explained, sipping on coffee again. "For the past year, I've been travelling to most parts of the world and now I'm taking a break before I cull through the images and send them off to the various magazines and websites that commissioned them."

Carla sat forward, fascinated. "What a great job!" she remarked. "What kind of photos do you take?"

"Nature shots mainly—landscapes, plants, animals, that sort of thing."

"So you're like one of those National Geographic photographers?"

Rhys nodded, remembering this as one of the magazines he had studied extensively before travelling to Earth. "Yes, you could say that. I freelance and sell off my work. Sometimes, though, clients commission me for certain assignments."

Carla sat back, regarding him with interest and thinking how this seemed to fit him right down to the ground: artistic, a flamboyant appearance that was simply a part of him and not a put on, and his connection to nature. She knew by Tom's reaction that Rhys was someone special and she now found herself liking him intensely.

"And you, what is your work?"

Carla came back to attention; she hated it that she'd been caught staring again. "Oh, I... Well, nothing as exciting as what you do, but I happen to enjoy my job. I'm a freelancer, too, only I develop websites for businesses and such. In fact, one of my recent assignments was to develop a website for a dog grooming salon and pet hotel. Tom even had a modelling part in it," she announced proudly.

Hearing his name, Tom came back to join them and went straight to Rhys. "I think he wants to try some cheese," Rhys said.

Carla looked perplexed. "How do you know that?"

Rhys hesitated for the merest of moments, but then explained, "I've always been sensitive to animals, I guess." And then, "May I?" He picked a cube of cheese from the platter, which Tom eyed greedily.

Carla nodded and Rhys fed it to Tom. It was gone as soon as it went in his mouth and the dog looked at Rhys for more. Rhys shook his head. "Oh no, that was just a treat. You don't want me to get into trouble with your mother, do you?"

To Carla's amazement, Tom seemed to accept this and he stayed seated quietly by their visitor's side. "I'm also sensitive to animals," Carla commented, "but I'm guessing nowhere near as sensitive as you. Tom obeys you more than he does me."

They laughed easily at this and Carla felt more relaxed. Rhys seemed to be a nice guy with nothing to prove—the extreme opposite of Michael. In fact, if she compared the two she could not understand what she ever saw in her ex. He had been so materialistic and self-centred. He would never have sat across from her talking about nature and animals, and being sensitive to the whole thing. Michael only talked of money, shares, and finance in general. Carla frowned at the thought.

"Something wrong?" Rhys asked immediately.

She produced a smile for his benefit. "Not really, though you might say it was a ghost from the past, but it's quite gone now." She poured him more coffee. "Eat up, there's heaps left."

Rhys helped himself to a couple more finger sandwiches and some fruit. "You said when we met that you're also here on a break."

Carla nodded. "Only for a short one. I'm meant to get back to work the week after next."

Rhys felt his heart sink. He didn't have much time left with her. "So where do you normally live?" Of course, he knew it was the mountains because Tom had been feeding him information, but Rhys reminded himself he had to play the game the Earthly way.

"I base myself in the Blue Mountains, but I travel to Sydney sometimes. Many of my clients are located in the city. What about you?"

This caught him off guard. He had no plans other than to stay at Kioloa while he formatted his report for Commander and then he would return to Tyerra. He didn't know what to say in response to Carla's question so he went with her own explanation. "Same here. I meant to say not based in the mountains, but in Sydney. My clients are in the city while others are overseas."

Carla looked a little crestfallen when she remarked, "So you're off travelling again?"

Rhys couldn't help but feel encouraged by her reaction. "No. I decided to take a long break. Too much travel can tire one out."

"But you're not from this part of the world, are you?" Carla surprised him yet again.

"Why do you say that?" He searched his mind rapidly to see whether he'd made any slips.

"It's your accent," Carla went on. "You have a bit of a British accent."

Rhys relaxed. "Well, I'm from Wales originally," he replied, hating himself for having to lie. "I grew up in the UK."

"What's your surname? We haven't been properly introduced, have we?"

Rhys agreed and was ready this time. "Lewis." He'd travelled extensively through Wales at one stage and Lewis was a common enough name. "What about you? Carla is an Italian name, right?" He knew this to be the case.

"Yes. My father was Italian. My surname's Fiori."

"As in *flowers*," Rhys pointed out.

"Well, you have indeed travelled extensively, haven't you?" Carla admired his quickness and wondered whether he spoke any other languages.

"Mind if I make more coffee? I'm a heavy coffee drinker, I'm afraid." Rhys said in order to change the subject. He didn't want to reveal too much else about himself, not just yet.

Carla was up on her feet and Tom came alive and went to her. "I'll make it. I'm a bit of a coffee head, too," she informed him. "I really love the stuff. You sit there and relax and I'll be right back."

With Carla inside, putting the coffee on and chitchatting with Tom, Rhys sighed. He had to watch what he said and remember it for future reference. He also had to find a way to bring her round to trusting him; only then would he be able to confide in her.

***

Rhys tossed and turned in his bunk until he sat up feeling wide-awake and with no hope of sleep to come any time soon. He ran a hand through his hair, brushing back the long fringe that fell over his brow and sighed.

His lunch with Carla had unsettled him and he frowned as he thought over what Commander had told him about spending more time with her. The more he came to know her the more chance his judgement might be clouded by his evolving feelings. This could have a detrimental effect on his mission, Rhys thought, but only if he allowed it.

He glanced at the clock on the wall. It was just past three. He groaned, deciding he may as well get up and do some work. The temperature in the campervan was quite cold so he threw his cable-knit pullover over his pyjamas and put on a pot of coffee. He certainly hadn't been lying when he'd told Carla he was a heavy coffee drinker. Tyerra did not have coffee, but this was easily fixed if he took some seedlings when he returned home. Perhaps, when this was all over, he would become a coffee grower.

He shook his head at the silly thought and switched on his computer, bringing up the report he had been working on for the past year.

All the information was expressed in advanced mathematical language with a huge amount of statistics covering different aspects of life on Earth and broken up by regions and different demographics. Just taking in the number of observations he had made so far did not make any sense to him. Measuring humans and their actions was not as simple as the League of Galaxies had thought back on Tyerra when they commissioned him for the assignment.

Rhys frowned as if having an internal debate with someone over the behavioural patterns of humans. His point being, for instance, how could someone who does something bad or commits a violent crime still have love for a pet? Unlike the highly evolved beings on other planets, Earthlings tended to have a rather compartmentalised psyche. They may hate their ex-spouse but love their children. They may sacrifice anything for their family, but at the same time would not think twice about ripping off the company for which they worked. They got on with their neighbours, who might be of a different race, but protested when their nation issued visas to more refugees and migrants. The list of inconsistencies for every sphere in human life was practically unlimited.

The coffee was ready and Rhys poured himself a full mug—strong and black with one sugar. He went back to the computer and continued studying the report. He had statistics on all sorts of crimes including domestic violence, child abuse, sexual abuse, animal abuse, and so on. There were other atrocities, too, such as terrorism, wars, world hunger, racism, health epidemics, the whole gamut of discriminatory behaviour, corruption at corporate and government levels, refugees, climate change, pollution, divorce rates, religious bigotry, gender issues, sexual preferences, and on and on; the list seemed interminable.

The fact extraterrestrials had worked with humans many years ago to help them avoid total destruction of their race didn't seem to have made much difference to the way humans still treated their planet.

Rhys had been given this information for reference by the League of Galaxies even though he had been fully aware of the help humans had received in the past and the fact it hadn't generated any real change in their nature. Irrespective of this, help had been given, and one of the biggest projects where aliens and humans worked side by side had been during the Cold War era. A time when humans were not quite ready to handle atomic weapons and tensions between the US and the Soviet Union, as it was known in those days, hung in the balance. If aliens had not interceded at the time, humans would have blown themselves off the face of the planet.

Afterwards, governments had kept their collaboration with extraterrestrials top secret and any human who claimed to have information, conspiracy theories, or even proof of alien contact had been handled in such a way that ridiculed them to the public so people thought them crazy or attention-seeking. In cases where this didn't work, many people simply went missing.

Police Departments the world over held huge numbers of files of missing persons who seemed to have vanished without a trace, but what they didn't know was that a certain amount of these individuals had not gone missing as a result of the usual reasons, such as not wanting to be found or because they met with foul play. These individuals had been repatriated and they now lived on a similar planet to Earth's level of consciousness, but in another galaxy without the hope of ever returning to their home planet.

Rhys finished his coffee and went for a refill. He'd been reviewing the stats that had been broken down by continent, nation, city, town, ethnicity, religion, gender, age, etc. The amount of data was so massive that it was difficult to take in and make much sense of, even for highly developed life forms such as his. The irony, however, was that among those highly evolved beings he knew to be members of the League of Galaxies, none had come up with a plausible explanation as to why humans were so changeable. "Compartmentalised" truly was the best word with which to describe them—and therein lay the mystery of this particular species.

Rhys wasn't sure how long he'd been sitting, thinking while he scanned the stats, but he suddenly became aware of the pale light outside the window and realised it was dawn. He stood and stretched, rubbing his neck muscles, which had become tense. He splashed water over his face and rinsed out his mouth with a solution he had brought with him from Tyerra. It was a rather advanced liquid version of what humans called toothpaste, but the solution kept his teeth from ever decaying and his gums from ageing or contracting any kind of disease.

The need for dentists back home had become extinct hundreds of years ago.

Rhys ran his fingers through his hair as if to clear all the information he had digested in the last three or so hours and then opened the door and went outside. The air was cool, but it didn't bother him. In fact, he found it invigorating. The temperature on Tyerra was colder than that on Earth and though Rhys managed to survive Earth's summer season, especially in humid countries, he much preferred the cooler climes.

He walked along the shore letting the icy ocean water wash over his bare feet and allowed his mind to clear from the complexity of his mission as he watched the sunrise. The ball of fire was just rising over the ocean, suffusing the sky with fingers of pink, grey and yellow. Once the sun was above the horizon, the pale sky started to take on a deeper hue of azure blue. It was going to be a perfect day.

Something caught Rhys's attention and he saw from the corner of his eye a red bundle of fur charging towards him. He smiled as he watched Tom running through the surf in his direction and his heart quickened when he observed Carla following at a sedate pace wearing black track pants and a white wool pullover with a tan shawl wrapped around her shoulders. Her brown hair blew freely in the breeze and the smile on her lips was serene and yet filled with excitement. Rhys forced himself not to focus on her reaction at seeing him, but knowing she welcomed it filled him with hope.

Carla waved and before Rhys could return the greeting Tom threw himself at him, making him lose his footing and almost bringing him down into the water. Rhys steadied himself and patted the dog's ears.

"Good morning to you, too, Tom," he told the dog. "But I don't fancy a bath with my clothes on." He laughed to himself and then remembered he was still wearing pyjama pants. Luckily, they were made of plain white linen and could have passed for casual pants even though they were a bit on the light side for the chilly weather.

By the time Carla caught up with him, Tom had settled down from his excitement at seeing Rhys and the dog amused himself by chasing after some seagulls that kept circling around him.

"You're up early," Carla remarked when she finally reached him. She took in his dishevelled hair, mainly blowing across his face and momentarily hiding his eyes, and a sensation akin to desire spread from her stomach down to her pelvis. She dismissed this as pure fancy, especially because it was too soon after her breakup to think of another man. Despite this, she acknowledged her attraction to Rhys, but of course she told herself she was still on the rebound and therefore had no intention of acting on it.

Rhys had shut himself off to her thoughts as much as possible, but the energy emanating from her body gave him a good indication of what was going on in her mind. Again, he thought how much he hated having to do things the Earthly way. If they had been on Tyerra right now he would have thrown her down on the sand and made love to her as humans did.

This stopped him short for a moment and he re-examined the thought. It had been eons since Tyerrans had sex in a physical way and why this concept came into his mind in the first place was beyond him. He gave a mental shrug of dismissal —Earthly ways could be tempting at times. He smiled to cover his confusion. "Actually, I've been up and about for hours. I couldn't sleep."

Carla looked somewhat surprised. "Funny that. I woke up around three after a bad dream and couldn't get back to sleep, either, so I ended up doing a bit of work on a current project and then decided to clear my head by going for a walk and catching the sunrise."

A sudden realisation filled Rhys with alarm. What Commander had warned him about had come to pass. No matter what he did now it was simply too late. He loved this woman in such a deep and passionate way that it scared him deeply. Xaye had been his soul mate, but Carla was more than this—she was a true twin soul. She reawakened in him not only the spiritual connection that existed between two people on the same level, but also the physical, earthy side of love that Tyerrans only knew to be a part of their ancestors' culture.

5

Rhys and Carla stood in silence for a few moments and watched the sun rising above the horizon, turning the sky a clear blue.

Already feeling the mild warmth from the ball of fire above them, Carla turned her face upwards with her eyes closed, but she still held onto her shawl as the sea breeze sent a shiver through her.

Rhys watched her enjoying such a simple pleasure and he couldn't help himself when he took a step closer and without thinking of potential repercussions, he drew her to him so her back rested against his chest and his arms wrapped themselves around the front of her body. He was shocked at the intense surge of desire that shot through him as their bodies made contact.

Carla's eyes flew open and her first impulse was to pull away from him, but she didn't. Much to her surprise, she felt herself relax within his arms and she let her head rest on his shoulder. This was absolutely crazy, she thought, but she didn't care. It wasn't like she was going to have sex with the man—this stranger she'd only met a couple of days ago. She merely felt the need to be held and with Rhys she felt safe and protected. Not for one moment did she get the feeling that he could turn out to be a weirdo. She fully trusted Tom's instincts about people. If Tom took to the guy so quickly it meant Rhys was not a danger to her person. Of course, Carla ignored the fact that Tom had failed to sense Michael's psycho tendencies. Well, Tom had been too young to know better back then, but now he was a bit older and wiser, Carla smiled at the thought.

"What's the smile for?" Rhys spoke softly near her ear.

"How do you know I'm smiling when you can't see my face?" she threw at him rather than have to explain what was on her mind.

"Just a feeling," Rhys replied. His arms tightened slightly around her and she enjoyed every second until even by her own standards she realised she must put an end to this, delicious as it was. She didn't want to encourage anything with Rhys. This was not the time.

She gently disengaged herself from the embrace and turned to face him. "Thank you for sharing the sunrise with me, but now I have to go and feed Tom."

At the mention of his name, Tom, who had been preoccupied with the gulls until now, gave up on the annoying birds and bounded back to where Carla and Rhys stood.

Carla reached down to hug the dog, but pulled back instantly. "Tom, you're wet right through!"

Tom simply wagged his tail and tried to lick her face. Rhys laughed.

Carla stood and said, "I think he's hungry and so am I, for that matter."

"I'd offer you coffee and something to eat, but I don't have any dog food," Rhys invited, although he would rather Carla did not go inside his campervan lest she see some of the equipment he had brought with him from Tyerra and ask questions.

He needn't have worried, though, as Carla declined. "That's sweet, but I really must get back. I want to finish the work I started this morning. Perhaps, next time?" She gave him a quick wave and before he had a chance to say or do anything she started on her way with Tom following her.

Rhys stayed put and watched as she walked in the direction of Merry Beach and he told himself he had to get away for a couple of days, for if he saw her again too soon he would surely mess up everything. The plan was to get to know her a little at a time before he took her into his confidence. He saw no other way in which to gain her trust and he was not even sure he would be successful, either. He would obviously gloss over the real reason as to why he was on Earth, but how did one explain they're from another planet to someone who has never had contact with extraterrestrials?

***

Carla spent the rest of the day finishing the project she had been working on and prior to dinner she took Tom out for a walk to their favourite spot on the ledge. She sat there, looking pensively towards the horizon and it wasn't until Tom nudged her on the shoulder that she realised it was dusk and if they didn't hurry, they would be climbing down the cliff in the dark.

She made her way carefully along the path leading to the beach with Tom walking ahead of her with a rather rapid gait and stopping now and then to wait for her to catch up. While walking, Carla thought about the events of the morning and she tried to figure out how she felt about Rhys. He was an unusual man with an air of detachment, as if he somehow didn't belong, and yet he engaged easily whenever he was in her or Tom's company.

All she knew about Rhys was that he was a nature photographer and he travelled widely; beyond this, he was a mystery. His looks were quite unusual, but for some reason they seemed to suit him. He also carried himself with an unpretentious air of confidence that communicated he was comfortable in his own skin.

Carla had also noticed his hair colour was natural; the orange suffused with yellow and brown streaks did not come from a hairdressing salon, she thought. Up close, the roots of his hair were exactly the same colour as his hair—the orange, yellow and brown reached into his scalp, so unless he had just had his roots dyed very thoroughly, it was impossible for him to have natural roots in three different colours. And on top of this, there were his eyes—more purple than blue; very rare.

Carla would have thought little of his colouring if Rhys

had been in a rock band. Even so, his looks were undeniably unusual and she had a strong conviction that they were natural rather than contrived. Perhaps, it had something to do with his Welsh background; she remembered a few months back having done research for website content for a site on Celtic mythology in places like Cornwall, Wales, Ireland, and Scotland, to name a few. These places abounded with tales of pixies, fairies, sprites, and such. In Wales, the *pwca* was known to be a kind of nature spirit; one that lived near ancient stones and was considered a bringer of both good and bad fortune. Nature spirits were said to be able to change shape and turn into horses, goats, and rabbits —and they could also take on a human form. Carla smiled as she mused about Rhys having derived from one of these creatures. The world was full of mysteries, and Rhys seemed to be one of them.

On a more serious note, Carla thought about how she felt at his touch. When he first put his arms around her while they watched the sunrise her first instinct had been to flee. At the same time, she could not bring herself to step away from him. She had wanted him to hold her. Moreover, she somehow knew she belonged there. Yet she could not explain why she felt this way about a relative stranger she met on the beach a couple of days ago when she was still dealing with emotions of grief and lack of trust from the breakup with her ex.

Tom's bark dispelled her musings and Carla realised they had arrived at the cabin. Tom was looking at a piece of folded paper that had been left wedged into the sliding glass door. Carla knew instantly it would be from Rhys even before she retrieved and read it. The note said he had been called away to Sydney for a couple of days; he signed off with his initials, RL, and left his mobile number alongside.

Carla folded the note, trying to stem her disappointment. She then unlocked the door rather forcefully and headed straight for the kitchen to prepare Tom's dinner. She left the note on the kitchen bench, but read it several times while cooking her own dinner before she finally placed it close to her mobile phone to remind herself and add his number to her contacts list.

Around nine, as Carla sat down to watch a film, her mobile rang. She picked it up instantly, thinking it could be Rhys, but then remembered he had not asked for her number, he had only given her his. The caller ID told her it was Jana.

"So sorry to call this late," Jana apologised when Carla answered the phone. "It's been so busy here, and I worked overtime four days in a row now."

"What's happening?" Carla was glad to hear from her friend; it stopped her thinking about Rhys.

"It's the MMG account. They're in a hurry for their website, and you know this is one of the more complex projects we're working on."

"Well, no," Carla replied. "I'm not working on that one."

Jana sighed tiredly. "You may well soon be. They're looking for extra hands so we can meet the deadline."

"What are you saying?"

"I'm saying if you could cut your holiday short, it would be great."

Carla's heart sank. She didn't want to leave just yet. "I'm still working on the MakeFace site," she informed Jana. "It's actually turning out to be a bigger job than I originally thought. They recently introduced extra product lines and have the new season lipsticks and eyeshadow tones, so they asked if I could incorporate this into the site straight away."

Jana sighed again, this time in frustration. "Okay. I'll tell the boss. But you know what an arsehole he is. He'll try to pull you off that one and give it to someone more junior."

Carla felt her blood pressure rise. "I'd like to see him try! I committed to this project and I'm going to finish it. I hate it when this guy gives me stop and start jobs. It really breaks my focus, plus he thinks he can pull me in ten different directions at the same time."

"Remember who pays your bills," Jana tried to pacify her, but this had the opposite effect on Carla.

"Look," she said in a stone cold voice, which was how she

sounded when angry. "I realise you guys are my biggest client, but I still pick the projects I work on. This was part of the agreement. I do have other clients outside Meyers Media, you know. So you can tell Mr Meyer to stick it up his arse. I'm staying with MakeFace, and that's final!"

"Whoa!" Jana's tone turned to one of amusement. "You must've given Michael a really good whatfor."

For a moment Carla did not understand what Jana meant, and then she remembered. Her voice returned to normal when she spoke, "I was going to get back to you about him. He called me, and this time he got through. I simply told him to keep the money and never call again."

"And you meant it?" Jana sounded astounded.

"Of course I meant it."

"Well, I'm impressed. I don't know what happened at that magic beach of yours, but whatever it is, I want some."

Carla laughed. "Don't be silly. Nothing happened," she lied, picturing Rhys's face and knowing very well that something had happened. What had actually happened was Rhys himself. She didn't exactly know how or why, but it seemed too coincidental that the moment she met him, she somehow started to feel at peace with everything. At first, she thought it truly was the magic of Merry Beach, but now she wasn't so sure. "Look, Jana," Carla changed the subject, "just tell Meyer I'm up to my eyeballs in work. In fact, I spent most of today working on the MakeFace site. I'll probably be finished in a few days and then, if you're still busy, I can lend a hand, all right?"

"Sure, I'll tell him," Jana said. "But what happened with Michael?"

Carla didn't want to talk about Michael. It was as if Michael had never existed. "Nothing happened," she replied, hoping to end the conversation with very little explanation. "I just moved on. He gave me some cock and bull story about wanting to return the money and that he only borrowed it. Look, I really don't care anymore. He can keep the bloody money as long as he doesn't contact me again."

Jana said with admiration in her voice, "Oh man! You sound so normal."

"Yeah, well. I guess I reached the limit of my patience and came to my senses. I really don't have time for liars and thieves in my life."

"True," Jana replied. "And good on you, girl!"

"I'll ring you next week sometime and give you an update on my workload," Carla told her friend. "I'm rather tired now, so I'm going to turn in. You have a good night."

Jana said her farewells and Carla disconnected with relief. One thing she hated was to relive the past and waste the present. She had fallen into that trap with the breakup, but thankfully she managed to overcome it. Although technically she was still grieving, she felt comfort at the thought it was no longer Michael she was thinking about. It was natural to grieve the death of a relationship, and this was the stage she had now reached.

***

While Rhys was away Tom moped around the cabin and even going for walks with his mistress did not excite him as much as it used to. Carla missed Rhys, too. She still could not bring herself to admit that he was fast becoming someone she cared about, but she did miss his enigmatic presence and unassuming company. He was easygoing, relaxed, and didn't try to impress. He didn't put pressure on her to talk about herself, either. Carla liked his manner and felt they could become good friends. In fact, it occurred to her that she didn't even know whether Rhys was married or had a partner of sorts. Since he had always been alone from the time she met him, she automatically assumed he was single.

Carla managed to finish the work for MakeFace by the third evening of Rhys's departure and she decided to celebrate her achievement by making a zucchini and pumpkin quiche with bocconcini and basil. She opened a bottle of red wine, even though she was not a big drinker and would only have one glass, and she decided to treat Tom to steak—the thing he loved most of all, but only got to eat on special occasions. At least, his favourite dish had the effect of perking up his low spirits and his tail couldn't stop wagging.

It was a lovely evening out, not too cold, so after their meal Carla took Tom for a walk along the beach, and without thinking she headed towards Kioloa. She knew Rhys hadn't returned yet, otherwise, she was sure he would have dropped by to say hello. Going to Kioloa, however, was an unconscious move on her part and one she didn't particularly want to change when she realised this was her destination. Besides, Tom ran like the wind in the direction of Rhys's campervan and there was nothing Carla could do to stop him.

The moonless night gave way to an indigo sky studded with millions of twinkling stars and planets, and Carla paused to take in the gorgeous backdrop this made against the dark water on the beach. The ocean sparkled here and there with the reflection of the brighter stars, and for a while Carla enjoyed the solitude of being the only person out and about, appreciating the show Mother Nature had put on for her.

A sudden scraping noise against metal caught her attention and she turned away from the beautiful vista to catch Tom scratching at Rhys's door. "Get away from there, Tom!" she called out.

Tom ignored her and kept scratching at the campervan door.

"Okay. You're being really naughty now, so no more steak for you for a whole month!" she threatened.

The dog still ignored her and Carla sighed and started in his direction, but stopped short when the door opened of its own volition and Tom flew straight into the van. Carla hurried her step and poked her head in the doorway. "Hello! Anyone home?"

There was no answer, except for a happy bark from Tom.

"Tom, come away! You can't go breaking into people's vans."

Tom was too busy sniffing around the place, his tail wagging excitedly. Carla sighed again, not knowing what to do. She looked around the caravan park and felt a little spooked. The place was quiet and although the public lights were on, all the caravans were in darkness, which meant the place was devoid of occupants.

Carla felt goose bumps on her arms, and on impulse she joined Tom inside Rhys's cabin and shut the door behind her as she switched on the interior light. She took a quick look around, but saw nothing out of the ordinary. The van was clean and uncluttered. At first, Carla thought Rhys had left for good, but on closer inspection she noticed a few of his clothes hanging in a small closet with its door partly open. She reached in, pulled out his cable-knit pullover and brought it to her face, taking in the fresh scent of the sea mixed with a subtle soapy vanilla aroma. She felt her face grow warm at the intimacy of what she was doing and replaced the garment immediately.

Tom had finished exploring the small place and simply sat waiting for his mistress. Carla did not see anything of interest. No computer, no photographic equipment. Nothing. But then, Rhys had said he was attending to business in Sydney; therefore, it made sense he would take his equipment with him. And good thing, too, she thought. After all, Rhys had either forgotten to lock his van or the lock was faulty, so anyone could have walked in and taken anything of value.

"Come on, boy, let's get out of here," she said to Tom at the same time as she happened to catch a glimpse of an object resting on the dinette seat. She picked it up and held it in the palm of her hand. It looked like a USB stick with a small black screen. There were no buttons on the device nor was there a lid she could pull off. It simply looked like a shiny black domino piece minus the white dots. She turned it around in her hand for a few moments and almost dropped it when the screen suddenly lit up to a bright green colour. "What can this be for?" she asked herself aloud. Something about the object made her feel she was being listened to, but there was no evidence of a microphone or speaker on the device, either. A wild thought crossed her mind that Rhys was not, as he said, a photographer, but some kind of spook working for ASIO.

"Nah." Carla dismissed the thought, talking to herself, "That's just too weird. It's probably some fandangled meter to measure the light intensity when Rhys takes his photographs." She placed the device where she found it and turned to Tom. "Come on, boy. Time to go home."

Tom, bored because he hadn't found anything exciting in the van, didn't need a second prompting and he shot out of the vehicle and went for a run down the beach while Carla switched off the light and locked up. She slammed the door with force and this seemed to engage the lock properly. She was glad she had done Rhys a small service by ensuring his van was now secure until his return.

6

Rhys returned to Kioloa the following morning and instantly knew someone had been in his van, and who it was. He didn't have much time to think about this, though, because the moment he put down his travel bag and equipment he spotted the thumb communicator with its screen lit up. He had thought it was in his pocket when he left, but he never checked and now he realised the device probably slipped out onto the seat while he had been sitting at the dinette. He picked up the device and placed it on the kitchen counter while he prepared some much-needed coffee.

"I warned you about his," Commander's voice rang inside Rhys's head. "You're already losing your focus."

"The communicator slipped out of my pocket," Rhys explained, although he knew his excuse sounded lame.

"Only because you were in such a rush to get away from your friend," Commander chastised him. "She was in your van last night, you know. Apparently, you didn't lock your door properly and the dog managed to get it open."

Rhys did not respond. Instead, he blocked any thoughts of Carla while he communicated with Commander. It was almost impossible to hide anything from him.

"I'm thinking of replacing you on this mission, Rhys. You've lost your objectivity," Commander sounded disappointed.

Rhys forgot all about hiding his thoughts then. "No! You're wrong. I haven't lost my focus at all. The situation's complex on Earth. The League of Galaxies doesn't realise the most important thing about humans."

"And what is that?"

Commander was merely humouring him; after all, he knew exactly what Rhys was going to say. Knowing this, however, Rhys still said it. "Their psyche is highly compartmentalised. It's not a black and white issue with them. There always seems to be a huge grey area in between. So we must be sure about the whole thing before we proceed with a decision."

"You're not telling me something I don't already know," Commander replied in a more understanding manner. "Don't forget we, too, descend from Homo sapiens."

Rhys put one sugar in a mug and poured the strong coffee to the rim. "I've been reviewing the data," he reported, "And I'm just not convinced humans are the entire problem."

This time, Commander seemed surprised. "What do you mean?"

Rhys took a few sips of the scalding drink and waited for a few moments. It felt so good to get the hot liquid into him —it also gave him time to formulate his response. "The League thinks what we're doing is for the greater good of other evolved planets. But has anyone stopped to think the negative energy we ourselves emit is partly a result of the fact that the League annihilated other planets in the past, just like this one? And they honestly believe the evil energy now eating at the fabric of consciousness solely emanates from what Earthlings are doing to their own planet?"

There was a long pause from Commander and Rhys waited. Finally, Commander responded brusquely, "You're getting ahead of yourself, and let me remind you that the decision is not yours to make."

Rhys slammed down his mug on the kitchen bench, spilling hot coffee onto his fingers. "None of you have been living among humans for any length of time. It's easy for you to wrap this up in a neat little package and blame conditions on Earth for the erosion of the fabric of consciousness. Let's not forget, however, the past actions of the League. Do you honestly believe destroying other so-called evil planets in the past scored any positive energy for united consciousness?"

Rhys rinsed his fingers in cold water and then went on drinking his coffee while Commander replied, "You would never have thought like this before. Don't forget you were involved in some of those decisions."

"Yes. I haven't forgotten, but I'm not proud of what we've done."

"It's Carla, isn't it?" Commander brought the topic back to her. "She's too much like Xaye. Your love for her is blinding you."

Rhys didn't bother to hide the extent of his feelings for Carla this time. Let Commander make what he liked of it. "She's much more than Xaye. She's truly a twin soul, and no matter what happens, I'm staying with her. This is the first time in decades since I have the opportunity to find happiness and even if it's short lived, I'm definitely staying on Earth if she'll have me." His defiant response made Commander pause in thought for a while, but Rhys could not read his mind. Commander was far too powerful.

When Commander communicated again he sounded more like the father Rhys had known since he was young. "You know you're the son I never had, and I was honoured when I was allowed to adopt you. You're not only gifted, but you're intensely sensitive to others' feelings and emotions. I guess this is what makes you so special and I don't want to lose you."

Rhys sighed. "And I don't want to lose Carla."

"I have nothing against her, you know that. I felt her energy when she was in your van and it was beautiful, although she's suffered greatly. But now she's healing inside and you were responsible for this in a big way. She's a strong woman and she's the right one for you, I give you that much. You forget, though, that she's not evolved like us and she would never be able to survive on Tyerra."

Rhys nodded as if Commander were standing in front of him and not light years away. "I agree. But there's nothing stopping me from staying on Earth to be with her."

"Despite the fact the League might vote to annihilate?"

Rhys nodded again. "Yes, despite that."

Commander went on, "And even if Earth were spared, you'll have a short lifespan like all Earthlings. You won't live the long life we have on Tyerra."

Rhys sighed, tired of having to justify himself. "I'd rather live the next thirty or forty years with Carla than be eight hundred years old and still feel empty and alone."

Now it was Commander's turn to sigh. "We'll discuss this another time. Meanwhile, send what you can of the data. We must find a solution to see if we can repair this weakening of consciousness. I'm already getting reports from some of the planets in the League about violence, sudden episodes of climatic change, and even war activity. This hasn't happened in hundreds of years."

Rhys didn't want to know any more. He wanted to end the discussion so he could go in search of Carla.

Commander read him loud and clear, and said, "Go to her and tell her the truth about who you are. I think she loves you, my son, but you won't know how much until she knows where you come from."

Commander shut off his signal and Rhys watched as the thumb communicator screen went black. It had been a while since Commander had called him 'son'.

***

Carla finished breakfast on the veranda and felt sleepy. The weather had turned mild and the sunshine enveloped her in its warmth. She lay back on a deckchair and rested her head against the back support, her face turned towards the sun with eyes closed.

She had probably dropped off because all of a sudden she was startled into wakefulness by Tom's mad barking. Her eyes flew open just in time to see the dog take off in the direction of the beach towards the lone figure walking on the sand.

Carla tried to compose herself as her eyes rested on Rhys, who was being greeted by Tom most effusively. She smiled at Rhys's attempts to calm down the dog while he wiped off the sand clinging to his pullover—the one she had sunk her nose into the previous evening.

Rhys waved to her as he started to make his way in her direction with a very excitable Tom, who kept jumping on his hind legs every now and then to try and lick Rhys's face. Carla waved back and went into the kitchen to put on some coffee.

By the time Rhys reached the veranda, Carla was coming out of the kitchen with the coffee things and a platter of mixed fruit.

"Welcome back," she greeted him. "I see Tom's happy of your return." She laughed as she took in the paw marks on Rhys's pullover. "Apologies for those," she said, a little more seriously. "I'll launder it for you. Tom got sand all over it."

Rhys smiled and patted the dog. "No problem. It'll come off easily enough with a bit of water. The fact you made coffee makes up for everything."

Carla invited him to sit and he took the chair opposite hers. She served the coffee and offered him fruit. Rhys took a bunch of green grapes from the fruit platter and munched on them in between sips of coffee. Carla noticed how Tom sat down on the floor next to Rhys's chair and put his head down for a snooze.

"Well, at least he's calm now," she observed.

Rhys glanced at the sleeping Tom. "It looks like he missed me."

"Yes," Carla admitted. "He sure did. In fact, last night he broke into your campervan. I hope you don't mind. I assume the lock didn't engage properly when you left, so I went inside in search of Tom and then relocked the door."

Rhys appreciated her honesty. Anyone else might have kept quiet in case he thought they had gone in to snoop around. Of course, he knew Carla had sniffed the scent of his pullover, and she also found the thumb communicator, but he wasn't going to embarrass her by telling her this. He had a more important thing to tell her; although right now, he was not sure how she would take it. Chances were she'd freak out and never want to see him again.

"Thanks for doing that. I did notice the faulty lock, but I was sure I locked it properly. Anyway, good thing you happened to be around."

"I found myself walking in that direction and Tom took off and started pawing at the van's door." She took a sip of her coffee and waited a few moments before continuing. "Did you have a good trip? You must've been busy because you look a little tired."

Rhys finished his coffee in one gulp and picked an apricot from the fruit platter. "I'll have an early night and catch up on my sleep. I needed to focus on a big project and thought my home office would help. Out here, I simply feel like going for long walks, plus now that I discovered you're an excellent coffee maker, I can't keep away." He smiled as he gazed into her eyes, trying for once to read her thoughts.

Since he had left, she had undergone a transformation. She now acknowledged to herself that she wanted to be his friend. She felt comfortable with him and even trusted him to some extent, mainly thanks to Tom's senses. She found him attractive, but was resisting the impulse of further involvement. While all this boded well for him, the problem now was that he was going to risk losing her trust when he told her the truth of his origins.

While he thought about how to broach the subject, Rhys kept his eyes on Carla and after a few moments he sensed she grew uncomfortably warm.

"More coffee?" Carla offered in order to break the spell his intense gaze cast on her.

Rhys reached across the table and took hold of her hand before she had a chance to pick up the coffee pot. She looked at him in surprise.

"Carla," Rhys plunged in, hoping for the best. "There's something really important I need to tell you about me. In fact, there are a number of things I wish to share with you, but I need you to keep an open mind and hear me out. Some of what I say will be difficult for you to believe."

Carla left her hand in his. It felt so good to be touched by him. To cover her sudden confusion, she said with jocularity, "Don't tell me, you're married with ten kids."

Rhys regarded her with laughter in his eyes. "Not at all, but I used to be married until I lost my wife in an accident. And no, there were no kids."

Carla gave his hand a comforting squeeze. "I'm sorry, Rhys. That must have been so tough on you."

Rhys shrugged, a little unsure of how to continue. "It was a long time ago." In fact, it had been something like three Earth decades, Rhys thought. Time on Tyerra passed much more slowly than on Earth, but he wasn't going to go into this right now.

Still with her hand in his, Carla prompted, "So what is it you want to tell me?"

Rhys looked for a way to start and realised this was going to go down like a lead balloon, no matter how he put it. He sighed as Carla waited with a look of expectancy in her eyes. "Carla," he finally spoke, his tone soft but direct. "I'm not who you think I am. I'm not really a nature photographer, either; although I do take photos." Rhys saw the query in her eyes, but her hand still stayed in his and she waited for whatever else he had to say. "The thing is, I work for a high profile organisation and I'm here gathering data for a major project."

The beginnings of a smile showed on Carla's face. "So you are a spook after all!" she exclaimed, confirming her earlier thoughts. "You're with ASIO, right?"

Rhys sighed again. "It's... It's a little more complicated than that."

This time, Carla withdrew her hand and leaned back on her chair. "So who are you?" Her tone reflected the fact that she did not like playing games, not that he was trying to play a game. Carla was a straightforward kind of person and Rhys knew she favoured the black and white of a discussion and disliked the grey areas.

He pressed on, trying to make the explanation more direct. "You've never heard of this particular organisation, but they gather data from all over space—you know, like NASA." Carla nodded. It looked like she could relate to this. Encouraged, Rhys went on, "Well, I'm one of their operatives or you might call me a field agent. Basically, I'm an information gatherer. I look at everything in the world—events, natural and human conditions, statistics on a whole bunch of things..." Rhys paused when he saw a light of doubt in her gaze. For once, he could not pick up on her thoughts. He was too emotionally involved to focus on what she was thinking.

"Okay," she said. "You're some kind of observer gathering info. So what? At least you're not a criminal or some sort of double agent selling secret information to the highest bidder, right?"

Rhys hesitated, but forced himself to continue, "You're right. I'm none of those things." Now to the crux of the matter, he thought. "I guess it's not so much who I am or who I'm not—it's more where I come from."

"From Wales," Carla filled in for him.

Rhys shook his head. "Not quite. That's just my persona. It's my Earth identity, you might say."

The sudden look of astonishment in Carla's eyes told Rhys understanding had dawned on what he was trying to say, but as he predicted, Carla was having trouble processing it. She didn't speak for a few moments and gazed at him as though for the first time. It was like she was looking for something quite out of the ordinary with his appearance. He knew she thought his overall looks were a little strange, but he still descended from exactly the same species as hers. The only difference was that his ancestors had evolved much more quickly even though their DNA makeup was identical to that of humans.

Carla leaned forward from across the table and looked more closely into his eyes. "Your pupils are not dilated, which means you can't be on drugs," she stated in a serious tone that verged on anger. "So are you trying to tell me that you're not from this planet?" Putting it into words made it sound even more preposterous than thinking about it, and Carla decided that in hindsight she would probably have chosen the vampire theory instead. At least, vampires were from Earth.

Rhys went to take her hand again, but she drew back from him. He sighed, feeling disappointed for not handling this at all well. At the same time, he hadn't expected her to accept it first time around. She needed time—time they may not have. "I know how this must sound, but please believe me when I tell you there are many of us who've come and gone from this planet since the beginning of your civilisation."

Carla threw him a suspicious look. "And are you some horrible little creature hiding inside a human body like in the movie 'Alien'? Is that it? Are you going to suddenly turn into some slimy organism and attack me?"

Rhys felt laughter bubble up, but forced it back down. Laughing would be inappropriate at this most delicate of moments. "No. I'm just like you," he pointed out with sincerity, wanting her to see he was telling the truth. "We share the same DNA. We're also Homo sapiens, only our DNA was picked up eons ago by other extraterrestrials exploring this part of the galaxy, and they ended colonising Tyerra with it."

Carla's tone was cold when she replied, "Is this some big joke at my expense?"

Rhys went to reassure her this was not the case, but she didn't give him the chance to speak. "Do you know what the word 'tierra' means in English?"

Rhys nodded. He also thought it ironic. "Although it's spelled differently in your alphabet 'tierra' is the Spanish word for 'earth'."

This didn't seem to appease Carla. "And you're still serious. You're not putting me on?"

Rhys gazed at her with an open and honest look in his eyes. "I swear to you I'm telling the truth. I realise this is difficult to take in, seeing as most Earthlings haven't made contact with space visitors. But the universe is infinite, with billions of planets, so how could anyone believe Earth is the only planet that holds humanlike life?"

Carla stood so abruptly that her chair scraped loudly against the timber deck and the sound awoke Tom. She glanced at the dog and then at Rhys. "I have no idea what to believe. But I do know you can speak with animals. Tom's been talking about me to you. Good god! For all I know, you can read minds, too; and you know all about me! How mortifying for me and how very interesting and amusing for you!" She was on the verge of tears, but hell if she was going to let them fall in his presence. "Leave now!"

Rhys stood, his hands extended in supplication. "You're right in that I can read minds and speak with animals, but I made a point of not focusing on your thoughts. I didn't want to intrude. You must believe me, Carla. I have nothing but the warmest regard for you. In fact, it goes deeper than that, and I have feelings ..."

But he didn't get to finish what he was going to say, because Carla stepped in the doorway of the cabin, ordered Tom inside, and then said to Rhys, "I thought Earth men were bastards, but it seems you males are all the same, all over the friggin' universe: liars and cheats!" She then slid the door shut so hard that Rhys thought the glass would shatter.

He stood there for a moment, feeling the fury emanating from her. Then, he turned to go. Hopefully, when she cooled down, she would give him another chance to explain.

The last thing Rhys saw as he turned one last time towards the door were the tears rolling down Carla's face and a very subdued Tom, his butterscotch eyes pleading with him not to go from their lives.

7

Carla drove as though the hounds of hell were after her or in this case, the aliens from who knew where.

When she shut the door on Rhys's face, after he dropped his bombshell news, she packed her bags, loaded the car with all her and Tom's belongings, bundled a confused Tom into the backseat and set off for home to the mountains.

She skipped lunch, too upset to eat, and by the time she left Merry Beach it was late afternoon, which meant she should have eaten something before tackling the four-hour drive home. It was now close to seven in the evening and her stomach grumbled. She still had a couple more hours to go before she reached the Blue Mountains.

Tom had so far stayed in the backseat through the trip, which was most unusual as he loved riding up front with her. Carla knew he was upset at their hasty departure, but this could not be helped. She had to sort out her feelings about what had occurred and this meant she needed to put some distance between Rhys and herself.

She took a quick peek in the rearview mirror. "Are you hungry, boy?"

Tom regarded her with sad eyes, but he did not respond. Carla sighed and made a point of keeping a lookout for the next service station where she could stop and buy coffee and something to eat. She had Tom's dinner with her and would feed him then. The dog had not eaten anything all day, just like herself, and they made a poor looking pair—both sad, tired, and still in shock.

Carla sensed Tom's energy so strongly that she was quite

surprised. Normally, she was sensitive to the feelings of animals, but Tom's emotions right now overwhelmed her. In addition to this, she had to try and keep her own feelings under control.

The shock she experienced at Rhys's disclosure shook her right to the core. It was bad enough being told that he was not what she believed him to be—a photographer—and that he worked for some secret organisation. But to discover he was not from Earth destroyed every belief she had ever held in the past about life in the universe—and she wasn't even religious! She could just imagine what someone who believed in God would have thought. The whole thing was too big to take in. It challenged everything she had ever been taught or thought to be true. It felt like she had lived her whole life without any real knowledge of the cosmos. Science, as she knew it, didn't make sense anymore. There was so much she did not understand, and it was no wonder she came away like a shell-shocked soldier after a war.

Knowing there were other life forms out there changed all paradigms in relation to her life on Earth. It was like she had been living in a small village during the dark ages with the strong conviction that it was the centre of the world. Then, rather abruptly, she would find herself transported forward in time to a major city with its hustle and bustle, the many conveniences, stores, theatres, restaurants, TVs, radios, Smartphones, computers and other high-tech gadgets, modern transportation, including those that fly through the air, escalators, elevators, and the list went on. Anybody would be totally overwhelmed if this happened. They would be shocked, frightened, and think it was some kind of a hellish nightmare or they would simply lose their sanity forever.

How could she hope to cope with the implications of all Rhys had revealed up to this point? To make matters even more complicated, she was sure he had been about to tell her how he felt towards her. In fact, she was certain he loved her. She didn't know how she knew this, except she felt it within herself and much to her surprise, she reciprocated the feeling. The knowledge spooked her. She had never known anybody for such a short time and come to feel this way plus sense his emotions at the same time. She had convinced herself that all she felt for Rhys was friendship and physical attraction, and while she was happy to be friends with him at the time, she had no intentions to act on the matter of her attraction for Rhys. Now, she realised in a kind of surreal epiphany that she had been foolish not to recognise her true feelings; what she and Rhys had between them went much deeper than mere friendship.

If she believed in soul mates, destiny, kismet, karma or whatever people called it, she would have been able to accept quite easily that Rhys was a twin soul—her other half. And if she'd been more open with her inner emotions she would have acknowledged the feeling immediately for what it was. Instead, she had played with the idea that it was simply an attraction to Rhys's looks.

So where did she go from here? Certainly not to another planet! This sounded so ridiculous that she didn't even want to contemplate the thought of it. She had at least admitted her connection to Rhys was spiritual or predestined, if such things were true, but she was not yet ready to entertain the idea that he was an extraterrestrial being. This was too far out, and yet she knew he had told her the truth.

Rhys had said something about his race descending from Homo sapiens and that their DNA was the same as humans. All this, however, went right over her head. She didn't even know where his planet was. Tyerra, he had called it. Where the hell was that? And how did Rhys get to Earth? Surely not in a flying saucer! This was just too corny; too preposterous; too unbelievable; and too weird.

Luckily, up ahead, Carla noticed the sign for a Shell station and she gladly focused on more mundane things like food and coffee. She turned into the station and parked the car near the building. When she opened the back door for Tom, he jumped out without being prompted and headed for a grassy area adjacent to the building so he could empty his bladder.

Meanwhile, Carla set up a dish for him with kibble near her parked car and filled a bowl with drinking water for him.

Tom came back from his toilet trip and after sniffing his dinner he decided to eat. Carla left him happily munching away while she went inside the building to buy coffee and a packed sandwich. She also purchased a couple of bottles of drinking water, milk, and bread so she would have fresh supplies for breakfast in the morning.

Carla rejoined Tom at the car and consumed her sandwich and coffee while the dog finished off the last of his kibble and drank a half bowl of water. He then went for another visit to the grassy area while Carla headed for the ladies toilet. When she returned, Tom had already settled himself in the backseat. Carla started the car and pulled out onto the road. Feeling refreshed and with her hunger sated, she made good time to the mountains without the need for further stops.

***

Rhys lay wide-awake in his bunk. It was still early, just after nine, but after the day's emotional turmoil plus his need to rest from his work trip to Sydney, he figured an early night would do him good. Thoughts of Carla's reaction kept haunting him, however, and he allayed his fears by telling himself she would need time to take it all in. If only she had given him another chance to explain. But this was not to be, at least not for the present. He was tempted to tune into her thoughts and had to force himself to think of something else. He wasn't sure he wanted to know what she was thinking right now.

As if on cue, the message notification on his mobile told him he had a text. Rhys knew this would be from Carla even before he read the message; it said: *Gone back home. This is too much to take in. It's best if we don't meet anymore. I wish you all the best. Carla.*

He put down the phone, feeling distraught. She didn't want to see him again, not even to give him a chance to explain fully. His disappointment hit him in the chest with a pain that was hard to bear. Why did she not realise they were meant to be together? They were like two halves of a whole, but she didn't know it.

Of course, Rhys had no intention of giving up on her. He knew exactly where she lived as he had followed Tom's energy while Carla drove home. Through the dog's eyes, Rhys saw the whole journey to the mountains. He purposely shut off his focus on Carla, but he picked up a lot from Tom, including the dog's own sadness at having departed so suddenly.

Rhys saw them stop at the Shell station, Carla eating her sandwich and washing it down with coffee, Tom eating his kibble. Later, when they pulled up at the mountain cottage, Rhys saw the name and number of the street where she lived and he decided to wait a few days to allow her to cool off before going to see her—and this time, he would do whatever it took to get her to listen.

The strain of the day plus his resolve to seek out Carla lulled Rhys into the deep sleep he needed. He slept straight through to the next morning and awoke feeling refreshed and full of optimism about his chances with her.

He showered and dressed before putting on a pot of coffee. When ready, he poured himself a mug and opened the door of his campervan to the beautiful sunny day. With coffee mug in hand, he made his way to the beach and sat on the sand. His mind was clear and for the first time in days he felt relaxed. This was until someone tapped him on the shoulder and he turned to see a tall, powerfully built, bald black man smiling down at him through emerald green eyes.

Rhys made to get up, but the man sat next to him instead. "You don't mind if I join you, do you?" said Commander in a deep, resonant voice.

Rhys shook his head in disbelief. "So you're doing this the human way now?"

Commander laughed good-heartedly. "You know what they say over here: *When in Rome, do as the Romans do.*"

Rhys couldn't help but smile with genuine amusement. He noted Commander was even wearing Earth clothes; a khaki green pullover and black cargo pants. "So did you come to fetch me?" Rhys remarked in a vaguely defiant tone.

Commander shook his head. "Nothing of the sort." He paused to take in the clear morning and the sparkling ocean in front of him. "You know, I forgot how beautiful this planet really is. Last time I was here, Australia had not yet been discovered by Captain Cook."

This was news to Rhys and he raised an eyebrow in curiosity. "You never told me you'd been here before."

Commander smiled enigmatically. "There's a lot about me you don't know."

"I guess you only told me what you wanted to reveal," Rhys quipped. "So why are you here?" This was said in a matter-of-fact tone. Rhys usually managed to hide his thoughts and emotions from Commander as long as he kept his mind busy with something else. In this instance, he simply thought of the ocean and its marine life.

"You really like dolphins, don't you?" Commander stated aloud, while telling Rhys silently that he knew what his son was trying to do.

"There was no need for you to come all the way simply to admire the dolphins in my head. I'm sure you're going to tell me what is going on sooner or later." Rhys kept his tone neutral and sipped his coffee.

"That smells good," Commander uttered, ignoring Rhys's smart remark. "You'll have to make me one and let me judge for myself."

Rhys stood up. "By all means. Come to the van."

They made their way back to the campervan and Rhys poured the still hot coffee into a mug and added one sugar. "If it's too strong I can mix it with milk; some people like it that way."

Commander took the mug from Rhys and had a sip; then another. He smiled. "Actually, this is just right, thanks. I guess I'll have to take some back with me now."

Rhys remained silent, waiting for Commander to tell him the reason for his sudden visit.

"Let's go back out to the beach. I like sitting on the sand." Commander led the way back to where they had been sitting earlier.

They sat side by side and enjoyed their drinks in silence. After a while, Commander spoke. "Rhys, I actually came over to make sure you're okay."

This surprised Rhys because it was the last thing he had expected to hear. "Why now?"

"We've grown apart for the past few years and I missed seeing my son." Commader's tone sounded sincere.

Rhys was touched. "I agree we've grown apart," he conceded. "It was when the League of Galaxies went against my advice to spare the planet Prima," he reminded Commander even though he knew he didn't have to.

Commander nodded. "You're right, of course. We didn't see eye to eye on that one, either, and perhaps we should have taken longer to reflect on it."

Rhys looked directly into his adopted father's eyes. "Are you saying you're having second thoughts about Earth?"

Commander savoured his drink before he replied, "I'm not saying anything as yet, except I recommended the League give you more time to submit your recommendations. I realise there are complexities with this species. The League understands this and they've agreed to wait a while longer given we share similar ancestry with them."

Rhys finished his drink before he spoke. "The species' ancestry is not similar to our own; it's identical. They just didn't evolve as quickly as we did."

Commander had to nod in agreement, but added, "Nor do they live as long as we do."

Rhys sighed. "They simply haven't developed the kind of technology we did to keep us alive for so long, that's all."

"And this is why life is cheap on Earth," Commander interjected with a frown.

"How can you say that?" Rhys argued. "They may not live as long as we do, but their feelings and emotions are the same as ours."

Commander sighed. "That may be so, but look at how they're treating the planet. They have massive issues with global warming, huge inequality in the standards of living, not to mention the violence—crime, wars, terrorism to name a few, and then there's the mass exodus of refugees from the Middle East and Africa; human trafficking of refugees, sex slaves, labour slaves; need I go on? The problem is no one seems to know how to stop this, nor do they seem to want to take responsibility for their fellow man. All this and more makes it obvious life is very cheap on this planet. Frankly, I don't know if there's a solution to the amount of negativity these issues generate, but the erosion to the fabric of consciousness is real and it's affecting other planets. So I hope for your sake we find a way to save Earth—if it's worth saving, that is."

"You hope?" Rhys uttered, a frown marring his otherwise smooth forehead. "There's a solution to every problem if we try hard enough to find one."

"That may be, but the League doesn't always agree."

Rhys stood abruptly. "The League! Who made them the decision makers, I'd like to know? It's easy for them to vote for annihilation when they don't like something about a planet, so they destroy it at the press of a button and never have to worry about it again."

Commander stood, too, towering over Rhys by a head. "You forget yourself sometimes," he berated his son. "This is not something the League takes lightly. They don't make decisions without thinking things through properly."

Rhys shrugged and turned towards the campervan with Commander following behind him. "That's your opinion."

Commander sighed with frustration. "You've been here too long, Rhys, and you're under the spell of an Earthling, which means your judgement is clouded."

Rhys stopped short and Commander almost slammed into

him. "Don't bring Carla into this!" Rhys replied heatedly. "My thoughts about the League are well known to you, and we had the same argument prior to Prima's destruction. I assure you my judgement is not at all clouded."

Rhys continued striding towards the campervan and when he reached it he placed his mug in the small kitchen sink. Commander leaned in and rested his on the counter. The men stood outside the door of the van, facing each other.

"Let me remind you our decisions are made for the greater good," Commander stated tersely. "Annihilating those planets stopped the erosion to the fabric of consciousness and doing the same thing to Earth now may stop it again."

Rhys felt hot anger rise up from his stomach and spread through his chest. "Has it ever occurred to you that the evil energy we're experiencing at present could be a remnant of the League's own actions in the past?"

Commander seemed taken aback. "What are you saying?"

"I'm saying this whole problem may have nothing to do with Earth. The causal effect could be the result of past actions on behalf of the League," Rhys stated hotly. "You know what they say on Earth? If you kill a person, you annihilate a whole universe. So ask yourself what the effect would be if you destroy a whole planet with all its living organisms!"

Commander went to respond, anger flashing in his green eyes, but he held back and took a deep breath instead. Rhys stood his ground and waited. When he recovered his composure, Commander gazed at Rhys with sadness and love in his eyes. "You're young and inexperienced compared to those in the League, and like the young everywhere in this universe you think there's a simple solution to everything. It's not that easy, Rhys. Look at us now, we're arguing—full of anger and resentment. This is exactly how Earthlings behave in a disagreement. I thought we were more evolved than this, but being on this planet is affecting us, too."

Rhys went to reply, but Commander held up a hand for silence. "No, my son. Don't say anything we'll both regret later.

I'll leave you now. Take good care and we'll await your report."

Commander took one last look at the young man he had loved as his own son for so many years; then, he turned and walked away.

8

After his argument with Commander, Rhys spent the next couple of days feeling guilty at having disappointed his only parent. Commander had brought him up as his own son after the loss of Rhys's own parents, and now Rhys had let him down.

Despite this, he admitted that what he said to Commander had merit. The League was ready to condemn Earth for the problems they faced with the fabric of consciousness, but in reality no one had really stopped to think as to whether some of this negative and destructive energy resulted from past annihilations favoured by the League.

Perhaps, Commander was right in saying Rhys was taking too much upon himself, but Rhys felt strongly about his position, and this had nothing to do with his love for Carla. In his opinion, Earth was not necessarily responsible for the outbreaks of violence and other catastrophes taking place on other planets. After all, no one was perfect; no matter how much more evolved they were than Earthlings.

The weather turned after Commander's departure and the past two days had been quite cold with grey skies and lashing rain. Rhys stayed mostly inside the campervan working on his report and trying to justify why Earth should be spared, but his mind was not on his work and his thoughts kept turning to Carla. He missed her so much it hurt. The strange thing was that even though they hadn't known each other long it felt as though they had been together forever.

Rhys knew this to be the result of their strong connection, and perhaps the fabric of consciousness had not broken down altogether, he mused. All beings were connected at some level, only they didn't know it unless they were highly evolved—and even then it was difficult to know for sure. With Carla, however, he had known the moment he'd set eyes on her—and it wasn't because Carla could have been Xaye's twin. This had been a strange coincidence, to be sure, but not the reason why Rhys recognised Carla as a twin soul.

When he went to sleep that night, he had disturbing dreams of being separated from Carla. Earth had been destroyed and somehow Commander managed to save him, but Carla had perished along with her planet. Rhys felt overwhelmed by the loss and grief, but much to his relief he awoke, finding himself sitting up in bed.

He glanced at the clock on the wall and saw it was almost five in the morning. The prospect of spending another day without seeing Carla was too much and suddenly he was up and getting ready to leave. He showered and dressed, had breakfast, packed his clothes and equipment—this time ensuring he left nothing behind—and then dropped off the van keys through the mail slot at the Caravan Park Office before he set off for the mountains. He was paid up in advance for two more weeks, but he wasn't coming back. His only thought right now was to see Carla and convince her to give him a chance.

***

Carla had all the heaters going in her cottage in order to keep warm from the raging storm outside. There had been a sprinkling of snow in the early morning and the main highway running through the mountains was closed, but by now the snow melted, even though the mountains were being lashed with torrents of rain.

It was just after lunch and Carla sat at the desk in her study with Tom curled up in front of the heater. She had made coffee and sipped on the hot liquid while she dealt with some of the extra work Jana had sent to her subsequent to their last discussion regarding the MMG account. Now that the MakeFace project was finished, Carla could spare a few days to help out.

The sound of the wind blowing furiously and driving the rain against the window panes in the cottage made Carla want to curl up in bed and have a long sleep. She sighed and forced herself to keep working, however, knowing at the back of her mind that sooner or later the power could go out and she would have to stop.

It was a good thing she had gas heating and cooking; at least she and Tom would be comfortable and well fed even if there was a blackout. She also owned a small generator to keep the hot water heater operating in the bathroom in case she wanted to take a shower, but working with the computer and having lights on would eat up the fuel in the generator too quickly, so she didn't use it for any other purpose. If the lights went out, she favoured candlelight.

By around three in the afternoon the intensity of the storm turned the sky a dark slate grey and Carla pulled down the blinds in the cottage and switched on her desk lamp. She had not seen such a wild storm in years and was amazed that the electricity was still going. She continued working, totally focused on what she was doing, but within minutes the power failed and she lost her internet connection. She wasn't sorry this happened; she had managed to get through a huge load of work and was now due for a break.

"Wake up, Tom." She patted the sleeping dog and switched off the heater in the study. "You can move to the loungeroom and keep napping there."

Tom did not argue and made his way to the lounge only to flop in front of the even bigger heater in there while his mistress went about lighting hurricane lamps and candles. Although the storm was blowing a gale there was thankfully no thunder, which frightened Tom so. Carla closed the doors to contain the warmth in the room, leaving the kitchen door ajar, and went to put on more coffee. She felt rather peckish and was debating on whether to make herself a sandwich when she heard a faint knocking coming from the front door and Tom's loud barking.

She poked her head in the lounge to find Tom scraping at the closed door that led to the front door foyer. Even before she opened the lounge door to let Tom out, she knew who it was standing outside in the raging rain. She sighed and made her way to let him in.

The moment she opened the door she found a dripping wet Rhys being welcomed by a delighted Tom, who jumped up on hind legs while his front paws rested against Rhys's chest, almost knocking him off balance.

"Tom!" Carla called loudly. "Get off right now!"

Tom obeyed, but stayed by Rhys's side as Carla invited him inside the foyer. "Just stay here for a moment," she said to Rhys while she ignored her pounding heartbeat. "I'll be back with some towels. Take off your shoes."

Carla disappeared through the lounge door before Rhys could speak, but Tom was not giving him much of a chance to say or do anything, in any case. The dog was so happy to see him that while Rhys kicked off his shoes he patted the animal to calm him down and reassure him he was back—at least, for the present.

Carla returned with two towels; she gave Rhys a large one so he could dry himself and used the second one to dry Tom, who was wriggling like mad, wanting to stay close to Rhys.

"My bags are in the jeep," Rhys informed her. "I have to go back out to get some dry clothes."

"Not now," Carla replied. "It's crazy out there. I have some old clothes my ex left behind, so throw the towel around you and come through to the bathroom. You look as if you could use a hot shower before you put on something warm."

Rhys was silently thankful and towel-dried himself as best he could before he followed Carla through the warmth of the loungeroom, which was lit by a hurricane lamp, and through to the bathroom, which was located adjacent to the kitchen. Carla took out a dry towel from the linen cupboard and went in search of dry clothes, while Rhys had a hot shower by candlelight.

Tom, now calm, followed Carla as far as the loungeroom and parked himself in front of the heater once again. Carla went into her bedroom and rummaged through an antique timber chest at the foot of her bed, where Michael had left a few items of clothing. She drew out a pair of dark grey track pants, long-sleeved t-shirt, a fleecy navy blue track top and thick woollen socks. She didn't think it appropriate to give Rhys her ex's underwear so he would have to make do with the track pants alone.

With items in hand, Carla knocked on the bathroom door and opened it a sliver, enough to slip in the clothing and leave it on top of the vanity; then, she turned back to the kitchen, reheated the coffee and made toasted cheese and tomato sandwiches in the grill while she fished out another hurricane lamp for the loungeroom.

Rhys rejoined her moments later with slightly damp hair and wearing Michael's clothes, which fit him quite well.

"Thank you," he said as he joined Carla on the sofa and eyed the food in front of them.

Carla passed him a mug of coffee and a plate with a couple of sandwiches. "You're lucky you got through. It snowed here this morning and the roads were closed."

"I know," Rhys replied, digging into the food like he hadn't eaten in days. "I had to wait until the roads reopened and there was nowhere to go but stay in the car."

Carla smiled faintly. "So I take it you didn't get a bite to eat all day. What time did you leave Kioloa?"

Rhys took a few sips of his coffee before he picked up another sandwich. "Around six this morning. I only had a coffee and a few stale crackers for breakfast."

"I thought I told you not to come here," Carla chided him gently, but was secretly glad he had made the effort. "Of course, under the circumstances, I could hardly turn you away in this crazy storm. Besides, Tom went off his food a couple of days ago and I have a feeling it had something to do with you. But this morning he finally ate, and somehow I knew you were going to show up."

"Well, I'm glad Tom paved the way for me, if only until you hear me out." Rhys had finished eating and now leaned back on the sofa, sipping on his second coffee.

"That doesn't mean I changed my mind about things. If anything, you should thank Mother Nature. I wouldn't leave anyone stranded out there in this storm." Carla noticed the crestfallen look in his eyes, but she was not yet ready to make things easy for him. "How did you know where to find me, anyway?"

"I focused on Tom," Rhys explained. "The day you left, I saw the whole trip through his eyes. You stopped off at a Shell station to get something to eat. Then, when you arrived at the cottage, I saw the street name and number and knew exactly where you lived."

Despite the fact she now accepted Rhys was not from Earth, Carla still found it overwhelming to be sitting here, talking to an extraterrestrial over coffee and sandwiches. It had been different when he had arrived, cold and wet to the bone. Her pragmatic self had taken over and she had given little thought to him being from another planet. But now, the whole thing sank in again. For Rhys to be able to see through Tom's eyes was difficult to take in, and yet here he was.

Carla shook her head in amazement. "I'm sorry," she said. "It's just that this is going to take time to process."

Rhys leaned forward, closer to her, but not invading her personal space. "You believe me then?"

She gazed into his strangely beautiful eyes. "I've always believed you, Rhys. It's just that when confronted with the reality of it, it was kind of difficult to take in."

"I understand," he replied, hope tingeing his tone. "Of course, it must seem crazy for you, and it will take time to get used to the idea."

Carla shrugged her shoulders. "I'm really not sure what to think right now. But, Rhys, what you were trying to say to me before I left Merry Beach—even if you were an ordinary man from Earth, I'm still not ready to get involved with anybody." Rhys was about to speak, but Carla went on. "I'm not going to beat around the bush and play silly games, so I'll come right out with it. I know there's some kind of strong connection between us. I may not be as evolved as you, but I can feel it. I think you were about to tell me of your feelings before I left Merry Beach. Well, I have certain feelings for you, too; but now is the wrong time. It's too soon for me and it wouldn't make any difference even if you were a human from this planet."

Rhys didn't know whether to feel elated at what she said or concerned that she may send him away again. "Carla," he spoke softly, "you're right. There is a strong connection between us and I have deep feelings for you. I know you've been hurt by your ex, but I'm not like him. I don't hurt people. I love you. And whether you love me or not, my love is not going to go away."

Carla was stunned at his forthrightness, but then she had also been quite direct with him. "Look, let's just change the subject for the time being." She didn't think she could cope with intense emotions right now. "Am I right in assuming you're not going back to Kioloa?"

"Yes."

She sighed, not knowing what to do, but deep inside her she knew exactly what must happen, and before she could suppress it, she relented. "You can stay here awhile; at least, until we sort things out." She observed the radiance in his eyes and added, "But no more talk of love. I'm not ready to think past this moment, let alone the future. What I can promise you, though, is that I will listen to what you have to say and I'll try to keep an open mind."

Rhys felt happiness course through him despite the fact that even he didn't know how much time they had left on this planet. He was due to send in his recommendation report sometime in the near future and knew he could not take too long. The League was willing to wait, but not forever.

Whatever happened, though, he would try to win Carla's love and trust—he only hoped he did this before something catastrophic occurred. There was a small chance his recommendations would be taken to heart and Earth spared, but as with Prima, there were no guarantees.

9

A swarm of refugees from Syria floated on the Mediterranean Sea in overcrowded and old rubber dinghies, praying for rescue boats to find them. The waters became quite choppy and several hundred people—men, women and children —fell overboard. Those who could swim tried to make it back to their boats, but they were prevented from climbing back in by those in the dinghies.

Sudden screaming alerted people to a mother and child. The mother could not swim, but she was close enough to one of the dinghies and tried with all her might to keep her child's head above water. A few people on the boat tried to help her, but others pushed them overboard and they were not letting them back on.

The mother, meanwhile, grew exhausted from trying to keep afloat, and her head disappeared under the water along with that of her child's. The people in the dinghy watched in horrified fascination until the last thing they saw was a baby cap floating aimlessly on the surface waters. Expressions of shock marred their faces, but they had to think of the greater good. They still had a chance to reach land and the less human cargo onboard the more likely they could get to safety.

Those who were thrown overboard for trying to help the mother and child became exhausted after a long time in the cold water and even though they could swim they had no chance of getting back into a boat. After a while they, too, disappeared under the choppy waters and the thin remnant of empathy they had had for the woman and child disappeared with them.

Carla shot upright in bed, tears coursing down her face.

She wiped at her eyes and managed to stem a scream of horror lest she wake Rhys, who was sleeping in the guest room. Tom was nowhere to be seen and Carla guessed he was probably curled up next to Rhys.

Although it was still raining outside, the electricity came back on some time during the night because Carla could see the numbers on her bedside clock flashing zero as they went into default mode with the return of power.

She had no idea what time it was and didn't really care. She felt deeply disturbed by the vividness of her dream and the cruelty of those who didn't save the mother and child. Of course, it had only been a dream, or more like a nightmare, but she was aware from watching the news on TV of the plight of the hundreds and thousands of refugees trying to reach sanctuary in Europe. So many had died in the process—especially the more vulnerable, the old, the sick, women and children. It was horrible, and Europe was still divided in their pledge to take in these people and give them the sanctuary they sought. It was politics as usual. Governments could never agree on anything and meanwhile people died in vain. Carla was sure if there was a concerted effort to help the refugees no one need die, and those on the rubber boats would have helped the mother and child without fear of reprisal from fellow refugees.

The image of the mother and child going under still stayed with Carla as she got up and threw a robe around her. Fresh tears streamed down her face and she couldn't seem to stop them. She dried her face, but more kept coming. What was wrong with her? It was just a bad dream, and yet it was based on reality.

She went to the kitchen to check the time on the wall clock and saw it had just gone three. So what now? She knew she couldn't go back to sleep, not when she felt so distressed. She may as well switch on the heater in the lounge and keep warm. Perhaps she would read something until she felt sleepy again.

The heater warmed the lounge quickly and Carla settled down with a book, only to read the first sentence on the same page over and over as her thoughts returned to the dream, which she still couldn't dismiss. Then, her mind turned to the occupant in the guest room and before she had a chance to re-examine her feelings for him, Carla got up from the sofa and made her way quietly to his room. She had a deep curiosity to see Rhys at rest, with his eyes closed, totally unaware of her watching him.

Luckily, Rhys had left the door ajar in case Tom needed to go out and all Carla had to do was poke in her head to take a peek. She drew back in surprise, however, when Rhys's voice spoke out of the darkness. "You can't sleep, I see."

Carla sighed with mortification at being found out. "I... I..." She didn't know what to say.

Rhys flipped on the bedside lamp and Carla saw him lying on his back, wearing one of Michael's old pyjamas, one arm behind his head, with Tom alongside of him and now regarding his mistress as if he wanted to berate her for disturbing their sleep.

Rhys smiled, glanced at the dog for a moment and without any prompting, Tom jumped off the bed and headed towards the heater in the loungeroom. Carla looked on, amazed.

"You told him to go?"

Rhys nodded. "He's gone to lie in front of the heater in the lounge."

Carla shook her head in disbelief; the whole thing about Rhys being from another planet hitting her once again in a wave of surrealism.

"You look cold," Rhys observed. "Why don't you get in under the covers?"

Carla was shocked. "There?" Her gaze fixed on his bed.

"Why not?" Rhys seemed calm even though the prospect of her being physically close excited him. "I thought you might want to talk," he added, hoping to reassure her that he had no designs on her, at least not yet. "You look upset."

The latter comment made Carla burst into tears again and she felt like an idiot as she made her way straight to the bed and into his arms.

Rhys held her while she cried against his chest. He

caressed her hair and guided her head into the nook between his shoulder and neck. The close proximity of her body to his infused him with a wave of heat he hadn't felt in many years. In fact, he had never been in this position. Tyerrans did not touch each other like this. Hugs, kisses, making love, all this happened via a mental process. Tyerrans' bodies reacted to mental stimulation, which could be just as powerful as touch. But lying here next to Carla and physically touching her, Rhys was surprised to discover that his whole race had been very wrong and they should have preserved the ways of the ancients.

Carla's body shook against his as she wept and this stirred him to such a height of sexual arousal that he had to force himself to focus on something other than the new sensations surging through his body. Instead, he tuned in on Carla's thoughts and instantly relived the dream she had had. It was as if it were happening to him in the present. He felt the distress and helplessness of the mother and child struggling in the sea while others watched. He lived the pain of drowning and the final release from suffering; he smelled the shock and fear of the refugees watching on, and sensed the exhaustion of the ones that were pushed in the water for trying to help. Finally, he experienced Carla's own emotions of despair for what she had witnessed. While it had been a bad dream, it was also reality. It was the united consciousness in the cosmos that had acted as a conduit to her subconscious and produced the dream.

Rhys had absolutely no doubt there was a real mother and child out there who had drowned; their fear and pain had been absorbed by the collective consciousness in the universe, and this was why Carla had dreamt it. Something she may have seen or read about the refugees opened the door of her subconscious and she then dreamed the mother and child episode because at her level of evolution she would not have been able to withstand the emotional pain of feeling it as he had felt it just now. Even so, the dream had been quite vivid and Carla seemed more sensitive than most people he had met on Earth. This was what made her so special.

Carla stopped crying after a while and pulled back so she could see his face and look into his eyes. She did not try to break away from his arms altogether, even though she now felt more composed. "I'm so sorry," she said, her voice rather hoarse from all the weeping. "I don't know what came over me."

Rhys caressed back a lock of hair that fell across her face. "Don't apologise," he replied gently. "I saw your dream. I felt it. And at least, I can share it with you."

Carla propped herself up on one elbow, but Rhys still kept one arm around her. She suddenly felt an uncontrollable desire for him. This rare man, who could see into minds and feel what others felt; who could speak with animals; who was gentle and compassionate—this man; this stranger; who had entered her life only days ago and changed it forever—this was the man whose love she felt so strongly as if she could literally touch the emotion.

She regarded him in wonder while he lay back on his pillow, looking straight back at her. Aside from his arm, which rested casually across her waist, he had not touched her in an intimate way even though she was aware of his arousal. Carla had never been with an extraterrestrial; at least, she didn't think so, she mused, but if this man was truly descended from Homo sapiens, then he was a hot-blooded man like any other. And yet, he had respected her feelings and comforted her despite his own desire. Carla knew the whole episode must be just as awkward for him as it had been for her, but Rhys's first concern had been to comfort her.

Something inside her being broke through at that moment and she knew without the need for explanation that they were truly connected. It was a spiritual connection so strong that she felt she was Rhys and yet she was a separate entity from him. Rhys did not move, he merely held her gaze and probably read her thoughts at the same time, but Carla didn't care anymore. She simply leaned over him and brought her mouth to his.

Her kiss assaulted him before he had time to register

what was happening. Rhys felt like a physical virgin, and yet so experienced in lovemaking at a mental level. He was comfortable with his body and what was expected in the sexual act, but what he hadn't counted on was the effect physical lovemaking would have on him.

It was a hot, wet, passionate affair that involved not only the body, but all the senses and the soul. It was almost like an out of body experience, even though he was still in his own body and Carla in hers. He felt every touch, tasted every taste, heard every sound, smelled every scent, and saw the beautiful human form moving in the one ancient art nobody on Tyerra had practised for millennia.

While still engaged in that first kiss from Carla, they had somehow divested themselves of their nightclothes and as their tongues explored each other's mouth, she was on top of him, touching him all over and only breaking from their kiss to taste the skin at his neck and chest while her hands moved lower over his abdomen until they found what they sought.

Carla gave him a gentle but firm squeeze and he felt his body arching towards her. It was then she straddled him and guided him inside her. She rode him, softly at first, and he felt the wetness between them as the scent of sex assailed his nostrils. His urge for release was so strong he knew he couldn't hold out much longer, and as if she sensed this, Carla started moving faster and within moments Rhys came into her with an orgasm so deep that it left him shuddering, even after release.

At the height of his passion, Rhys still felt Carla's own orgasm pair with his own and her muscles contracted around his penis as she spasmed a number of times. Their release was simultaneous and later, while he waited for the shuddering sensations to ebb, Carla stayed lying on top of him, with him still inside her. They kissed and touched each other for a long time until their bodies calmed into a languid kind of satiety and they fell asleep with Rhys's arms entwined around Carla's body.

They were awakened hours later by a hungry Tom, who jumped right on top of them and took turns at licking Carla and

Rhys's faces to see who would get up first and feed him breakfast.

Carla did not have time to register the fact that she was naked, her legs still tangled with Rhys's and her head resting on his shoulder. Rhys was the first to disengage and sit up to try and control a very demanding Tom. He threw on his nightclothes, which he had to retrieve from the floor, and he kissed Carla's lips softly as he gazed down at her, taking in her dishevelled demeanour after their passionate lovemaking. He felt an urge to make love to her once more, but restrained himself.

"I'll feed Tom and make us something to eat. Coffee's going to be very strong this morning."

Carla smiled, bashfully, and snuggled under the covers while Rhys and Tom headed for the kitchen. She must have dozed off again because a short time later she heard her name being called and Rhys announcing breakfast.

She gathered her nightclothes and dressed hastily on the way to the bathroom. She smelled Rhys's scent on her and a wave of desire hit her all over. No time for a cold shower, but she splashed water on her face while she brushed her teeth and ran a brush through her messy hair. She then joined Rhys in the kitchen.

He had made scrambled eggs and grilled Roma tomatoes with thick slices of toasted sourdough bread. The wonderful smell of freshly brewed coffee pervaded the entire place.

"Eat it while it's still hot," Rhys stated, filling her cup with coffee.

"Where's Tom?"

"Sunning himself in the backyard."

Carla looked out the window and noticed for the first time that last night's rain had given way to a sparkling day with blue skies and full sunshine, not a cloud to be seen. Then, she noticed the time on the wall clock. "Good God, it's past ten already!"

Rhys grinned while he buttered a piece of toast. "Taking into consideration the kind of night we had, I'm not surprised." Carla blushed and Rhys laughed. "Don't go shy on me. If anything, I'm the one who should be feeling that way."

This caught Carla's attention and she forgot about her inhibitions. "What do you mean?"

"This is the first time I've had physical sex," he confessed.

A stunned Carla looked at him with eyes wide open. "You mean you're a virgin?"

Rhys shook his head, laughingly. "No. I was married, remember? What I meant to say was that everything on Tyerra is done via mental processes—even lovemaking."

Carla, who started to sip coffee, almost spilled some down her chin. "You're joking, right?" Rhys shook his head in response and Carla went on. "I thought you said you guys are like us, same DNA structure, that sort of thing."

Rhys wore a serious look on his face when he addressed her. "There is so much I need to tell you, Carla. We'll talk later. Right now, we should enjoy each other's company and the aftermath of our lovemaking experience."

Carla's stomach turned and her appetite suddenly left her. She simply nodded and went on sipping her coffee. Rhys's tone sounded serious and the implications of what had happened suddenly dawned on her. She had crossed the line she promised herself she wouldn't cross and made love with another man— and an extraterrestrial to boot! But she didn't want to think about this right now.

One thing she asked herself, though, was whether she was capable of getting pregnant by Rhys. If, as he said, Tyerrans had the same DNA as Earthlings, then there was every chance this could happen. The only reassurance she had was that she had not yet ovulated. She had practised rhythm contraception for years as she was very much in touch with her cycle and up until now her body had never failed her.

The other thing that nagged at her was the fact that Rhys had come to Earth for a reason. This meant when this reason no longer existed he would return home. The thought of him leaving now tore at her heart and she shot him a furtive glance, wondering whether he was reading her thoughts.

Rhys ate contentedly and gave a piece of buttered toast to

Tom, who had come back to join them. As far as Carla could tell, Rhys had left her alone to think privately.

10

Carla was in the shower when a flash of the previous night's dream came back to haunt her. The vividness of it hit her just as it had before and she experienced a deep sense of unease. She hurried through her ablutions and turned the bathroom over to Rhys while she escaped to her room to dress.

Although the day was sunny, the breeze was quite cold, and Carla dressed warmly in woollen leggings, long-sleeved T-shirt under a long black and forest green pullover that reached to just above the knees, and thick socks inside black hiking boots. She pulled back her hair and tied it into a short ponytail and then went in search of a scarf, gloves and a hat. Rhys had expressed a wish to walk along one of the bushwalking tracks in the Jamison Valley and Carla wanted to be sure she rugged up against the cold.

Once she had the items she wanted, she pulled out her overcoat from the wardrobe and took everything into the lounge to wait for Rhys. She made sure her mobile phone was fully charged and as she waited for Rhys she scrolled through the news. She skipped the political items, crime, abuse, protests, and strikes—the usual dose of violence and bad news, she thought; then, her thumb stopped scrolling as her eyes caught a piece about Syrian refugees stranded in the Mediterranean sea. She tapped on the screen to open the item and while she read the contents she felt the hairs at the nape of her neck stand on end. She read the entire story in stunned silence as it described her dream of last night, right down to the smallest detail.

She almost jumped up from the sofa when she felt a hand rest on her shoulder. "Hey," said Rhys, "take it easy."

He sat next to her, also dressed for their bushwalk in heavy khaki cargo pants, his usual cable-knit pullover and holding a heavy black cashmere jacket in one hand, which he tossed aside as he took and placed Carla's phone on the coffee table and then held her hands in his.

Carla drew comfort from their warmth. "It really happened, Rhys." She felt tears rise to her eyes, but managed to keep them from spilling down her face.

"Perhaps, it's a good idea if we have that talk now." Rhys gave her hands a reassuring squeeze.

She nodded and waited in silence.

"For some reason," Rhys began, "you seem to be open to events not happening in front of you. I see this in you, and I think I'm responsible."

Carla didn't quite understand what he was getting at. "How do you mean?"

"I think my being near you affects your level of consciousness. You're starting to get thoughts and images that filter through my mind and they enter your subconscious. I knew you were sensitive before, but now that we're together you're somehow picking up a lot more."

"But you didn't have the dream," Carla argued. "And you didn't mention you were thinking about the refugees."

"That's because I automatically filter out things. It's what I was trained to do," he explained. "If I didn't filter out all the horrible stuff that happens every day on this planet, I'd go mad, you see. I wouldn't be able to take it all in, even at my level of consciousness. It seems to me what's happening with you is that as I filter information I don't necessarily need, you're starting to pick up on bits and pieces of it. I believe this has something to do with our connection."

Carla regarded him, a hundred questions written in her eyes, and Rhys took a moment to tune into them before he spoke again. "You already know I communicate via thought; I can read minds and such. All people on Tyerra can do this at different levels. Some are born with a gift—although I guess it's sometimes an unwanted gift because it only brings on mental anguish; but that's how it is."

"But you said you can filter out things at will," Carla reminded him.

"Yes, thankfully, I can. The process is rather complicated and I don't want to bombard you with too much information right now, but let's just say I'm not aware of every bit of information I discard. It happens automatically and your subconscious is picking these up; at least some of them, anyway."

Carla took a few moments to mull over what Rhys said, but more questions popped into her head and she could not stem her curiosity. She wanted to know more about him and his elevated mental process. "Can you tell the future?"

Rhys shook his head. "No, thank heaven. It's bad enough knowing the past and what people are thinking and feeling in the present."

"So why are you really here?" Carla remembered what he had told her before, about gathering information. "And how did you get here? Where is Tyerra? And if you have sex via thought process, how do you reproduce? How did you learn to speak English and, I suspect, other languages? How come you're so much more advanced than Earth people? Why do you..."

Rhys gently placed his index finger across her lips to stop her from speaking further. He knew she had more and more questions building up inside her, and one of those was about them and their future, although she had not yet voiced it. Carla was too afraid to ask in case he said something she could not live with. He sighed, for once not knowing where to start, except to simply reassure her.

"I'll tell you some things," he stated, "but not all at once. There's too much to take in and you're going to need time to process it. The one thing I do want you to know, first and foremost, is that I love you, and I'm not going to let you go."

It was so simple the way he put it that Carla felt like sobbing with relief. He wasn't going to abandon her after all. He would stay with her no matter what. She moved into his arms and this time it was Rhys who initiated the kiss. It was long and passionate, but he controlled his desire because he felt they still needed to talk.

Carla had hundreds of questions crowding into her mind and at the same time she felt like a child, afraid of what some of the answers might be. She was vulnerable and fragile, and Rhys wanted to protect her for as long as he had the power to do so. He took comfort in the thought that if Earth were to be destroyed he and Carla would perish with it together. He was going nowhere without her, no matter what the consequences.

He pulled back gently from their kiss and Carla rested her face against his chest as he went on holding her. She said, "I know you tuned in on my thoughts just now, so you know I love you like I've never loved anyone before. It's a love so deep and spiritual that it defies explanation, but I believe it was meant to be; I know this now." She echoed his own sentiments and he held her closer to him in response. They stayed like this for a while, just resting contentedly in their closeness, both feeling the strong bond they now shared. But Carla could not stay still for long; she was bursting to ask more questions and she could not stop herself from blurting out, "How old are you?"

Rhys thought it was time to indulge her by answering a few of her questions. He had to start somewhere. "In Earth years, I'm thirty-three."

"And in Tyerran years?"

"Three hundred and thirty."

Carla looked at him in astonishment. "You mean to say you've been alive that long and there's not a single wrinkle on your face? So one of our Earth years is like ten years over there?"

He nodded in amusement. "Yes."

"So if you lived to, say, eighty years here on Earth, you'd be like eight hundred over there."

"That's right. Our technology is far more advanced and we can live to a great age and keep looking young a lot longer than Earthlings," Rhys explained. "But in the end we, too, must die.

Everything dies." His tone held a trace of sadness all of a sudden.

"Your wife died, you said."

Rhys nodded. Carla was fast beginning to tune in on his feelings. "Her name was Xaye. She died as a result of a volcano eruption. We didn't get away fast enough. You know, she looked very much like you." He didn't want Carla to know Xaye had been identical in looks because he didn't want her to think his feelings were based on this fact. Xaye, he knew now, had been his preparation for meeting Carla. He couldn't explain why this was so or why he knew this, but for the first time in his life he wondered whether there really was some kind of creator in the universe with a divine plan.

Tyerrans believed life had evolved by accident. Despite this, for a long time Rhys had experienced too many coincidences that led him to believe there might be something more powerful out there. What this was, he didn't know, but he felt something was guiding events, or perhaps he was just being too sensitive for his own good, he mused.

"I am really sorry about Xaye," Carla interrupted his thoughts. "I remember you mentioned it was an accident. It's not morbid curiosity that makes me ask this, but when did you lose her?"

"Three years ago in your time, but it's really thirty years in mine. This is why it's so long ago. The one disadvantage about living for too long, though, is the mental anguish that comes with emotions. We have to carry ours a lot longer than Earth people."

Carla caressed his face and rested her head on his shoulder. "Death is horrible," she uttered in a haunted tone. She was thinking of her own parents, now long gone; pets she'd loved and lost; relationships that had ended, which were a kind of death, too. Death was final and not just on Earth, but throughout the entire universe. "Do you still have parents?"

"No. My parents passed on when I was a kid. They were quite mature when they decided to have me; they were very career oriented, you might say, so they waited to have a child.

Anyway, they passed on when I became what you call a teenager. That's when Commander adopted me."

"Who's Commander?" Carla was so curious about Rhys she wanted to know everything at once.

"Commander is both my adopted father and the man who sent me here. But this is definitely a story for another day," Rhys replied. "Now, how about that walk you promised me?" He didn't want to go on talking about himself. He wanted to live every minute with Carla in case this was all they had.

"Wait. What about your ability with languages? I mean, I'm assuming you speak more than English."

Rhys gave in. "Okay, a couple more questions and then we're going for that walk. Just as I read minds and see through others' eyes, I can get into their heads, no matter what language they speak. We think in pictures, even though some people may not realise this. So I can see how the pictures translate to language and I'm able to process the language instantly."

"You'd make an awesome translator if you ever decided to get an Earth job," Carla observed.

Rhys smiled. He supposed she was right, and he may even do something like this if Earth was spared. "Right. About that walk..."

Carla pressed him back on the sofa as he was about to rise. "Hey, you said a *couple* of questions. There is one other question I have for you."

"Shoot." Rhys couldn't help being amused by her enthusiasm. If he allowed it, they'd be here all day talking.

"You said you do everything on a mental level in Tyerra. So aside from being a very quiet planet where no one needs to talk, which sounds a tad boring, how do you reproduce?"

Rhys laughed at her wit. "Yes, I guess it is a quiet planet, but don't forget we can tune in on thought, so our minds become just as confused as yours do on Earth when you hear people talking aloud. As for reproduction, it's an external process."

"You mean like test tube babies?"

"Yes. When a couple wants a child it's all done in the lab.

This gives the birth lab a chance to watch the development of the fetus and ensure nothing goes wrong. They can often alter DNA to prevent birth defects, you see. But people can still choose to have a natural birth if they wish, only we just don't it this way. Over millennia, it's become a rarity to have a natural birth."

"It sounds so... clinical somehow. I understand about ensuring the child grows healthy. That's a great advantage, of course, plus producing the baby in a birth lab is painless and safe. But think of what you're missing out on—the wonders of a child coming out of the mother's womb—the strongest bond possible between mother and child."

This time, Rhys stood and brought her to her feet. "That's enough questions for one day. Now that you find our race boring because we miss out on the wonders of nature and physical lovemaking, we must seem like a bunch of cold-blooded beings to you."

Carla knew Rhys meant this in jest. He was not chastising her in any way, but there was an element of truth in what he said. Things on Tyerra seemed too cold and clinical for her liking. In any case, she decided to respond with humour at his comment and uttered, "I don't think you're boring; just different. But Rhys, after last night, let me assure you there was nothing at all cold-blooded about you."

Rhys had no comeback and felt his cheeks blush instead.

Carla enjoyed scoring over him for once. As far as she was concerned, in the lovemaking department, she was the more evolved of the two.

11

Days turned into weeks for Carla and Rhys as they settled into their love relationship quite naturally. They pretty much did everything together, like most couples in love, and the only activity where they differed was work. Carla worked on her website designs and Rhys reviewed his recommendations so he could finalise the report for submission to the League of Galaxies.

Tom, meanwhile, became an even happier dog. He loved Rhys to distraction, and it finally dawned on Carla why this was the case—the two talked to one another. The dog loved Carla, too, she knew, but her communication with him was mostly one-sided as Tom could not reply to her via thought. With Carla, he was limited to wagging his tail or to the different tones of his barks. Carla still had a silent kind of understanding with Tom, but not to the level Rhys enjoyed. In many ways, she envied their comradeship. Sometimes, when they went for a walk, Rhys and Tom sat together looking over a cliff or they played fetch at the park, but at the same time they conversed.

One evening over dinner, Carla brought up the subject. "What is it that you and Tom find to talk about? Surely, he's not evolved like humans."

Rhys took a peek inside the lounge to ensure Tom was asleep in front of the heater as usual and then returned to the kitchen. "I don't want him to hear me," he explained. "You see, animals may not be as evolved as humans, like they don't read books or discuss the state of the nation, but they do possess refined senses. They know when a person is friendly or hostile; they have a wonderful affinity with all things natural, especially the weather and geological events. On the whole, they live with a built-in instinct for survival. So sometimes we discuss the weather, natural disasters, or some of the people Tom met through you. For instance, he has a great ability to recount things that happened with your ex because he's good at sensing the whole gamut of human emotions. This is how he knows when you're happy or sad."

"Wow!" Carla remarked. "And all this time I thought he didn't understand what had happened with Michael."

Rhys smiled. "Oh, he knew all right. In fact, he tried to warn you in his own way that Michael was going to leave you on the night of your argument. Apparently, when you were attempting to talk to him about trying to work things out, Tom tried to grab your attention by making out like he wanted to play. It was the only way he knew to shift your focus from what was to come, but of course he couldn't talk to you or tell you what he sensed."

Carla put down her fork and looked down at the vegetarian lasagna on her plate. "I was so stupid to trust that guy. If only I had the ability you have."

"You weren't stupid, you just trusted him. You thought he loved you." Rhys patted her arm to lend comfort. "If you had my ability you would never have become involved with someone like him in the first place."

Carla put her hand over his. She couldn't stop touching this man who had become so special to her in such a short time. "You're right, of course."

They went on eating and Carla thought briefly of Michael as though he had been someone from a previous life. She had changed into a different person since she had become involved with Rhys. Just knowing him had raised her to a different level of consciousness altogether, and though she considered herself to be an average human, her mind seemed to have expanded tenfold and she was much more sensitive to things. So much so, that despite the fact Rhys had not told her very much about himself, although he made a point to answer any questions she asked of him, Carla sensed he was preparing her for something bigger to come, so she tried not to pester him too much. She knew if an important issue came up he would tell her. Besides, having such a strong connection with him, oftentimes Carla discovered that answers to questions she wanted to ask simply popped into her head.

For instance, she discovered Rhys preferred vegetarian food, as she did, especially because of his sensitivity to animals. Carla knew on Tyerra they did not use animal products, as their ancestors had, and modern Tyerrans rarely kept animals for anything other than companionship.

Rhys's ancestors had evolved eating animals and all kinds of plant life, much like on Earth. Modern Tyerrans, however, had developed a stronger sense of responsibility towards the animal kingdom and they no longer consumed animal protein. Curiously, they seemed to have retained their slightly longer canines even though they were not needed to bite on flesh. When Carla had teased Rhys about their first meeting and how she thought him to be a vampire due to his slightly longer canines, he had explained that a lot of the plant life their ancestors consumed was quite fleshy and fibrous, and difficult to bite into. Therefore, like many flesh-eating humans, modern Tyerrans still had their canine teeth, but nowhere near as long as those of their ancestors.

These days, Tyerrans tended to take a healthy approach in order to optimise their longevity and they stuck to pure plant food in their diet. Of course, unlike Rhys, many Tyerrans had not discovered the magic of good coffee, Carla mused.

Thinking about all she had learned so far about Rhys's race, she remembered there was one thing she had wanted to ask for some time and as Rhys did not think to mention it, she put it to him now. "You never really told me how you travelled to Earth. Tyerra must be very far and I know if you'd travelled by the conventional method, even close to the speed of light, it would've taken millions or even billions of years for you to get here."

Rhys had finished his meal and was sipping on his usual coffee. He smiled. "I was wondering when you'd get around to that one."

Carla had also finished eating and cleared the table. Then, she rejoined Rhys with her own coffee. "There's nothing secret about that, is there?"

"Not at all," Rhys replied. "It's just rather complex to explain. But to put it in simple terms, we're able to warp space so we can reach any part of the universe in a relatively short time. Tyerra's in a different galaxy to the Milky Way and conventional space travel, as you've just said, wouldn't have made it possible for me to get here in my lifetime."

"So when you say 'a relatively short time', how short is short?" Carla's eyes were wide with fascination. For her, this was the stuff of pure science fiction.

"It's pretty much instant or a few minutes, depending on conditions in space at the time. We use a warp drive, you see, and this allows us to bend space. It's like folding a blanket. When you do this, the two edges come together, but the minute you unfold it the edges are far apart. Same thing with warping or bending space, so when space is bent we pass through the shortcut, you might say."

"And how does the warp drive work to bend space?"

"The drive uses negative energy density," Rhys explained, and added when he saw the confused look in Carla's eyes, "It's a kind of material found in the universe. By using this energy, we can travel from one point to the other without it taking us millions or billions of years to get there."

Carla smiled. "I think I'm sorry I asked. I do understand what this means in simplistic terms, as you put it, but it's mindboggling. So did you just get dropped off on Earth?"

"You might say that. Tyerra's in a galaxy that's approximately eight billion light years away."

"Excellent," Carla stated as if they were discussing the local taxi service. "I take it when you need to get a lift back to your planet you make some kind of phone call." She couldn't believe this conversation even though she knew what Rhys told her was true, but it was so surreal.

Rhys couldn't help but laugh and then explained about the thumb communicator and how he was able to reach Commander, or anyone else, via thought process with the aid of the device.

"Okay." Carla nodded as if she understood the whole thing. "I take it we're talking about that little rectangular thingy I found in your campervan. I have a feeling you sensed that I found it when I told you I was there that night."

"Yes, but I wasn't about to bring it up. There was no harm in you finding it."

"Anyway, the thing went green," Carla remarked. "Does that mean someone was listening to me? I remember getting the feeling I was being either watched or listened to."

"Commander was at the other end, tuning in on you," Rhys admitted.

"Ah, so he was sussing me out." Carla found this whole conversation too incredible for her own good and, though she wanted to know more and ask about this Commander person, she silently agreed with Rhys's earlier suggestion that she should take time to digest all new information she learned bit by bit.

"He likes you, you know," Rhys stated.

"Oh, so the stepfather approves," Carla remarked lightly, but didn't want to go on with the subject. She felt the need to earth herself (no pun intended) by going back to normality—whatever this meant since meeting Rhys.

"Enough questions for one evening?" Rhys queried, knowing exactly how overwhelmed she felt.

Carla nodded and crossed over to where he was sitting. She stood by his chair as Rhys waited, not wanting to read her mind. Most of the time, he shut off from her thoughts unless he sensed she was upset about something and needed for him to listen to her, but the impish smile that appeared on her face now told him she was just fine.

Rhys regarded her with curiosity as she stood over him. Carla placed a hand on either side of his face and brought her mouth down on his in a searching kiss. His arms encircled her waist and he pulled her onto his lap without breaking the kiss. The hunger he had for her was insatiable and he grew hard as their kiss deepened.

Somehow, Carla divested herself of her pyjama bottoms and she straddled him on the chair, her fingers working to unbutton Rhys's own pyjama pants. When she achieved this, she broke the kiss and gazed straight into the passion in his eyes. Then, she lifted her body slightly and lowered it again, taking him inside her. Within moments, their passionate movements culminated into a simultaneous orgasm that left them breathless.

***

The flames raged through the Jamison Valley as they made their way around the entire Blue Mountains National Park, flanking the township of Katoomba in an arc of fire that engulfed most of the forest. It was almost impossible to breathe out of doors and Carla looked out through the study window to see ash raining down from the sky as if it were snow and settle silently on houses, gardens and streets.

"This can't be happening. It can't be!" Carla uttered aloud, ran to the back of the house and hugged her dog, who was pawing at the back door. She saw the fear in Tom's eyes. "Don't worry, boy. We're safer inside." She tried to comfort him in a soft voice while they crouched together on the kitchen floor of the cottage. She thought of the sandstone embankment that lay behind her back garden and prayed the rock walls would provide a safeguard against the advancing bushfire as they had done for the past 110 years of the weatherboard cottage's existence.

Outside, the only things that could be heard were the deafening sounds of the advancing inferno drowned by the sirens of fire engines as they sped past on the way to meet the monster fire. Overhead, the rumble of helicopters and helitankers kept getting louder as a number of them amassed in the airspace above the township in case they had to release water in order to save the town; others flew past on their way to the raging fire to dump thousands of litres of water in the hope of containing the killer flames. It didn't help that wind gusts blew in from the Megalong Valley at around 100km per hour and creating more force for the fire to keep on burning.

Carla switched on the radio sitting next to her on the floor just in time to catch the tail end of the latest news update. "... and the battle is proving to be a tough one. This is an unprecedented disaster never before recorded in the history of Australia. It seems the prediction of the worst El Niño event to date, due to global warming, is now a reality. Record lows of rain plus dry winds created this tinderbox scenario; one that even the most hardened of firefighters has ever experienced. Weather patterns around the world have been unpredictable in the last couple of decades with mammoth superstorms, superfires and other catastrophes that..."

Carla switched off the radio. She didn't want to hear any more. This was the end. It was what humanity had brought upon itself due to its arrogance, greed and the exploitation of planet Earth. There was no respect for Mother Nature and no respect for the planet—and now mankind was paying the price.

Carla buried her face in Tom's silky neck and held onto the dog, hoping for a miracle. It seemed nothing could save them and this was how they would perish. Carla coughed while Tom whimpered at the burning smell drifting inside and penetrating the entire cottage. Carla tightened her arms around the dog and closed her eyes.

A loud cracking noise followed by the sound of something smashing made Carla's eyes fly open at the same time as Tom broke into a frenzy of barking. The roof over her loungeroom had collapsed into itself and the ceiling gave way to the burning support beams as they crashed through into the room. The flames spread so quickly as to give them no escape, except through the back door, but as Carla turned to open it she saw the whole backyard dripping with flames that had engulfed the trees and shrubs from the houses on either side of hers and from vegetation behind the sandstone walls. There was no way out of the ring of fire that began to close in on them at such a rapid pace.

Carla screamed for Rhys, knowing deep in her heart that he was dead. He had gone out only minutes beforehand to check on what was happening outside and had not returned. She tried to tune into him to no avail. Only an image of his charred body flashed into her mind and she screamed again in both pain and fear.

Her body writhed violently and Carla knew death had now come for her. The flames were at her feet and the pain that shot through her was unbearable. To her horror, Tom was overcome by the flames, and he lay dying next to her, his body burned beyond recognition. Again, Carla screamed and shook like a leaf in the wind. She waited for death to claim her, but the shaking continued, on and on.

"Carla!" Rhys's voice called out to her, but she did not understand how this could be when he was dead. "Carla! Wake up! Wake up!"

Carla opened her eyes and upon seeing Rhys leaning over her in bed she collapsed into his arms and cried inconsolably. Surely, this could not have been a dream. It felt so real she had to pull away from Rhys for a moment to check on Tom, who was lying fast asleep at the foot of their bed irrespective of her screaming. She then lifted the bedcovers and checked her feet— her skin was untouched and unblemished.

Rhys kept a hold on her, looking concerned, and Carla turned to him for reassurance. He was alive and well. It had been a dream after all—or more like a horrible, unfathomable nightmare of apocalyptic destruction. Carla collapsed into Rhys's arms once again and her relief at discovering they were all safe left her feeling exhausted.

12

"Please tell me this isn't some kind of prediction," Carla pleaded, still within the circle of Rhys's arms.

After her maelstrom of weeping, Carla dozed off for a short time while Rhys held her. He stayed awake, worrying about her ability to handle the dream visions she started to experience since they had been together. For once, he was unable to explain how something he automatically filtered out at a subconscious level could transfer itself into her mind. The worst part was, as in the case of the refugee mother and child, that this, too, could become a reality.

Rhys was sure Commander would provide an explanation to this mystery, but he was loath to contact him. They had already argued about his mission and Commander had tried to talk him out of staying on Earth if the League decided to proceed with annihilation. So the last thing he needed now was to get into another argument about what was happening with Carla. Commander would only illustrate the point that she, like every other human, could not handle their level of consciousness and in the end, if Rhys stayed with her, she may end up going over the edge as the dreams became more frequent and got worse.

Rhys chose not to entertain this possibility. There was a chance that whatever transferred into Carla's mind was coming from the recommendations report he was putting together for the League of Galaxies.

He had reported on so many atrocities to date—and had had to filter them out of his own mind in order to stay sane—that it was just possible some of this reached Carla's subconscious because of their connection. The solution, therefore, was for him to submit the report immediately and firmly shut it out of his mind for good. Whatever happened afterwards with the report was up to the League. Rhys intended to spend the rest of his life with Carla, loving and protecting her, no matter what the outcome. If the League chose to destroy them, so be it. But if they spared Earth, Rhys and Carla had a real chance at a life without further thoughts of atrocities or vivid nightmares.

"Well?" Carla's sleepy voice brought him out of his reverie.

"I'm sorry. I was thinking about what you said." Rhys gently kissed the top of her head. "I don't think your dream is necessarily a prediction."

"But the refugee mother and child did drown, the same way as in my dream!" Carla argued.

"Yes, you're right. Except you dreamed it *after* it happened, and only found out when you read the news. So the dream wasn't a prediction. As for this latest dream, you can see there's no fire in the mountains, especially with recent rainfall. Everything's okay and I feel it'll remain this way. El Niño hasn't even shown any signs of arrival as yet, but in your dream you said the strong, dry winds fanning the fire occurred as a result of this event. So it doesn't match."

Carla remained thoughtful for a while, mulling over what Rhys had said. Rhys, in the meantime, re-examined her dream in his mind. When he had shaken her awake after she started screaming, he had instantly tuned into what happened and seen her whole dream. Now, he ran it again in his mind as if he were replaying a film.

"It was spring." Carla's voice intruded into his thoughts. "So maybe it's yet to happen."

"And Earth could get hit by an asteroid at any moment," Rhys returned, trying to qualm her fears. "I don't believe you're seeing the future in your dreams, Carla. I think you're picking up on some of the stuff I've filtered out automatically. Somehow, it intruded into your subconscious. Remember when I said I couldn't predict the future? Well, no one can as far as I know, because when you look at the future in the face, if you're able to, it changes."

Carla became intrigued. "Is that really so?"

"It seems to be. Have you ever heard of the observer effect?

Carla had touched upon this in one of her science subjects at university. "You mean something like a form of reactivity, where the researcher's cognitive bias causes them to unconsciously influence the subjects of an experiment?"

Rhys gazed at her in admiration. "Yes, something like that. There's a school of thought on Tyerra that thinks this applies to those who claim to see the future. Their argument's based on the observer's effect. So if you claim to see the future, they'll say it's impossible because once you see it, it changes forever."

"Perhaps you're right, and I'm just receiving images from whatever you filtered out. They say when two people are together for a long time or, as in our case, when they're closely connected at a higher level, they tend to share each others' thoughts to a large extent."

Rhys smiled mischievously. "So since we share our thoughts to a large extent, as you say, what am I thinking right now?"

It was clearly obvious what Rhys was driving at and despite her desire for more sleep Carla felt her body come alive. At that exact moment, however, Tom raised his head from where he had been sleeping and with a couple of playful barks he threw himself on Rhys for a cuddle and much face licking.

Carla laughed so hard she had tears rolling down her face, while Rhys struggled to get Tom off him. "I bet even you didn't see that one coming, Rhys Lewis!" She couldn't stop laughing. "I think Tom's trying to tell you that you took to physical lovemaking like a duck to water, and you've ignored him for far too long. But dogs rule in this household—so keep it in your pants and take him out for his morning walk."

***

While Rhys walked Tom, it occurred to him that he had not been in touch with Commander lately, and he knew he could not delay sending in his recommendation report any longer. Since living with Carla in the mountains he had almost forgotten why he was really on Earth, and this suited him just fine. His life had changed almost immediately the moment he met her and for the first time, he felt truly alive since the passing of Xaye. He had been twice blessed in love. First, there was Xaye, whose passing left him so distraught he didn't have any intentions of looking for anyone else. But when he thought all was lost, love touched him a second time with Carla. This was his chance to live a happy life, no matter how long both he and Carla were destined to live.

Rhys was fully aware that on Earth he would age just like all Earthlings because he no longer had access to the advanced nutritional supplementation that kept him living hundreds of years, as it did to all the population on Tyerra. Besides, medical technology on Earth was in its infancy compared to where he came from, and it was not conducive to a long life by Tyerran standards. In all the years Earthlings had researched cures for degenerative diseases including cancer, they had come up with very little.

This was one of the first things Rhys had tuned into when he first arrived. Back then, he had been more open to people's emotions and it seemed almost every person he came across lived in their own private nightmare—most often with a chronic illness or a fatal condition. He had passed faces in the streets, anonymous faces, full of inner pain and the struggle to remain alive. Rhys's heart broke at the intense pain he absorbed into his being from people—both the physical and emotional feelings they experienced. After a while of this kind of absorption, however, he couldn't stand it any longer and had trouble coping. This was compounded by the fact that he had been powerless to save his own wife's life, albeit from a catastrophe rather than a health condition, but this did not matter. He felt responsible for not having been able to save Xaye; and on Earth he felt responsible for not being able to save humanity.

This was the one golden rule he'd had to abide by before he'd been allowed to embark on this mission—no interference. In essence, this meant even though Tyerran technology could save humanity's pain in all sorts of ways, such as showing them how to avoid ill health, starvation, poverty, wars, and so on, advanced races were not encouraged to interfere.

Rhys had asked Commander at the time why this was so and he responded, "Because the only way for any race to advance themselves and reach a higher level of consciousness is to learn from past mistakes and suffer the consequences of their actions —and until their consciousness is lifted to such levels, they will stay buried in the dark ages."

Rhys remembered his indignation when he lashed out at his stepfather. "How can you stand there so calmly and say that? What about when the League helped them during the Cold War?"

Commander regarded him with a kindly look in his eyes. "We made an exception that time. If we hadn't, they would have surely blown themselves up."

"But now you're sending me on this mission to see if Earth is worth saving," Rhys's cynical response burst into Commander's mind.

"You're still young and idealistic," Commander replied. "We gave Earthlings a second chance that time. Did they learn from it, though? No. They're simply continuing to create their own negative destiny."

At the time, Rhys had not been able to find a comeback for this so he dropped the topic and agreed he would not interfere. He even understood, to a certain extent, that growth and development of mind and spirit came from hardship and negative events. The balance of what Earthlings called Ying and Yang applied to the entire universe—you couldn't have one thing without its opposite.

Tom's bark intruded into his mind and Rhys happily shut

off his thoughts and engaged in play with the dog. They made their way to Carrington Park, a small reserve overlooking the majesty of the Jamison Valley, and there they spent the best part of half an hour running around and playing fetch with a sturdy stick Rhys found.

There wasn't much communication between him and Tom today, except that the dog sensed Rhys's preoccupation. Rhys did not bother to hide it from him. If anything, he reassured the dog he would be staying with him and Carla for good. This was all Tom had been waiting to hear and after a few happy barks he ran around the park, fetching the stick Rhys kept throwing for him and bringing it back to his master.

Rhys had to smile at this one—Tom now considered Rhys his master. Carla was still Tom's mistress, but when it came to disciplining, it seemed Rhys had the upper hand these days.

"Don't you tell your mother about this," Rhys cautioned the dog. "If she gives you a command, you obey, okay?"

Tom responded by nuzzling Rhys's face when he bent down to sit on the grass. Rhys patted the dog and ruffled his ears and with playtime over, they rested side by side drinking in the beauty of the valley before them.

***

The appetising smell of breakfast and strong coffee met Rhys when he opened the front door of the cottage a while later with a very hungry Tom in tow. He felt his stomach grumble in tune with the dog's and was grateful Carla had breakfast ready.

Tom charged towards the kitchen leaving Rhys to take off his boots in the foyer. So much for Tom considering him the master, Rhys thought with amusement. The little critter would have sold him down the river for a yabby when it came to breakfast. While Rhys took off his boots, he heard Carla's voice talking to Tom.

"Tom, stop jumping up on me or you don't get any

breakfast. I made you some of those sausages you like," she scolded him good-naturedly. Tom responded with a couple of happy yips and all was silent.

When Rhys walked into the kitchen, he noticed Tom's face buried in a bowl of diced sausages. The dog was oblivious to everything while he munched away. Carla had just finished cooking scrambled eggs and served them on sourdough toast with mushrooms and grilled Roma tomatoes sprinkled with freshly grown oregano from the cottage's herb garden.

Rhys helped her with the coffee and poured it into two earthenware mugs. He took his coffee black with one sugar as usual; Carla simply added a dash of milk. "Have a good walk?" Carla enquired as Rhys set the coffee pot on the table and she set their plates down.

"A vigorous one," Rhys responded and suddenly pulled her to him before she had a chance to take a seat. He kissed her so thoroughly that for a moment Carla thought they would skip breakfast and move into the bedroom, but Rhys was ahead of her and smiled when he released her.

"Oh no, my girl," he said with humour. "This is revenge for kicking me out of bed this morning without letting me have my way. Besides, while lovemaking is great there's nothing like a nice, hot breakfast." Still with a smile on his face, he sat down and tucked into his food.

Carla took the seat opposite on the small round table and made out like she was indifferent. "You're too funny, Rhys, if you think I was thinking about sex at this time."

He only responded with an all-knowing gaze that told her he had already read her thoughts. *Damn!* she thought. *It's not fair when he does that.*

"I know it's not fair," Rhys said between bites, "it's just that when I'm excited my filtering system doesn't always work."

Carla laughed despite having been caught out by him. "Oh, what a lame excuse coming from an advanced being. So I suppose this gives you every reason to listen in on my thoughts, is that right?"

He winked at her. "Only the sexy ones."

She regarded him with love in her eyes and thought it was almost a sin to be so happy. At this thought, she felt a cold shiver spread through her, but was relieved Rhys had shut off his focus on her thoughts. At least, she assumed so as she stole a glance his way and saw him eating happily. She didn't want to worry him if she could help it, but something told her that very soon Rhys would have much more to contend with. Whatever it was, it felt quite serious to her, but she hoped when the time came Rhys would share it with her. Together, they could overcome almost anything.

When he finished breakfast and sat back sipping his coffee, Rhys regarded Carla thoughtfully. He had pretended not to be conscious of what had just gone through her mind, merely for her benefit. He watched as she finished eating, then her eyes met his.

"There *is* something wrong, isn't there?" Although she posed this as a question, it came out sounding like a statement.

Rhys sighed, knowing it was time he told her the truth. There was no longer any point in hiding the purpose of his mission as he had taken the decision to stay on Earth and suffer the consequences, whatever they may be. If he and Carla were to live however much time was left to them in happiness, he owed it to her to tell her everything, no matter how frightening or painful. He loved and respected her too much to hold back. Besides, she was growing more sensitive to his thoughts on a daily basis and it was only a matter of time before she guessed.

The longer he took to reply to her question, the deeper the concern in her eyes. Rhys hated to see her like this and knew the time to talk was now.

13

They sat side by side on a garden bench out in the backyard under the warming sun while Tom ran around, trying to catch their attention. Carla experienced a moment of déjà vu and was transported to the evening when she and Michael had been in exactly the same situation—having coffee and about to discuss the serious matter of their relationship. The only difference now was that the sun shone down on her and Rhys, and this somehow had the effect of softening whatever blow was to come. Despite this, Carla waited anxiously to hear what Rhys had to say. She rested her coffee mug on a small table close by and remained silent.

Rhys placed his mug next to hers, ran his fingers through his hair, and turned to her. "The only reason I can tell you this now is because I'm not going back to Tyerra. I no longer consider myself a part of this mission and even though I'll submit my recommendations to Commander, I have no more say in what happens."

Carla noticed Rhys seemed to be searching for words to expand on this point and before he could continue she blurted out, "It was never about gathering information, was it? Whoever or whatever this organisation is, they want to destroy Earth." Her tone was filled with certainty rather than accusation.

Rhys did not look surprised. "Our connection's getting stronger every day. You read me like a book." He frowned, wondering how she was going to react to the rest of what he had to say. He went on to explain, "The group I work for is called the League of Galaxies. Commander is the representative for Tyerra and also the unanimously voted Head of the League. There are at least two hundred other representatives, each from a different galaxy with evolved life."

Carla's shock when Rhys confirmed the League of Galaxies wanted to destroy Earth did not give her time to feel fear, at least not at this stage. She merely felt a neutral curiosity about the whole thing. "They're kind of like NATO in a way," she remarked.

Rhys nodded. "Yes, you might say that. But Carla, the decision hasn't yet been made. The whole thing hinges on the report I send back."

She felt a little relief at this, but knew they were still not entirely in the clear. "Why do they think Earth should be destroyed?"

"This is the complex part," he replied, reaching for his coffee and taking a few sips. He needed the caffeine and thought at the same time what a good thing it was that Tyerran life forms could not tolerate alcohol; otherwise, he would have been a fully-blown alcoholic by now. "The issue concerns the aspect of what holds the universe together. It's what we call the fabric of consciousness. This must always be held at just the right balance in order for everything to work as it should."

Carla interjected, "You mean like a collective consciousness that can send waves of thought and make things happen?"

"Right," Rhys replied. "It's exactly like that. It works on causal effect, you see, and..."

"And it's just like what we call karma here on Earth. Whatever we do carries consequences. So this is cause and effect, but on a universal level. The collective things we do as a race has a causal effect on the fabric of the cosmos."

Rhys regarded her with surprise. "How do you know all this?"

She shrugged. "It's pretty much the view most spiritual people hold," she explained. "I'm not religious and I don't believe in a creator per se, but I do believe in a kind of force that drives everything—just like the collective consciousness or as you call it, the fabric of consciousness."

Rhys nodded, surprised and yet relieved she had such a deep understanding of the concept. Carla saw this in his eyes and continued talking. "So if I'm right, this League of Galaxies believes the evil on Earth is upsetting the applecart, as it were."

Again, Rhys nodded. "Exactly the reason why they sent me here. I've been compiling data and statistics for them on absolutely everything you can think of. Then, I'm supposed to make recommendations as to whether Earth should be annihilated or not."

Now it was Carla who reached for her caffeinated drink, and she started to feel anger growing deep within her. This was not aimed at Rhys, but at the League of Galaxies. "How do they know the evil or negative energy's coming from Earth? Why single us out?"

"That's something I've already brought up with Commander," Rhys replied.

"So you think the same way I do on this?"

"Yes."

"Commander will say your judgement's clouded because of your involvement with me," Carla shot back.

Rhys smiled rather cynically. "He already has."

Carla had a feeling she was not going to like this Commander guy, if she ever met him.

Rhys read her thoughts and added, "But he's bought me more time to submit the report. I was supposed to submit it prior to leaving Kioloa, and since then he hasn't been in touch. Besides, he's of two minds about Earth contributing to all the negative energy. You see, there were other planets the League destroyed in the past because of the same reason."

"And your argument is that this is what unsettled the collective consciousness," Carla remarked thoughtfully.

"Exactly," Rhys agreed emphatically. "I've already told Commander of my views. Plus some years ago, I recommended against the annihilation of a planet called Prima. Unfortunately, the League did not agree with me at the time and they went ahead and destroyed it."

The anger inside Carla bubbled to the surface. "So who do these people think they are? Who made them judge and jury?"

Rhys couldn't get over how Carla's opinions echoed his own. All he did was agree with her. "You're using my argument verbatim."

"Well, they're not going to get away with it!" Carla stated with indignation. "Destroying Prima alone would have generated huge waves of negativity throughout the universe; not to mention any other planets they destroyed in the past. So I'd say the League needs to examine its own actions before they go around pointing the finger at Earth!" Carla was so worked up by now she shot up from her seat and paced back and forth. "They have no right to do this, Rhys. You did well to resign or whatever it is you do over there. They're killers, just like anywhere else—but they kill on a massive scale."

Rhys reached out for her hand and gently drew her back to the seat. "I'm afraid there isn't much we can do if they decide to destroy Earth," he spoke softly, taking the sting out of her tirade. "Carla, this is much bigger than two people like you and me. It's out of our hands now."

Carla found no words with which to respond so she squeezed his hand for reassurance.

"I had an argument with Commander last time I saw him," Rhys confessed. "He came to visit just after you left Merry Beach."

"He came to Earth?"

"Only to see me," Rhys replied. "He can't accept the fact that if the decision taken by the League is to destroy this planet, I'm still staying on."

Carla searched his eyes. "What does that mean?"

"It means I can't take you with me because Earthlings can't live on Tyerra for long. The energy from the high levels of consciousness is too powerful and Earth people wouldn't survive it without the right filtering system," he explained. "So I told Commander I'd stay here."

Carla felt the pinprick of tears in her eyes. "You'd do this for me?"

Rhys enfolded her in his arms. "Of course. You know how much I love you."

Carla pulled away. "But you can't give up your life because of me," she argued. "I won't let you do it. How do you think I'd feel if they're going to destroy us, and you die needlessly because of your feelings for me? You have the ability to live for eight hundred years or more, you said; so why kill yourself for a lost cause?"

Rhys brought her back into his embrace. "Because I don't want to live without you. And this is a point I won't discuss further," he stated firmly.

His tone took Carla by surprise. She had never heard him talk forcefully. He was always pleasant; he never got angry; he was too evolved for that. "I... I don't know what to say, Rhys," she whispered close to his ear. "I love you so much I'd give my life for you, too. This is why I say, save yourself. There's no need for both of us to die."

Rhys stood up, bringing her to her feet. "Please, let's not discuss this right now. The choice is mine to make and I'm not going anywhere. Besides, there's still some hope left that Earth might be spared."

Carla kissed his lips lightly. "I don't want to think about this horrible thing, either. I can't even conceive the League making the decision to destroy Earth. Right now, I can't wrap my mind around anything else except the fact we're together."

"You should rest a while. You didn't get much sleep last night," Rhys suggested, kissing her brow. "I'll clean up the breakfast things and then I'm going to submit the final report."

Carla nodded in agreement and they walked back inside the cottage with their empty coffee mugs. Tom stayed out in the sun, looking after them. Rhys communicated to the dog that Carla needed rest and he should stay and enjoy the warmth. Sensing they were not splitting up, like what had happened the last time with Michael, the dog felt reassured and obeyed.

While Carla rested, Rhys checked through his report and

ensured statistics and all pertinent information was in order. In conclusion, he recommended the League should examine past events, which revealed a high probability of causal effect on the erosion of the fabric of consciousness. He listed some of them, including the destruction of the planet Prima plus other planets. Then, he worked on a complex set of calculations to illustrate the small percentage of negativity generated by Earth's activities and its causal effect towards the erosion issue. In the end, Earth's causal effect measured approximately 2.5% of the overall negative energy when past destruction activities by the League were taken into consideration.

Rhys felt a kindling of hope for the first time when he examined the result of his calculations. Surely, the League would consider this low percentage of negativity negligible in comparison to past corroding events that contributed to the erosion of the fabric of consciousness, and they would hopefully spare planet Earth.

With no more to be done, and after checking and rechecking his calculations, Rhys submitted his report to Commander, who would in turn check the report before he tabled it for discussion at the next meeting of the League of Galaxies.

Totally lost in what he had been doing, Rhys was surprised when Carla called him from the kitchen to lunch, just as Tom walked into the small office for a cuddle. Rhys ruffled the dog's ears and patted him. "Did you hear that, boy? Lunch is ready."

Tom barked happily and took off for the kitchen with Rhys following. Carla set down a bowl of kibble for Tom and then turned to the stove for the espresso maker. Rhys caught the aroma of freshly brewed coffee and smiled. "That smells great!" He stole a quick kiss from Carla and, before he could go back for more, she handed him the coffee pot.

"Here you go," she chided him gently. "Make yourself useful while I finish with the other things."

Rhys set down the pot and cups on the table while Carla brought over a platter of antipasto with slices of fresh Italian bread. Rhys poured the coffee and they sat down to eat.

"Did you finish your report?" Carla asked, reaching for a couple of bocconcini pieces, which she placed on her plate alongside sundried tomato slices and fresh basil.

"I have." Over lunch, Rhys explained what he had done and how he felt optimistic about the results.

"I don't want to be negative, of course," Carla remarked when he finished speaking, "but unless the League recognises their own past actions they'll still go on blaming Earth."

"That sounds very grim," Rhys observed.

Carla laughed. "Now I can tell you're a real extraterrestrial. Trust me, if you'd been an Earthling who had to deal with real arseholes out there, you'd be saying the same thing as me. With corporate companies, as with governments worldwide, it's all about their ego and how much more money they can make. It's the power over people they have that gives them a rush of excitement. Meanwhile, they don't give a crap about the population and the daily problems we face in our lives. So if members of the League are anything like Earth governments and corporate businesses, then we're doomed."

Rhys was struck by the cynicism in her voice. "But surely there's good on Earth to balance this kind of behaviour you're speaking of."

Carla nodded. "Sure, there's good. This is how over time people have managed to bring about change—but it's always a tough struggle. In any case, I'm not sanctioning the League's reasons for wanting to destroy Earth when I say bad things about humanity. All I'm trying to point out is that we could do a lot better for ourselves."

"Then you're an optimist after all," Rhys remarked.

"I try," Carla said with hope. Perhaps, she thought, she was attempting to convince herself that there was basic goodness in mankind. Oftentimes, however, one had to search very hard to find it.

***

Carla watched the tide ebb beyond its usual stretch of beach, leaving exposed the sandy bank that led to a deeper indentation on the ocean floor. A variety of fish flapped around violently while a myriad of marine life lay marooned on the wet ground. Seeing this spectacle, people on the beach approached and children rushed to pick up starfish, sea snails and other molluscs that were stranded to the elements of sun and wind.

A feeling of dread hit Carla in the stomach as she stood at her usual cliff ledge with Tom. The dog had started to whine and he shuffled with his front paws while moving away from the cliff. He then made eye contact with her and returned to doing his routine all over again. This went on for a few minutes as Carla looked on in fascination; first at the receding shoreline down by the beach and then at Tom.

She could not figure out what was going on and as she looked around her, she merely noted the tranquil day. The sun was out, the sky a bright blue, the waters their usual azure colour, and the birds... Carla's heart jolted as a wave of panic rushed through her, leaving her legs feeling weak and rubbery. Where had the birds gone?

Again, Tom did his whining and shuffling routine and Carla looked down towards the beach. Some people collected clams while others picked up flapping fish to take them closer to the water's edge. Kids were still going around with brightly coloured sand pails, gathering and storing sponges, starfish, shells and whatever other creatures they could find.

Tom came back to her side and this time bit down hard on the bottom part of her trouser leg as he started to drag her away from the ledge. Carla couldn't move at first and stood rooted to the spot as understanding suddenly dawned. She resisted Tom's pulling force, however, and looked out to sea, where in the distance she noticed a long wave starting to roll towards the shore. The wave did not look big, but the moment she saw it Carla knew exactly what it was. She started to yell at the people down by the beach while she waved her arms, trying to point to the oncoming tsunami, but no one could hear her.

The wall of water moved rapidly and grew larger as it started to get closer to the shore. Carla watched, horrified, as the monstrous mass of water suddenly became the size of a large mountain and crashed down on the people at the beach, sweeping them to their deaths.

Tom barked wildly and then bit down on her trouser leg again, this time pulling with all his might. Carla's mind had enough time to register the second wave coming in just behind the one that had swept away everything. The wall of grey-green water was massive, even higher than the cliff Carla stood on. She knew it was too late. There was nowhere to run. She looked up at the crest of the wave just as it was about to crash down on her from its great height. Then she jumped up and her eyes took in a frightened Tom, watching her from the foot of the bed. Rhys sat up next to her, knowing immediately what had happened, and he flipped on the bedside lamp. Carla waited until her heartbeat slowed down so she could draw deep breaths.

The panic that infused her swamped all logic out of her mind and though she knew she had just had another one of her dreams, she could not yet function. She simply remained sitting up in bed, wide-eyed and unable to speak. A shiver of fear rushed from the bottom of her feet to the top of her head and she started to tremble with a bone-chilling coldness that made her teeth chatter.

Rhys enfolded her in his arms and brought her back down to lie next to him as he drew the blanket right up to her chin, covering every bit of her while he tried to warm her with his body heat. There was no need for them to speak. The image in her head was his, and the emotions she felt, he felt.

The horror of what she'd seen etched itself into the recesses of her mind forever along with all the other disasters she had dreamed about. Carla did not sleep for the rest of the night. She simply stayed in the safety of Rhys's arms and as the warmth of his body communicated to hers, she was able to relax a little. Nothing, however, could take away the haunted look on her face as she lay in the semi-darkness with eyes wide open.

14

During the days that followed Carla had no more nightmares and she and Rhys put it down to the fact that now the recommendation report had been submitted, and Rhys had completely shut off from thinking about its contents, nothing else could filter into Carla's subconscious.

Until Rhys heard back from Commander, the waiting turned into an idyll in time for Rhys and Carla. This was their season together, no matter how long or short. This was all they might have to take with them beyond consciousness if Earth was destroyed. Whatever the case, Rhys and Carla agreed not to think or talk about anything to do with the pending situation until word came through after the League of Galaxies held their meeting.

Carla telephoned Jana and put a hold on all her project work. She was loath to lie to her friend, but did not want to disclose any of what was going on. She simply told Jana she needed more time to think about things, but she did not mention having met anyone, even though Jana made a joke about Carla holding out on her and that she probably had a man stashed away somewhere at Merry Beach. Carla laughed at Jana's remark and told her the only male in her life was four-legged and furry, plus she allowed her friend to believe she was still at the cabin.

By isolating themselves to this extent, Rhys and Carla were able to express their love for one another without the world intruding in on them. This was all they had at present and they refused to think about a future that may not exist. So they took pleasure in the simple things in life as if they were on a holiday. They went for long drives to explore the wonders of the Blue Mountains National Park; had picnics in lush green grounds near waterfalls; walked many of the bushwalking tracks; stargazed from the Jamison Valley at night, taking in the millions of stars in the velvety black sky while Rhys shared his superior knowledge of the universe; but above all, they expressed their love at every level—physically, mentally and spiritually.

For Carla, this time became the chrysalis that led to her transformation as a being not only of Earth, but one of the cosmos. In essence, she was still Carla, but from a mental perspective she melded with Rhys and through him to the totality of the fabric of consciousness. For the first time, Carla felt truly alive and connected with all living things.

Rhys, on the other hand, found himself on a voyage of discovery of what it meant to be an "earthed" being. His experience with the physical taught him once again that all things must have a balance, and his ancestors had known this. It became a humbling experience for him to discover that no matter how evolved, Tyerrans and other superior beings in the universe could not fully appreciate life without the diversity of the senses. For instance, imagining touching something or someone became a lot more powerful when the sense of touch was used—and the same applied to all other senses: sight, taste, smell, hearing. In many ways, Rhys became the perfect human—evolved enough to know better than to do harm; full of empathy and with the desire to advance humanity in a positive way; but at the same time, to appreciate life fully through his senses.

Rhys's lovemaking with Carla intensified as they both became more familiar with each other's rhythm. As a result, they often ended up with tears in their eyes at the beauty of this most intimate expression of unity between two beings.

One night, after they made love and lay in each other's arms, Rhys remarked, "What people call 'fucking' must be so empty—so self-centred in many ways."

Carla swept back the fringe of hair that fell across his face so she could see his eyes more clearly in the semi-darkness of the bedroom. "What makes you say that all of a sudden?"

"It just occurred to me," Rhys replied as he caressed the side of her face. "I simply think fucking seems calculating and unemotional. It's just a means to an end. A person wants to relieve themselves by achieving orgasm, so they simply fuck whoever they can find and once the act is over they move on, and more than likely never see the other person again."

Carla found herself nodding in agreement. "You're right there. Fucking is what people use to express lust, which is often confused with love. They use it for power and control over others. This type of behaviour carries a huge component of self-gratification and narcissism; or simply, as you say, people use it to relieve themselves—like when someone needs to relieve their bladder by emptying it."

Rhys didn't reply, but waited for Carla to go on. He knew she had more on her mind when it came to this topic.

"Fucking tends to give some people a sense of entitlement over another person, so they can dominate or manipulate them by conning them into thinking they care while what they're really after is something the person has, which they themselves want." Her tone sounded neutral when she expressed this point, but Rhys knew immediately she was referring to her ex.

"Everything must have a balance though," Rhys remarked. "Good and evil; light and dark; making love and fucking."

Carla pushed herself up on one elbow. "What is it that really brought this up in the first place?"

"Only the fact that being so close as we are teaches us the spiritual side of life. And this is what truly matters."

Carla leaned down and kissed his lips lingeringly. "There is another dimension to fucking, however, but this is something for another day. Meantime, you changed my life completely, and for this I'm so grateful. No matter what happens in future I'll always know we're a part of each other forever, and nothing can erase this because matter itself can't be destroyed. So our love and existence will go through changes, but in essence it will still be there until the end of time."

They remained silent for a moment and although they agreed not to think about what may happen, they could not help facing the reality of their love and how it would still go on in another form, even if their bodies were destroyed.

At that precise moment, a huge explosion deafened them and the room shook violently. Tom scrambled under the bed as Rhys and Carla jumped out of it and reached for their clothes.

"What the hell was that?" Carla uttered in the dead silence that followed the explosion and before they heard sirens going off all around them. People were screaming out in the streets and the smell of smoke permeated the cottage. Carla had an instant flash of her bushfire dream, but knew this could not be it. The explosion had been like a bomb or something that had the power to shake the ground.

She thought of the extinct volcanoes all around them, but this was not a possibility. The last known volcanic eruption in the Blue Mountains occurred approximately fourteen to twenty million years ago.

Rhys rushed out to the street and Carla followed close behind. Even though it was past midnight, the street was full of people who had come out of their homes to see what was going on. Carla heard some of them screaming about flames just before she saw plumes of fire and smoke rise over the town, cordoning them off from any form of escape. The flames encircled them.

Fire engines sped past as people rushed in all directions to check their homes and prepare to protect them from the advancing fire if need be. Some people stood in the street, still in shock, wondering what had happened, while others went to their aid and helped shepherd them out of harm's way by taking them away from the road.

Carla held on to Rhys. She was still trying to process the shock of what was happening, but her heart jolted in fear when she caught the look on Rhys's face. It was the look of someone who knew exactly what was going on. No shock, no surprise, just resolute anger flashing in his eyes.

"It's them, isn't it?" Carla shook his arm so she could get his attention. "They're going ahead with it and didn't even warn us!"

Rhys grabbed hold of both her arms and drew her away from the street and into the front garden of the cottage. "Come inside," was all he said.

Carla allowed herself to be drawn by him and Rhys led her to the loungeroom where he made her sit on the sofa. Tom came out to join them, but his head was down and his tail between his legs. He was still shaking with fear. Rhys called to the dog and gave him a reassuring hug. Whatever he mentally communicated to Tom had the effect of making him look normal again and the dog lay in front of the heater, which Rhys switched on to warm the room.

"Rhys," Carla reached out for his hand to pull him down next to her, "tell me what's happening!"

Rhys remained standing. "I have to contact Commander. Something's gone wrong."

Carla released his hand. "You think they're destroying us?" The concern in Rhys's gaze unsettled her.

"I'll know more when I reach him," he replied and walked out of the room towards the study, where he kept the thumb communicator.

Carla switched on the TV and put up the volume so she could hear above the din of the events taking place outside. She hoped the flames did not reach the town. Then, it occurred to her that if they were under attack by the League they could be destroyed at any time and the fire would not matter at all.

"... it was reported as a ball of fire," the news announcer's voice said as Carla turned to the news channel. "It is believed to be a small asteroid, but one with force enough to do damage" the announcer went on. "The object, which was first seen by Sydneysiders, hurtled through the skies in the general direction of the Blue Mountains. Reports coming in confirm this is what happened. The object hit the Jamison Valley floor, causing a large explosion on impact and resulting in raging fires around the national park. Thankfully, we do not have any reports of loss of life. Residents are urged to stay indoors while the fire department attends to the scene. As we speak, helicopters and helitanks are on their way to douse the flames in the hope of getting the fire under control. Please stand by for another update in ten minutes."

Carla switched to CNN news, which was reporting the same thing; she then tried the ABC and Sky News, and it seemed the incident was an isolated one as there were no reports of any other destructive events around the world. She turned down the volume, but left the TV on, and went in search of Rhys.

Shivers ran down her spine when she recalled the similarity of this catastrophe to the dream she had had about the bushfire. Although in her dream the fire had been a result of climatic change combined with the effects of El Niño; the fire caused by whatever projectile the League had deployed was doing the same damage and flanking the town of Katoomba. Fortunately, the night was still and without the wind to fan the flames it was likely the fire would be brought under control that much sooner and the town saved.

Rhys was in the study, gesticulating with his hands, but not actually talking. At first, Carla thought he'd gone mad, but then she remembered he was communicating via thought process. It was strange to watch him have a discussion without actually speaking and yet employing the same body language everyone used when communicating verbally.

Rhys threw a quick glance her way but kept up his discussion, and Carla drew away. There was no point in hovering if she could not hear what was being said.

She went to the kitchen and put on some coffee. No one was going to sleep tonight. The screaming in the streets had ceased and the only sounds now were those of fire engines, helicopters and the crackling of flames coming from the national park. Carla hoped again that the town would be saved. Her cottage was right in the middle of the Katoomba CBD, which was one of the best locations to be in during a bushfire. If the fire reached this far, though, there was no hope for anyone else.

While the coffee was on the stove, she fixed some sandwiches and all the while kept an eye out for flames in the backyard. The smell of smoke became stronger, but so far no flames were to be seen. This gave her reason to hope that things would turn out well, and the fact that this seemed to be an isolated incident strengthened that hope.

When the coffee was ready she took everything into the loungeroom, just in time to catch the news update. She put up the volume on the TV as the announcer explained the firefighters were struggling with the fire, but it seemed to be under control. Carla then did a sweep of all other news channels and thankfully no other reports came in regarding catastrophes around the world. If it weren't for Rhys, having the feeling something had gone wrong with the League, Carla would have thought this to be the work of arsonists, except they did not use explosives, at least not of this magnitude. Additionally, in order to start a fire in the middle of winter, and especially after such heavy rain, it would take some kind of huge force to set one off.

Reassured that they were in no immediate danger of annihilation, Carla switched off the TV and waited for Rhys to return. He was back within minutes; a look of fury marred his face. He sighed with frustration and sat next to Carla on the sofa.

Carla put a cup of coffee in his hand and he accepted it gratefully. She knew he didn't trust himself to speak just yet so she offered him a sandwich, but he declined and sipped on his coffee instead.

She stroked his hair, imagining how angry he must be. Rhys allowed his head to rest against her shoulder, trying to relax. He stayed like this for several minutes with eyes closed and just when Carla thought he had fallen asleep he opened his eyes and sat up. He seemed calmer and she refilled his cup. This time, he accepted a sandwich.

"It's going to be okay," he finally spoke. "Thankfully, the fire will be put out in a few hours and there's been no loss of human life."

Carla wanted to cry with relief at his words, but then she thought of the poor animals in the bush and felt like screaming at the horror of it. No one remembered the animals until it was too late. Rhys put an arm around her and drew her to him.

"I'm so sorry about the animals," he said, having read her thoughts. "Many didn't make it, but if it's of any consolation, they died instantly. This was not a regular bushfire and it surged so quickly upon impact that anything in its path perished immediately."

Silent tears rolled down Carla's face. It didn't matter whether they died instantly or not; the fact was they were dead. She buried her face against his chest and cried for the creatures, for nature, and for the reality of the planet she lived in. Life was so harsh that sometimes it was better to simply die.

Rhys tightened his hold on her and kissed the top of her head. "I know what you're feeling, but that's the way life is—and not just on Earth. Sometimes, despite our best intentions, things happen and those we care for suffer." As he said this he thought of Xaye. "I'm sorry this had to happen as it did."

Carla pulled away and sat up facing him while she dried her tears with a tissue. "What did happen exactly?"

"Believe it or not someone got trigger happy and decided to send us a warning."

Carla was stunned, but her tongue seemed to work when she exclaimed, "So they're not as evolved as they make out to be!"

Rhys shook his head in wonder. "I can't think of what the hell is going on over there right now. Commander told me the meeting didn't take place yet. He just keeps harping on about the negativity, making people do crazy things." Rhys's tone reflected his earlier anger.

"Well, this might make them realise they're not as perfect as they like to believe," Carla remarked. "From my point of view, they seem so smug about everything."

Rhys had to smile at her comment. "Don't forget I'm one of 'them' too."

Carla leaned over and kissed his lips lightly. "Yes, but

you're more informed than they are. You can see the difference between what they think and what's happening here on Earth. You agree the balance is upset, not necessarily because of Earth, but because of their own past actions."

"Spending time on Earth gave me more perspective, I guess."

"Anyway, what was that thing, a missile?" Carla referred to the so-called asteroid.

"Yes. It was a small one, but you felt its power."

"But why fire it over here? I checked the news and there are no accounts of anything catastrophic anywhere else."

Rhys looked thoughtful for a moment. "I think it was meant for me."

"What! Why do you say that?" Carla regarded him in shock. "What have you done to them to get this sort of response?"

Rhys shrugged. "Who knows? I think someone's pissed off because of my report and the argument I made about the League's past actions contributing to what's happening now. They already have me marked as a bit of a troublemaker because I always speak my mind, plus I really pushed for Prima to be spared last time, and they didn't forget it."

Carla couldn't believe what she was hearing. "These people are just as bad as Earthlings. I told you about their egos. Good grief, it seems it's the same thing all over the universe!"

"Not every being's like that. In the past, they were fair in the League. I think this consciousness erosion is having a psychological effect on everyone right now."

"Is this what Commander says?"

Rhys finished his coffee in one gulp before he replied, "Yes. And I agree. It was never like this before. But I pushed the point that this is exactly why they can't blame Earth for what's happening. It seems the League's past actions are starting to have an effect on everything."

"And Commander agrees?"

"I think he's beginning to see my point of view."

Carla shivered. "These people scare me, Rhys," she said, taking hold of his hand. "You have enemies out there."

Rhys replied with reassurance in his voice. "Don't worry. Commander has a good idea it's someone from one of the galaxies that recently joined the League. He'll uncover the whole thing, and there will be repercussions. I'm only sorry they caused a huge fire over here simply to make a point."

Carla moved into his arms. She wanted to bury her face against him and stay there forever. The shock of the night's events was beginning to wear off, leaving her exhausted. She wanted to sleep, but she was still worried something else might happen even though Rhys seemed of the opinion that all would be resolved.

15

The bushfire was extinguished, just as Rhys had predicted, and although thousands of hectares had been affected, no human loss resulted. Wildlife, however, did not fare very well and all sorts of animals were rushed to vets by residents and park rangers. Vets gave freely of their time to treat the animals and many locals opened their homes to foster wildlife until the animals recovered and could be released back into their natural habitat.

Carla volunteered as a foster parent and came home holding a joey that she decided to name Rhys Junior. Both Rhys and Tom were surprised when she walked in holding the joey wrapped in a blanket, just like a baby. The baby kangaroo looked a little startled and tried to burrow down into the blanket pouch in Carla's arms.

"Meet Rhys Junior," Carla announced to the two in front of her. "He was found in his mother's pouch with slightly singed ears and much in shock." Her voice turned croaky when she added, "The mother didn't make it."

Rhys looked at the little fellow and Carla envied his ability to communicate with the joey. She would have loved nothing better than to reassure Rhys Junior that he was here to recover and would be safe with them. But it seemed Rhys did the job of telling him this because within seconds the joey looked at Carla and accepted the milk bottle she had been holding in one hand. The joey clamped its mouth around the rubber teat on the bottle and started to suck greedily and Carla sat down with little Rhys on her lap while he fed.

"You'd make the ultimate vet," she told Rhys.

Rhys switched on the heater in the loungeroom and Tom plonked his bulk in front of it after he sniffed Rhys Junior and satisfied himself that the joey was not here for the long term.

"Young Rhys is a bit cold," Rhys explained. "He likes a warm environment."

Carla nodded. "Yes, I know. We'll have to make up a snug bed for him in some kind of box. I have old blankets in the linen cupboard and a large piece of sheepskin that should come in very handy."

"Leave it with me," Rhys said and went off to the kitchen to make coffee while Carla fed their baby. He smiled at the thought —their baby. The joey was so cute with his curious eyes and slightly singed ears, he looked adorable, and it was so like Carla to make him a part of their family immediately. Tom, in the meantime, accepted he had a stepsibling for a short while and he took this in his stride after Rhys explained the situation to him.

The pain Carla felt at the death of the joey's mother ran through Rhys's mind, too. Carla was heartbroken, but she tried to keep her feelings to herself. She probably didn't want to overwhelm him with so many emotions. After all, the whole time of the bushfire had been traumatic for all of them. Rhys, in particular, felt extra sensitive; first taking on the pain of all living beings around him and then trying to contain his anger at finding out the fire had been started on purpose by some lunatic from the League.

"Hey," Carla's voice intruded into his thoughts as she called from the lounge, "I forgot to tell you; I read in the news that the fire almost reached the secret canyon of the Wollemi pines. Thankfully, the pines were spared."

Rhys knew where the secret canyon was located, even if Carla did not. The Wollemi pine was one of Earth's oldest and rarest trees, thought to be extinct until in 1994 a national park ranger discovered a bunch of them. There were less than one hundred of these trees left, which were known to be living fossils with the same genetic make-up as those in existence about 200 million years ago. The national park kept the location of this remote canyon a secret so the pines would remain undisturbed. Some of the trees were thousands of years old, with the oldest known fossil being around 90 million years. Since their discovery, measures had been taken to grow new pines in different locations in order to keep the species alive for future generations. Each tree's location was now recorded on GPS so rangers knew exactly where to find them.

"Did you know the tallest Wollemi is over 130 feet tall? That's like 40 metres or so! But of course, you probably know all this, including their location," Carla called out again from the loungeroom.

Rhys finished with the coffee and brought it into the room just as Carla was done feeding the joey and was now wiping its bottom with a baby wipe. "The vet told me I have to toilet him or he may hold onto his pee because he's under stress," she explained as Rhys put down the coffee things on the table.

Rhys softly patted the joey's head. "He's fine. He feels safe with us."

Carla finished cleaning the joey's bottom and threw the soiled wipe into a plastic bag. She then put the joey back into his blanket pouch. "He's only about ten months old."

Rhys nodded. "I know." Then, he handed her a mug of coffee and took the joey out of her arms so she could relax for a while.

Carla looked disappointed.

"What's wrong?" Rhys asked.

"I just wonder what you see in me," Carla confessed, casting him a look of sadness. "You read my mind, you know my thoughts, and you seem to know practically everything there is to know in the universe. How can I compete with that to keep your interest?"

Rhys reached out with one hand and caressed the side of her face. "Don't say things like that, Carla. I love you for your uniqueness. I may be able to read thoughts, but the caring and sensitivity you show, that's genuine love and caring that comes from inside you, plus your empathy for all the suffering in your world is what makes you the person you are. I had nothing to do with any of those things."

Carla put down her coffee mug on the table and moved closer to him. She caressed the joey's soft head and then leaned across and kissed Rhys's lips in the same manner as her touch on the joey—softly. "I'm sorry," she said, feeling contrite. "You must think I'm a real whinger, when I have so much to be grateful for. Meeting you gave meaning and purpose to my life. It's just that I sometimes think you'll get bored with me."

Rhys gave her a reassuring smile. "Don't be silly. It's not like I'm constantly reading your thoughts and you can't surprise me as a result of this. You surprised me plenty of times, trust me," he said, thinking about their physical and spiritual union. "Besides, you, too, gave meaning and purpose to my life. We're a true pair. Don't ever forget that."

With the joey between them, they kissed long and lingeringly and when they drew apart the joey was fast asleep in Rhys's arms.

***

Rhys spent the afternoon building a timber box in which to house little Rhys and he lined it with the blankets Carla had mentioned. He then fashioned a pouch-like form with a piece of fleecy sheepskin so the joey could sleep in the cocoon and feel safe and warm.

Tom helped Rhys in the project, mainly by keeping him company and asking for reassuring pats every now and then. The dog was envious of the cute kangaroo even though Rhys had explained the 'roo was only going to be with them for the short term.

Rhys smiled at Tom as he worked and kept up a lively conversation with him about taking him for a long walk after he finished his work, and how they would play catch in the park.

Carla went to have a nap after lunch while Rhys worked out the back, making Rhys Junior's new bed. She slept fitfully, waking at the slightest noise in the house. For some reason, she felt on edge and yet she had nothing to worry about—at least, not for the present moment.

She lived with the man she loved and who loved her in return; she was surrounded by the love of Tom and Rhys Junior; the bushfire had been pretty much extinguished, and with rain predicted for that evening it would more than likely be put out altogether. The animal victims of the fire were getting help, and the world seemed a better place for once. But for how long? Carla asked herself.

After tossing and turning for a long while, she gave up trying to get any sleep and went to the study to do some work; at least, when she focused on her work she felt calmer. She checked her emails and noticed one from Jana, asking if all was well. Carla replied, telling her friend she was now home in the mountains and back at work. She also reassured her that the fire had not affected the town. The last thing she wanted was for Jana to drive up to check on her wellbeing and come face to face with Rhys.

At present, Carla kept Rhys a secret. If the League of Galaxies settled the future of the planet in a positive manner there would be plenty of time to introduce Rhys to all and sundry. Right now, though, Carla was not ready to explain Rhys's role in her life. She did not want the outside world to intrude in on them, not until they knew for sure what the fate of Earth would be. Besides, she was being selfish and wanted to keep Rhys all to herself for as long as possible, especially if their time on the planet was limited.

This brought thoughts of the League and the outcome of their decision. Would they really sanction the destruction of Earth? They had done it with other planets in the past, so what was so special about Earth that they would spare it? Carla agonised about this and hoped Rhys could pull this one off and save the planet.

The world was a cruel place where atrocities occurred every day, but Carla deeply believed in the beauty that counteracted the evil on the planet. She was sure the positive energy was much stronger than the League believed and that Earth truly was worth saving. The miracle of nature was the biggest testament to this whole situation and no one, not even the League, had the right to destroy nature. This in itself would have a detrimental effect on the fabric of the cosmos and if only the League could get this through their heads—and if Commander could help the process along and convince them of the fact—then Earth had a chance for survival.

As if on cue, Carla noticed the thumb communicator glow green and she knew who was at the other end of the device. If she could talk through the thing she could tell Commander what she really thought of the League and their high-minded attitude.

She picked up the device and pondered on it for a few moments, knowing all the while Commander would be reading her thoughts. She may not be able to talk to him in a two-way conversation, but he would be able to read her mind. Of course, she would not get a reply from him unless he somehow made it so the device could talk back to her or he managed to send her some sort of telepathic message.

She knew she should be rushing outside to call Rhys so he could communicate with Commander, but she stalled a little longer. "I know you can hear me at your end," she suddenly said to Commander with her voice, realising that whether she expressed herself verbally or via thought he would hear her all the same. The only negative was that she would not be able to hear him unless he spoke or planted a reply in her mind via thought. "Anyway," she continued, "I'll hand you over to Rhys in a moment, but first I want you to know I love him so much that I would give up my life for him. So I'm pleading with you to convince him to leave Earth if the League decides to destroy it. I don't want Rhys to lose his life simply because he wishes to stay with me. And while on the subject, I don't think you guys have the right to make such lofty decisions as to what planet should or shouldn't be allowed to exist. I mean, who do you think you are? Take a good look at all the wonderful things we have over here. Even if humanity's tainted, there are plenty of people who'll lay down their lives to save someone else, even a stranger. People sacrifice so much to make this world a better place, but the League doesn't seem to be aware of this—or perhaps they simply want to use Earth as the scapegoat for what you yourselves have done in the past.

And yes, I know all about Prima and the other planets the League destroyed. So are you going to make the same mistake again now and justify Earth's destruction with your cock and bull story about the negative energy coming from here? I'm not religious, but I tell you one thing I learned—before you go casting fault on others look at your own faults first; and as far as I'm concerned, this applies to you extraterrestrials as well!"

Carla ended her tirade when she felt tears spill down her face and onto the hand that was holding the communicator. She only had enough time to berate herself for being so outspoken to a being far superior than herself. She then said in a calmer tone, "Hold on a moment, I'll go and get Rhys."

She placed the communicator back on the desk, quickly dried her tears, and then made her way past a sleeping joey in the loungeroom and through to the backyard where Rhys was working on the box for Rhys Junior while Tom kept him company.

Rhys turned when she appeared at the door and the look of concern in his eyes told her he sensed something was amiss.

"What's wrong?" He noticed Carla had been crying, but he had switched off his focus from her earlier to give her some privacy. "Did you have a bad dream?"

Carla went up to him and straight into his arms. He held her close and quickly scanned her mind. It was a jumble of chaotic thoughts and emotions, but the one thing he picked up straight away was that Commander was waiting to speak with him. Normally, he knew when Commander wanted to communicate, but between concentrating on building the box for the joey and chatting with Tom, Rhys had shut out everything else.

Carla pulled back so she could look up at him. "Nothing's wrong. I didn't mean to worry you. I was working in the study and the communicator light went on. Commander wants to speak to you... but... but..." Carla did not quite know how to tell him.

Rhys placed a hand on each of her shoulders and gazed into her eyes. "But what?"

"Well," she said, wincing, "I... uhm... Well, I kind of got carried away and think I let him have it."

Rhys laughed suddenly, surprising her. She thought he would be upset. Her eyes looked questioningly at him.

"Don't worry about Commander," he reassured her. "It's good for him to hear from an Earthling, especially from you. I don't know what you said to him, but I can feel him snickering already. I think he likes your fighting spirit, my love."

Carla felt relief flood through her. Rhys was obviously tuning into Commander even as he spoke with her and it seemed she hadn't made matters worse after all. "Go to him," she said eagerly. "He's waiting."

Rhys took one long look at her, kissed the tip of her nose, and hurried inside the house.

16

"Commander's paying us a visit," Rhys announced when he rejoined Carla.

Carla was sitting with little Rhys and Tom who were both asleep in front of the heater. The afternoon had turned cold and cloudy and the expected rain that was predicted had arrived early and was now falling quite hard.

Rhys detected a tone of concern in Carla's reply. "Is that good or bad?"

He frowned for a moment. "I'm not sure. His ability to shut off his thoughts is far superior to mine, so I couldn't pick up on anything."

Carla sighed, feeling exasperated. "This waiting game is driving me crazy. I hope Commander took note of what I said. I know I blurted it all out. But hey, I'm fighting for the survival of my planet."

Rhys took a seat next to her on the sofa and smiled. "Actually, Commander said you were a spirited little thing."

"Well," Carla remarked begrudgingly, "at least he seems to like me."

Her nuance was not lost on Rhys. "But you don't like him."

Carla's eyes flashed a look of defiance. "How can I like the guy when he wants to destroy my planet?"

"He didn't say he wants to do that. He's simply putting my recommendations forward to the League." Rhys hoped to placate her.

Carla did not want to judge, but right now she disliked Commander and what he stood for. "Whatever," she said dismissively. She didn't want to talk about the situation. Let

Commander come to see them face to face first. "By the way, does his visit mean he's going to be our houseguest?"

Rhys shrugged. "I don't know. Last time he came to see me he only stayed for a couple of hours."

"Well, I hope he doesn't think he's welcome in this house; that is, unless he has good news."

Rhys gazed at her, but in her mood he decided not to try and cajole her in any way. "And if he wants to stay?"

Now it was Carla's turn to shrug. "I don't know. I never had an extraterrestrial for a guest."

"What about me?"

Carla's bad mood flew out the window when she saw the love in his eyes. She leaned towards him and put her arms around his neck. "I'm sorry. I didn't mean to sound so horrible. It's just the stress getting to me." She ran a hand through his hair and caressed his face. It was like she wanted to make sure he was real and not just an illusion in her mind. "I'm still worried about that maniac starting the bushfire to get back at you. I know we agreed not to talk about the situation of Earth's fate, but it's all moving so fast somehow. Our time together may be coming to an end; and how can I lose you when I just found you?"

A tear escaped from one of her eyes and Rhys wiped it away with his thumb as his hand curved itself around the contour of her cheek. There was no need for words of comfort. Rhys's gesture alone communicated his deep love for her. Carla closed her eyes and wished for the thousandth time that Earth would be left alone. Then, she could spend the rest of her life with Rhys, loving him and being loved back.

***

It rained for two days straight and finally the fires were fully extinguished. On the third day, the sun made an appearance and the azure blue sky gave Carla reason to hope. The day was what locals called a magic mountain day; crispy clear, not too cold, and with the colours of nature creating a vivid panorama of greens, browns and reds. The thousands of Eucalypt trees in the national park emitted their special oil into the atmosphere, expelling the blue hue for which the Blue Mountains were renowned.

Carla sat out in the sunshine with little Rhys on her lap feeding on his marsupial milk formula while Tom sat at her feet, throwing the occasional look of envy at the joey for monopolising his mistress's attention. Carla smiled now and then at Tom, knowing full well how he felt about the presence of the baby kangaroo, but still accepting him in his own way.

Rhys had gone to do the grocery shopping and Carla experienced a momentary sense of the surreal, as she sometimes did when it hit home that she lived with an alien. And yet, Rhys was human in so many ways; the longer he spent time with her, the more human he became. Sure, he still read minds, but aside from this everything he did was like a normal human. He ate like a human, bathed like a human, and made love like a human. The latter was something he'd latched onto immediately, Carla mused with a smile on her lips. The moment they became involved in a physical relationship was the moment Rhys's real education into human behaviour began.

It wasn't so much the sex, because all humans had sex and yet could still behave like arseholes; her ex being a case in point. It was more the essence of their lovemaking that had changed Rhys. The connection of two beings at all levels: the physical, mental, and spiritual. This was something so rare to find, even among humans, and Carla felt both humbled and grateful that she had been fortunate enough to discover this depth of loving. And to think it had taken an extraterrestrial to show her how magic love could be, where all senses were engaged—physical and in the ether.

The sun lulled her into a state of peace as she thought of her life with Rhys. The joey fell asleep on her lap and Tom napped by the side of her chair. All was quiet in the back garden, except for the sound of bees buzzing among early spring flowers, until Carla heard a footfall and Tom's low growl. She opened her eyes and her heart jolted with shock at the man standing in front of her.

Exotic green eyes the colour of emeralds regarded her from a rather handsome black face. The man was bald, very tall, and sporting an athletic build. He looked ageless, but Carla guessed in Earth terms he would be in his early fifties.

She placed the joey in his box and threw a glance at Tom so he would stop growling. The dog sensed the man was not a threat, after all, and although he didn't take his eyes off their uninvited guest he remained quiet.

Carla, who stood at 5'4 ft, felt dwarfed by the man who was well over six feet, but she was not fazed. "So you're the man Rhys calls his father," she said in a cool voice.

"And you're the woman who took him away from me," replied Commander, but not without admiration for her response.

Carla felt herself prickle and at the same time realised Commander did not mean this as a condemnation, but was instead paying her a compliment, albeit in an offhand manner. She was awed by his presence, although her shock at first seeing him had dissolved and she felt no fear of him. In fact, she liked what she saw despite her feelings of enmity.

"Rhys is out right now, but you're welcome to come in and wait. I'm sure he'll be along soon. So how did you get here; dropped out of the sky?"

Commander smirked at her impertinence. She was the true spitting image of his son's late wife, Xaye, but he could see why Rhys felt closer to Carla. Her soul shone pure light and her capacity to love seemed endless. Xaye had also loved like this, but the connection between her and Rhys had been slightly different. Xaye had not been on the same spiritual level as Rhys. Carla, on the other hand, was an exact match for him.

As he kept gazing at the figure in front of him, he noted not once did she flinch or look away. She stood her ground, waiting for a response to her question. "I arrived last night and was dropped off near the Jamison Valley. I waited until morning and then walked. Your side gate was open, so here I am."

Carla noted the way he was dressed. Long-sleeved black pullover and charcoal grey cargo pants; very classy for an alien. She then saw Commander smile, for he obviously read her thoughts. "You have me at a disadvantage," she stated rather firmly, "and I would really appreciate it if you would shut off your focus on my thoughts."

Commander chuckled this time. "Well, you certainly don't mince your words, do you? I know how direct you are, especially after our little one-sided conversation the other day."

Carla blushed. "Yes, well. I thought nothing ventured, nothing gained."

Commander did not respond, but did as she requested. He shut off his focus and decided to get to know her the human way. "Aren't you going to ask me in for coffee?"

The abrupt change in conversation brought a smile to her lips and the tension she felt in his presence suddenly dissolved. "Any alien who drinks coffee is a friend of mine," she said with reluctant humour in her voice, but this gained her a smile of approval from Commander.

Just before they went in, however, Commander crouched down to make Tom's acquaintance and, like Tom had done when he first met Rhys, he put his paw in Commander's hand. The joey kept sleeping, but Commander picked up the box with him in it. "We should take him inside. He's getting a little cold."

Carla nodded, already used to Rhys's ability to sense the feelings of people and animals. She led the way into the loungeroom where she left Commander with Rhys Junior and Tom, who followed in Commander's footsteps now they had become friends. Carla proceeded to the kitchen to make coffee and returned minutes later with a tray bearing the coffee things, including Scottish shortbread biscuits. Commander sat on the sofa, silently communicating with Tom while the joey slept near the heater, which Commander had switched on for him.

"How do you take your coffee?" Carla asked as she poured him a cup.

"Black, one sugar, thanks," he replied.

"That's how Rhys takes it."

"I know. He's the one who put me onto it and now it seems I'm addicted."

Carla smiled and handed him the cup. She offered a shortbread biscuit and Commander took one.

"So what's the food like on Tyerra?" Carla queried. Among the many discussions she'd had with Rhys about his planet, she never fully covered the matter of food, except to discover Tyerrans were vegetarians.

"A bit bland at times," Commander confessed while he savoured the shortbread and helped himself to another.

Carla was bursting to ask him about the purpose of his visit, but she felt this was best left for when Rhys returned. There was, however, one thing she needed to get off her chest. "Commander," she uttered, "the other day, when you heard me talking to you, I meant what I said about getting Rhys to go back to Tyerra if Earth is to be destroyed. Rhys explained to me why he could never take me to live on your planet, and I accept that, but I don't want him to stay with me if the League decides to destroy Earth."

Commander regarded her with a kindly look. "You love Rhys more than your life."

Carla nodded. "Rhys is everything to me. Without him my life would no longer have any meaning. And if I'm to die, there's no point in him dying in vain when he can save himself."

Commander sipped his coffee with enjoyment to hide the fact he was moved by what Carla had said. Loving Rhys as his own son, he understood love made a person do anything—even give up their own life, but actually hearing Carla verbalise it somehow drove the point home more powerfully. "Rhys feels the same way about you. He won't leave despite what happens to Earth. He says he has no life if you're not in it."

Tears threatened to spill down her cheeks as Carla heard this from Rhys's own father, but she made every effort to hold them back. "If we're to be destroyed, I hope you can convince

Rhys to leave." This was all she could say and knew Commander would try his hardest to get Rhys off the planet in case of annihilation. Knowing one was going to die was bad enough without having to bear the pain of a loved one dying because they didn't want to live without the person they loved. The problem was that while she was willing to give up her life for Rhys, he was also willing to give up his for hers.

Carla noticed Commander watching the interplay of emotions across her face at the complexity of the situation. She sensed he had turned off his focus on her, as she had requested he do earlier, and now he seemed to be trying to figure her out the old-fashioned way.

"I know humans seem rather contradictory to you in many ways," Carla remarked as if it was she who was reading his thoughts. "Whatever happens, though, I want you to remember this about humans: disaster is sometimes more powerful in bringing us together than love can be."

Commander's look of compassion unnerved her. Perhaps, he was about to tell her all was lost and that destruction would follow. Instead, he said, "Rhys explained humans are compartmentalised creatures. You can harbour love and hate at the same time. You show an uncaring attitude at the atrocities committed in this world, and yet you come together, as you've just said, when disaster strikes, and you help one another. The complexity of your psyche is not as black and white as the League thinks."

"And what do you think?" Carla suddenly felt hope beginning to grow inside her at the possible survival of her species, but before Commander could reply, the lock at the front door turned and Rhys walked in with a number of bags filled with groceries.

The look on his face was one of surprise. He put the bags down on the floor and took in the scene before him—Carla and Commander having coffee; Tom curled up at Commander's feet, and the joey fast asleep in his box. A cosy scene, but with some kind of tension in the air, especially coming from Carla.

Commander had obviously shut off his filtering system, making it impossible for Rhys to know he had arrived.

"I was wondering when you'd get here," Rhys said aloud for Carla's benefit.

"Hello, Rhys," Commander replied in the same manner. "Carla makes far better coffee than you do."

This was meant to lighten up the atmosphere, but neither Carla nor Rhys smiled. Now that Rhys had arrived, so had the moment of truth and Carla jumped up and went to the kitchen for an extra cup, which she then filled with coffee for Rhys. She wanted to delay matters, especially if Commander had come to tell them Earth was to be annihilated; she wasn't yet ready to hear it.

"Rhys, have a seat. We'll put away the groceries later," Carla uttered and handed him the cup. She then turned to Commander. "Another one for you?"

Commander nodded, still keeping his filtering system shut. Despite this, he knew what Carla was trying to do. He watched as she refilled his cup and added one sugar; then, she offered him another shortbread. Meanwhile, Rhys sat down, sipping his coffee in silence. Even with his barriers up, Commander felt the strong bond between his son and this woman who was so right for him. The love in the room was like something Commander could touch if he only reached out with his hand, and the realisation of this affected him deeply. He had never in his life come across such deep love between two people, not even on Tyerra.

He sighed and tried to gather his own emotions at such a discovery. Rhys had discussed with him the nature of humans, but not being as evolved as Tyerrans and other races, Commander had assumed Rhys's judgement had been clouded by his love for Carla. The last thing he had expected to find, therefore, was the kind of love two people breathed, felt, and lived so completely—so much in tune with one another.

Having lived for hundreds of years himself, and being highly learned, Commander had read about this kind of love, but he always thought it greatly exaggerated—simply something that was a remnant from Tyerra's own ancestors and who used to write about this emotion. They had defined love as the completeness of everything; the true fabric of the cosmos.

In fact, love *was* the cosmos. The ancestors had not been referring to physical love when they wrote about it, but to unconditional love. Love for the sake of loving. Love that had the power to overcome the impossible. Love that was willing to sacrifice unselfishly, without demands or conditions. Love that engulfed everything and everyone, good or bad, and fuelled the energy that was the cosmos.

This was the love that had the power to withstand the negativity created by the multitudes. And this love could not be destroyed, even if the beings of a planet were annihilated: for love was energy—and energy could not be destroyed. It could change and undergo all kinds of transmutations, but never, ever, could love be made to disappear because without love there was nothing, and by the laws of the universe 'nothing' did not exist. There had never been 'nothing', but there had always been love.

Commander suddenly became aware of Rhys and Carla's eyes on him and he felt tears rolling down his face for the first time in his long life.

17

"The League wants to hear from you, Carla." Commander informed a surprised Rhys and Carla over dinner.

After his earlier emotional state Commander had excused himself, claiming fatigue from the journey, and Carla led him to the guest bedroom so he could grab some sleep before dinner. When she returned to the kitchen she started making dough for homemade pizza while Rhys put away the groceries in silence. Neither of them spoke, each wrapped in their own thoughts.

Rhys had never seen Commander in such a state and he was not sure whether the evidence of his emotions was due to the League having decided on annihilation for Earth or because of something Carla had said to him while Rhys was out shopping.

When Commander retired to the guestroom, Rhys scanned Carla's mind. To his surprise, he wasn't able to tune into any relevant thoughts. She was simply preoccupied with the toppings she would use for the pizza. Rhys sighed and realised it would also be useless for him to even try to tune into Commander's thoughts, so in the end he was left to draw his own conclusions.

"What did you and Commander talk about before I came home?" Rhys remarked casually once he finished putting away the groceries.

Carla, who was mixing the ingredients for the pizza dough in a large bowl, stopped and regarded him with curiosity. "You mean you don't know?" Rhys shook his head and she added with a bit of a smug grin, "I bet you've been trying to scan my thoughts, right?"

Rhys didn't know where she was going with this, but he nodded rather than try to engage in a guessing game with her. "I confess I have, but all I got was your pizza toppings," he replied with a half-amused smile.

Carla threw him a smile of her own; this time feeling guilty she had teased him. She turned back to her task and responded, "I asked Commander to shut off his focus on my thoughts. Perhaps, this has something to do with you not being able to pick up on them, either. He's a very powerful man, your father, but I have a feeling deep down inside he's a real softie."

"Does this mean you're not going to tell me what you were discussing with him?"

"It's nothing secret, if that's what you're getting at," Carla assured him. "It was simply something I was curious about." She kept herself from thinking what she had asked Commander to do with Rhys in case of annihilation, and she did so by running through recipes in her mind just in case Rhys was scanning her now.

Rhys looked a little put out. "So you're not going to tell me?"

"Best ask Commander," she responded as if the matter was of no importance.

Feeling surprisingly frustrated with Carla for the first time, Rhys got on with feeding little Rhys, and then he took Tom for a walk before it got too cold. Carla saw them off with a bemused look on her face. She knew she couldn't keep her thoughts to herself for long, but it had been gratifying to learn that when she focused on something entirely different Rhys had trouble tuning in.

She loved Rhys with all her heart and soul, but she knew he would be upset if he found out what she had asked of Commander. For once, she would like to keep this particular thought to herself. Therefore, the best thing to do was to forget it so Rhys wouldn't pick up on it later. If Commander chose to disclose his and Carla's discussion to Rhys, so be it.

At dinner, Commander looked rested and back to his

businesslike self. So when he announced the League wanted to meet her, Carla was stunned. "Why would they want to meet me?"

Rhys stayed silent, waiting for Commander's response. He could not understand why the League had requested to meet Carla, either.

Commander took his time in finishing off a slice of pumpkin and zucchini pizza and then reached for another, this one a mushroom and onion with Kalamata olives. Rhys managed to control his impatience by reaching for a slice of pizza, too, all the while berating himself for becoming more human. He could not remember when he had ever felt impatience on Tyerra. At this, he noticed the enigmatic smile on Commander's face and knew his father had read him loud and clear.

"I think they became rather intrigued with you when I reported the message you sent to me via the communicator." Commander finally spoke, addressing Carla. "They seemed to think there was merit in what you said and suggested meeting you in person before a final decision is made."

Carla's eyes grew wide with excitement. "You mean they're going to spare us?"

"Not so fast," Commander replied. "They want to hear your argument first."

Rhys finally interceded. He could no longer contain himself and he stated in an accusatory tone, "I thought you said Carla couldn't go to Tyerra, that the level of consciousness over there would do her harm."

Commander turned to Rhys and put up a hand to stem his outburst. "Rhys, I said she could not live there. I meant long term. It would be too much for Carla and I wouldn't want her to come to any harm."

"So how does this change things if she goes to Tyerra to talk to the League?" Rhys controlled his tone so he would appear calm, although he still felt agitated and upset in his concern for Carla.

Commander was able to reassure him, "I'd be with her at all times, filtering on her behalf. She will be totally safe with me and when the meeting is over I'll bring her straight back."

"What about me?" Rhys protested, forgetting his resolution to remain calm. "I thought the League might want to hear from me. After all, everything they wish to know is in my report."

Carla turned to Rhys and put a hand over his to pacify him. "You have to look after Tom and Rhys Junior."

Rhys was taken aback at her remark, while Commander seemed to be enjoying her response to Rhys's impatience.

"My son," Commander uttered, "I would never let anything happen to her. You have my word on that."

Rhys sighed and ran fingers through his hair, his appetite gone. "Whatever." He sounded like a sulky teenager.

"You're picking up a lot of Earthly ways, I see," Commander chided gently. "But this aside, there is another reason why the League is being so thorough on this one and wanting to hear from an Earthling."

"And what is that?" Rhys decided to ignore Commander's remark about his Earthly manners.

"They want to be one hundred per cent sure of their final decision. Meanwhile, they're still working to discover why the ex-member of the League started the bushfire incident."

Carla shot a concerned look at Commander. "You mean you haven't caught him and he's still after Rhys?"

The look in Commander's eyes was a grave one. "Unfortunately, he escaped. But we don't know if he's really after Rhys. Perhaps, he's simply angry because Earth is getting a lot more consideration on the issue of annihilation."

Carla threw a glance at Rhys to see how he took this news, but he seemed unconcerned. "And what business is it of his if Earth is getting more consideration?"

"That's what we're trying to find out," Commander reported. "We thought he was with the representatives from the planet Hergon, but now we have reason to believe he's a survivor from Prima who's impersonating one of the Hergons."

"What?" Rhys became more alert at this. "How could the Hergons not know this? I realise their planet neighbours what used to be Prima and a number of Primans may have escaped their fate by taking refuge on Hergon. But even if he is a survivor from Prima, why take it out on me? I was the only one who argued to save the planet in the first place, remember?"

"Yes, I know. But right now I can't answer your question. It could be he thinks you voted for destruction instead. Anyway, we're looking into it," Commander replied.

Carla's hand pressed down on Rhys's again and she threw him a look of entreaty. "Rhys, I must go to Tyerra and talk to the League about saving Earth. Please understand how important this is, especially if it means they'll end up sparing the planet."

Rhys nodded, albeit reluctantly. "I'd rather be there with you, of course. But sure, I'll stay here and look after the animals."

Carla wanted to kiss him, but not in front of Commander. She gave him a warm smile and then turned to their guest. "Saving the planet is of the utmost importance, of course, but I will only go if Rhys is going to be safe while we're away."

"You need to trust me more, Carla. Rhys will be fine. We won't be away for long," he replied. "In the meantime, I need to go back to the ship and organise things for the meeting." He then turned to Rhys. "We're scouting the space around Earth for the Prima man, but we don't expect another demonstration from him."

Fear spread through Carla at Commander's words. "Won't this Prima guy pick up your presence if you're scouting Earth for him?"

"We're doing this via long distance. Besides, we know how to stay under the radar, as you Earthlings say. So please trust me and be ready for tomorrow evening." Commander left them after dinner, telling Carla he would call for her at eight.

Rhys cleared up the dinner things after their guest's departure while Carla loaded the dishwasher. They worked in silence and just after nine they turned in. Tom and Rhys Junior were happily asleep in front of the loungeroom heater.

"I don't think I'll get any sleep tonight," Carla remarked while she lay with her head on Rhys's shoulder. "I'm so nervous about tomorrow."

Rhys tipped up her chin slightly with his finger so he could gaze directly into her eyes. "You'll be okay with Commander. I promise."

"I wish you were coming along." Carla didn't sound too reassured by his comment. Rhys smiled. "But you told me to stay here and look after the animals."

"I didn't mean it. I can get Tom's sitter to look after them; she's really good and I always use her when I have overnight trips to Sydney. I'll ring her in the morning." The thought calmed her a little.

"I don't think Commander wants me on this trip," Rhys remarked, shattering whatever calm she had managed to muster.

Carla hoisted herself on one elbow and regarded him with concern. "Why not? It's silly for you to stay here all alone."

"When I turned in my report, I made it clear that I wanted nothing else to do with the League, remember? So if I come along now, they'll think I'm influencing you."

Carla frowned. "But that doesn't make any sense," she argued. "Okay, so you pissed off the League, but what possible motive could you have for influencing me? It's obvious that I want my planet to be spared; it's my home after all. So I don't need to be influenced by anyone."

Rhys softly traced the contours of her nose and face with his index finger. "They'll say that because we love each other my report is too one-sided."

Carla tried to focus on their discussion even though his touch awakened her insatiable desire for him. "That's preposterous," she uttered heatedly. "Sure, we love each other and want to be together, but that's not the main reason I want the planet to be spared. I'm fighting for all that's beautiful on Earth. Surely, the world is worth saving for what's good about it!"

Rhys caressed her hair, sending little shivers of delight through her. "I agree," he whispered near her ear and started to nibble at her earlobe.

All thoughts of the upcoming trip flew out of Carla's head along with her fears of facing the League. She told herself to live for the moment in case there was no tomorrow. Life was short and precious. It was mind blowing to think how tiny Earth and all of humanity truly were in the scope of the big picture. When she thought about people and their petty problems they became insignificant, especially after she met this man she loved so much. He had changed her paradigm of thought and many of her beliefs and values.

Since meeting Rhys, her consciousness had expanded to encompass the entire universe. Only love mattered in the cosmos, the love for all beings and all things—after all, this was the only energy that kept the universe alive.

Rhys's mouth moved from her ear to her lips and Carla met his kiss with a passion that went beyond the physical. Her mouth received his hungrily; it was as if she could drink in all the universal energy from his being and at the same time share her own with him so their love would live on forever. Making love so completely—with mind, body, and spirit—was an experience Carla had only learned with Rhys, and she felt humbled by the beauty of it.

They made love on and off through the night—slowly and mindfully—using all their senses, including their thought process and their spiritual love for one another. They tasted, touched, and smelled their love using mouth, tongue, hands, nose, and eyes, so they explored every part of their bodies and knew every taste, scent, look, and texture.

Their numerous sexual unions were slow rather than frantic, unlike the pace lovers use when overcome with lust. Rhys and Carla moved almost leisurely and fluidly, savouring the smoothness of skin-to-skin contact, the wetness of each union, the aroma of their lovemaking, and the lingering shudder of each orgasm.

Just as each time they had made love in the past, the two melded together, both in mind and body. But on this occasion, they reached a place that felt surreal—where they actually became the other. It was a place where their physical bodies disappeared and their souls united in a suspended and timeless plane of existence. They were no longer Rhys and Carla—they just were.

Towards dawn, the lovers finally slept in each other's arms; they were inseparable. Wrapped in each other's souls, they shared the same aura, and their experience transcended the natural law that two objects, or in this case two beings, could not occupy the same space—but somehow through their loving exchange they had achieved this, at least at a subconscious level, and now they could never be separated again.

18

The next evening found Carla walking along one of the bush tracks in the Jamison Valley, following closely behind Commander and with the smell of the recently extinguished bushfires assaulting her nostrils. She shivered at the memory and was grateful she could not see the devastation around her.

"Make sure you watch your step." Commander's voice intruded into her thoughts. "We can't use a flashlight if we want to remain undetected."

Carla was glad she had worn her hiking boots; at least, she felt sure-footed. "I'm okay," she replied. "Good thing the moon's out."

Commander walked at her pace so she didn't lag behind and they made their way in silence for almost an hour before they came off the track and into dense bushland that had somehow remained untouched by the fire. At this point, Commander paused and Carla ran into the back of him. He reached out to steady her.

"Do you want me to carry your backpack?" he asked.

"No," Carla said; glad that in the darkness he couldn't see her blush of embarrassment at being so clumsy. "I'm fine, really."

"Hmm," Commander remarked. "I just don't see what you have to carry in that pack. Didn't Rhys tell you there was no need to bring anything along?"

At the mention of Rhys, Carla's heart contracted with pain. She couldn't stand being away from him, especially when some space weirdo from Prima might be lying in wait to kill him. In addition to this, and although she knew she'd be safe with Commander, there was no guarantee they would have a safe trip.

Anything could go wrong and she may not make it back to Earth. The thought of never seeing Rhys again almost made her turn back.

"Are you okay?" Commander's voice cut through her thoughts once again.

"Sure," Carla replied casually, as if she wasn't aware she was on her way to another planet in another galaxy that was millions of light years away from Earth, in order to convince a pack of aliens that her planet should be spared. The whole thing was so unbelievable and surreal that she was not sure if she could cope with what was happening.

She almost jumped out of her skin when she felt Commander's hand on her shoulder. "Here," he said kindly. "Let me carry that pack." As he took it, Carla began to feel a sense of calm descend upon her.

Commander grasped hold of her hand. "We're going to climb down some steep steps now, so hang onto me."

While they made their way carefully down the steep descent, Carla felt stronger and more confident about the mission ahead. It struck her that when she had been on the verge of a panic attack a light touch on her shoulder from Commander stemmed the fear from spreading. Then, she remembered what he had told her and Rhys at dinner the night before.

"Yes," Commander spoke even before she had a chance to formulate the question. "I'm focusing on your thoughts and making sure I filter whatever threatens to make you feel anxious, afraid, or simply not being able to cope."

Carla wasn't sure whether she should feel grateful or annoyed. "Hey, I can handle my own thoughts while I'm still on my own planet, thank you very much."

Commander laughed. "Well, let's just say I promised Rhys I'd take good care of you."

Oh, Rhys! If only you were here with me now, Carla thought, and immediately felt embarrassed when Commander spoke again. "Rhys is thinking the same thing right now. But don't despair; you'll soon be together again."

Carla sighed. She knew when she was beaten. "With all due respect, I'm beginning to find you very annoying."

Commander chuckled with humour. "I told Rhys you were a bit of a spitfire," he commented. "Anyway, you didn't need to bring this backpack. You look fine just as you are."

"Stop spying on my thoughts! Carla uttered heatedly. "I wanted to have a fresh change of clothes and some make-up, okay? I can't face a bunch of aliens without my war paint. And this is something neither you nor any male on Earth or in space, for that matter, would know anything about. It's a girl thing."

Commander simply chuckled again and kept leading the way down to the valley floor. Carla shrugged off her annoyance and focused on her footsteps. The lower they descended, the colder it got and she was glad she was wearing her Goretex jacket over a black Alpaca turtleneck and thick black ski pants she had chosen for the trip. She noticed Commander was similarly attired, except his legs were encased in cargo pants. Obviously, spacesuits were only worn by aliens in the movies.

"Stop thinking so much and focus on what you're doing," Commander chided her, which once again reminded Carla to watch her thoughts. "We're almost there."

Carla took a look beyond Commander, but saw nothing except trees and rocks over the rough ground and a star-studded sky above with a full moon. They walked on for several minutes through a patch of dense bushland until they finally reached a clearing, and then they stopped.

In the darkness around them, Carla noticed the outline of a triangular-shaped object the size of a rather large campervan. The object floated a few inches above the ground as if it were cushioned by the air. With the light provided from the moon, Carla espied windows at one corner of the triangle, very similar to those on a jet plane cockpit, except these were much larger. Aside from this, there was nothing remarkable about what was obviously some kind of space vehicle.

"This is it?" Carla's voice reflected the anxiety she felt at having to fly inside the small vehicle.

Commander returned the backpack to her. "This is just a shuttle to take us to the main ship."

"I knew that," Carla responded, trying to keep calm.

Commander remained silent for a few seconds and then a narrow door slid open from one side of the shuttle, displaying a couple of steps. "Let's go," Commander said, taking hold of Carla's hand again.

Carla stayed exactly where she was and Commander looked at her questioningly. "Is there a pilot in there?"

Commander sighed. "Yes. And I asked him to open the hatch so we can board. Now, are you ready or not?"

Carla shrugged her shoulders, took one last look around the clearing in case she never returned to Earth again, and allowed Commander to lead her inside the shuttle. The steps and doorway vanished into solid matter as soon as they boarded, with no evidence they had been there in the first place. Carla tried not to panic when she realised they were completely sealed inside the vehicle.

Before she had a chance to speak, however, Commander led her to a seat, very much like those found on private jets, while he joined the pilot upfront, taking the seat next to him. A quick look around the shuttle revealed an unremarkable interior with charcoal grey metal walls and a couple of seats behind the piloting area. The floor plan was completely open; there were no partitions between the front and back seats. It was similar to the seating arrangements in a car. There were a couple of cabinets built into the walls, each without handles, and Carla assumed this was some kind of storage hold area.

"Put on your seatbelt," Commander instructed. "We may have some movement coming out of the atmosphere."

Carla did as she was told and drew out a plastic water bottle from her backpack. Her mouth felt dry as hell.

Commander observed, "We do have water right here in the shuttle, you know."

"Well, I don't see it," Carla replied. "Don't worry about me, anyway. Just... just drive...or whatever it is you do."

She caught his half smile as he turned back to the panel in the piloting area, which resembled the sophisticated dashboard of an airliner, only it was more compact and slimline. Carla's eyes then rested on the pilot, who up until now had remained silent through her exchange with Commander. But then, she thought, perhaps not all Tyerrans spoke English.

The pilot looked young, somewhere in his twenties by Earth standards. He sported a haircut similar to Rhys's, only this guy's hair was platinum blond. His build was tall and slim and his features rather handsome. He was dressed in black cargo pants and a long-sleeved skivvy of the same colour; similar to what Commander wore. Carla wondered whether all Tyerrans possessed such a diverse and good looking appearance. So far, those she had met, being Rhys and Commander, possessed a flamboyant look about them that always had the power to arrest one's attention.

Commander turned back to her and in the dim light of the shuttle she still noticed his bright emerald eyes. She cast a furtive glance at the pilot, who was watching her and saw his eyes were the colour of deep amber. If it weren't for the fact that she loved Rhys beyond measure, Carla figured she would have a great time ogling the males on Tyerra, especially if they all looked so good.

"Are you ready?" Commander did not hide the sarcasm in his voice and Carla felt berated.

"Uhm... Yes. So sorry to hold you up." Carla waited until the two men turned back to the dashboard before she smiled— all the while knowing Commander knew exactly what was going on in her mind. She was nervous as hell, and a little flirting could go a long way to calming her anxiety.

The lights in the shuttle went off suddenly. Carla watched as the shuttle moved vertically upward, and within moments all she could see through the window was the dark sky filled with millions of stars. She had no idea what technology Tyerrans used, but it was far too advanced in comparison to what was available on Earth.

The two men remained silent, although Carla assumed they communicated via thought. So she sat back and felt herself relax a little. This was not as scary as she had imagined. The shuttle seemed to be suspended in the air, but in fact it just kept moving silently and smoothly in an upward trajectory. Carla only knew this was happening because she caught a quick glimpse of Earth, now far below them, and the horizon looked slightly curved.

They travelled for approximately fifteen minutes in this manner and just as Carla started to enjoy the experience, the shuttle shook and vibrated as if it had hit something. Commander turned just in time to catch the look of concern on their passenger's face.

"Relax," he told her. "We've just docked with the main ship."

Carla didn't know whether to laugh or cry at the craziness of the situation. Nobody would believe her if she ever had the opportunity to relate this tale to anyone. She would simply be considered another 'looney bin' with a UFO fixation.

Commander and the young pilot stood and Carla followed suit. She assumed they would now transfer to the main ship, and even as she thought this the sliding door and steps on the shuttle materialised out of nowhere and the exit waited for them to step through.

Carla clutched the backpack to her and stayed close to Commander as they made their way out and onto a kind of docking area with a walkway leading to a set of see-through doors. As the trio approached, the doors swished open to let them enter and Carla had just enough time to take a peek back at the shuttle, which in the light of the dock looked bright orange. A sense of déjà vu hit her like lightning then, but she had no time to process it as she tried to keep up with the two in front of her.

As soon as the trio stepped through the sliding doors, the doors swished shut immediately behind them and a jet of white, odourless vapour enclosed them. Carla knew they were going through some kind of disinfection process and she remained standing on the spot like her companions.

After a few moments, the vapour cleared and they proceeded through to another set of doors, these ones made of shiny metal. Carla found herself in a passageway that led to a large triangular common area filled with a control panel and seats for piloting. In the centre of the open plan there was a rectangular tabletop with built-in cabinets underneath and a number of seats surrounding the table. A few closed doors around the perimeter of the open area caught Carla's attention and she figured she was in the navigation bridge of the main ship, and the doors probably led to private areas.

Carla put down her backpack on the table and espied a couple of young men similarly dressed to the blond pilot. They were also alike in appearance, but with different colouring. One of them sported bright orange hair and had tawny skin, while the other had light skin and his hair was a mane of metal grey worn long and cascading down his back, almost to his waist. Again, from what she saw of them, they were quite good looking. Interestingly, there seemed to be no females on the ship.

The blond pilot threw a quick smile at her before he went to join his colleagues and Carla wondered if these beings could read her thoughts.

"No, they can't," Commander answered her silent thought. "Most Tyerrans have a certain ability to read the minds of those closest to them, such as family and friends. Rhys was born with the gift to read anyone's mind."

"And you?"

"I, too, have this gift; only I've lived much longer than Rhys and had time to develop it to a more powerful level."

"Well, it's good to know these guys can't see into my head. Firstly, because they'd be horrified at some of my thoughts and secondly, because I think between you and Rhys, this is all I can cope with for now."

Commander smiled. "Your sense of humour is your salvation. Most Earthlings would be freaking out by now."

"But you forget I've been with Rhys for a while and the idea of being with an alien grew on me."

"True," Commander agreed. "But I also detect a certain passion in you for truth and justice. So you're not really afraid to what lengths you have to go to ensure you get what you seek."

"You detect correctly," Carla affirmed, and then confessed, "but the reason I'm not freaking out now is because you're here, looking after me."

Commander did not reply at her sincere compliment, but Carla felt he was moved by what she had said. "Okay," Commander remarked instead in his usual businesslike manner. "That door to your left is the bathroom. Next to it is a bedroom where you can rest if you wish." He then pointed to another couple of doors. "There's a kitchen through there with food and a big tin of coffee, compliments of your loved one." Carla blushed at his reference to Rhys. Her loved one! "And through the other door there are a couple more bedrooms."

"So how long is this trip going to take?" Carla hoped she wouldn't be stuck here for weeks on end. Rhys had never actually told her how long it took to get to Tyerra.

"Oh, I expect maybe an hour or two." Commander surprised her with his response.

Carla's jaw dropped open even though she knew these guys had the technology to warp space and travel through wormholes. The enormity of it all was too much to take in so quickly. "I think I need a very strong coffee," she said, trying to bring normality to the situation with a mundane task.

"Good idea," Commander replied. "Make one for me, too. Black, one sugar."

Carla felt like spinning out. Here she was, somewhere in outer space about to travel through a wormhole, and she was going to make coffee. "What about the other guys, do they want any?"

Commander took a moment to respond and Carla noticed the guys nodding. He had obviously communicated with them via thought. "Yes," he turned to Carla. "The guys heard much about coffee from Rhys, and later from me, so they're all curious to try it."

"Do they speak English?" Carla wondered if they could vocalise their communication.

"They can if they have to, but they're shy of you."

Carla found this amusing. "Well, that's a first for me—extraterrestrials shy of little, insignificant me."

"Okay, pay attention." Commander was back to business again. "Just so you know, you can move freely about the ship. The atmosphere inside is set to remain as it is for the rest of the trip. It'll take us around one hour to reach the wormhole and once we pass through it we'll land on Tyerra in about thirty minutes or so."

Carla said nothing, still feeling rather spun out.

"Go make the coffee and then join us. I'm sure you'll enjoy the experience of this trip."

Carla found her voice. "I wouldn't miss it for the world."

In the galley-like kitchen with gleaming chrome benches and equipment she had never seen before, Carla managed to find the coffee and sugar. At first, she didn't see any cupboard doors, not even a pantry in sight. Then, after some reflection, she made herself imagine the cupboard doors were visible and much to her amazement they transformed into doors. "Wow!" she uttered in awe.

She then went through the cupboards one by one and found chrome cups, cutlery, and a pantry that held what looked like vegetables of some kind, although to Carla they looked like sea kelp. She recognised the can of Lavazza coffee, however, and felt like she had found an old friend. The other Earth object she came across was a much-loved Bialetti espresso maker. Carla could have kissed it for its wonderful familiarity.

The stove was another thing she had to imagine and an area similar to a convection stovetop appeared at the end of a bench. There were no cooking rings to be seen and no knobs to switch on the stove. So after adding the ground coffee and filling the Bialetti machine with water, which she found coming from a slim waterspout near the stove area, she simply set the espresso maker on the surface of the stove and watched as the metal turned a tinge of red, radiating heat.

Carla discovered that as she moved the espresso maker around the stovetop, the tinge of red became more marked or more faint and she worked out this was to control the temperature she needed to boil the water in the coffeemaker. She set the Bialetti pot on the hottest corner of the stove and within a few seconds the water boiled and rose into the upper chamber of the espresso maker, bringing with it the aromatic smell of coffee.

When Carla took the coffee out for the boys, Commander seemed pleasantly surprised. "What, you didn't think I could work it out?" Carla challenged him with a look of reproof.

Commander chuckled. "Not at all. I knew you'd work it out. You're a bright one for a human."

The other boys smiled and thanked her quietly as she handed out cups of the steaming hot drink. Carla then sat in one of the chairs by the dashboard panel and sipped her own much-needed caffeine. She then asked, "So where are the women? Don't tell me you guys have the same attitude towards women as most male Earthlings—you know: barefoot and pregnant."

"Nothing like that," Commander assured her. "We have exploration teams made up of both sexes." Then, he added in a teasing tone, "I guess you just got lucky on this trip with a team made up of good looking young men."

Carla was quick with a comeback, "Except for you, that is. Aren't you considered to be middle-aged?"

The look on Commander's face was comical and Carla grinned at his dumbfounded countenance.

19

Rhys lay awake with Tom and Rhys Junior as his bed companions. While he was tired and craved sleep, something did not feel right. He could not quite put his finger on it and this kept him awake, searching his mind for an answer.

At least, he knew Carla was safe and this reassured him. He had communicated with a very jovial Commander less than an hour before and was informed Carla had made coffee for the crew and that even though she found the boys quite attractive, her heart and soul still belonged to Rhys. This made Rhys laugh and miss her all the more.

"You never told me what a smartarse she can be at times," Commander chuckled and Rhys saw the big smile on his father's face in his mind. "You know, I'm beginning to really like your girl, despite the fact she called me middle-aged."

Rhys laughed really hard at this and his heart warmed at the idea that for all it was worth and whatever the future held for Earth, at least Carla had won over someone like Commander with his superior mind and old wisdom.

Commander informed him they should be back by the next evening, Earth time, which made it approximately four days in length on Tyerra. Carla would have a lot of time on her hands and Rhys wished once again he'd been asked to accompany her.

When Commander ended their communication, Rhys fed the joey, topped up Tom's kibble bowl, and got ready for bed. He was exhausted after the previous night's lovemaking and he looked forward to a long sleep to blank out the time he and Carla would be apart, even though he would see her in about a day. Despite this, he found it frustrating when he could not fall asleep because a feeling of unease began to creep up on him as soon as he switched off the light.

At first, he thought it was because he missed Carla, but the feeling was of an ominous nature and this unsettled him. He opened his mind and scanned the space above Earth, but nothing came to him. Then, he brought his consciousness closer and searched for signals inside the planet's atmosphere; again, nothing. Finally, he decided to bring his mind even closer and he scanned every nation on Earth, at the same time filtering out the collective misery of humankind and the animal kingdom. He was not sure what it was he was looking for, but when he found it he would know.

After he exhausted his search worldwide, he brought his mind to Australia and worked inwards from there. He scanned the country, each state, cities and towns, until finally he honed in on a very weak signal, but one that meant a threat nonetheless. He tuned in on the signal and much to his surprise he discovered it was coming from somewhere in Katoomba.

Rhys sat up in bed suddenly, his mind alert, and he scanned every single household in the town. Nothing. Then, he scanned the mountains, valleys, and all the bushland around. He picked up on an even fainter signal and shook his head in disbelief. Either, he was losing his powers of detection or someone was deliberately blocking their thought process to avoid discovery. If the latter, Rhys knew the threat would be extraterrestrial, and his mind flew directly to the fugitive from Prima. Surely, the guy had not come after him right here in Katoomba, and yet this was what Rhys's every sense told him. He sighed and lay back on the bed. The perimeter of the cottage was safe as was the town around him. The threat came from somewhere in the Jamison Valley.

Rhys did not think anything would happen during the night, but he set his mind on continuous scan of the signal. Though he would now be able to get some sleep, his mind would awaken him if the signal suddenly changed. First thing tomorrow, he would investigate and once he settled on this plan of action he fell into a deep sleep.

***

Carla sat, entranced, by the look of outer space. The Earth started to look smaller and smaller until she saw the whole planet just as someone would see the moon from Earth. Tears came to her eyes at the many thoughts that ran through her mind in no particular order: beauty, love, Rhys, animals, plants, humanity, misery, war, peace, evil, kindness, Tom and Rhys Junior, her dead parents, the mountains, the ocean... and on and on.

"Your coffee's growing cold," Commander reminded her gently. "I'll help you filter the pain." He gave her an understanding smile. "I need you to be clear-minded for the upcoming meeting."

Before Carla could reply, Commander placed a hand on her head and closed his eyes for several seconds. Carla's whole being became infused with a sense of peace and tranquility and when Commander opened his eyes, she felt relaxed and neutral. She could still appreciate the contrast between love and evil, beauty and ugliness, but she did so objectively and without bringing emotion into it.

"Better?" Commander asked.

Carla nodded and sipped her coffee.

"Okay. Rhys may have already told you some of the things I'm about to run by you, but I want to make sure you're clear on everything."

Carla nodded again, still entranced by the beauty in front of her.

"In about half an hour we're going to go into warp drive and enter the wormhole that will take us to Tyerra. You know about warped space, right?"

"Yes. Something to do with harnessing negative energy density and warping space. I assume you guys are old hands at it and that the wormhole won't collapse on us."

Commander smirked. "You've been watching too many sci-fi movies."

"Not at all. I read a lot, though."

"Well, it's more or less what you said," he continued. "Tyerra's approximately eight billion light years away from Earth. Ours is an old galaxy, much older than the Milky Way."

"What's the name of your galaxy?" Carla was curious.

"It's simply a series of letters and numbers. We don't have romantic names like you used for your galaxy."

"Is this because you guys never talk?" Carla half teased.

"Communicating via thought doesn't mean we don't have an imagination," Commander reproved.

"Fine." Carla didn't seem fazed. "So what are the letters and numbers? I'm just curious."

Commander sighed. "We're wasting time, but if you must know it's EDGE-021. And no, our system of writing is only based on mathematics. The name I gave you contains letters, I know, but I simply translated them for you in a format you'll understand."

"Thank you." Carla thought she'd better shut up and let Commander finish telling her whatever she was meant to know.

Commander went on, "Once we pass through the wormhole it'll take us under an hour to land. Then, we'll make our way to the League of Galaxies headquarters. I'm the Head of the League and, therefore, I chair the meeting. This is a special meeting, by the way, simply so the other members can meet and ask you any questions they may have. They will speak with you in English and the meeting may run for a few of your Earth hours. After this, I'll run you back home."

Carla couldn't help herself when she uttered, "What, no sightseeing at all?"

Commander ignored her comment and continued, "You'll be brought back to the ship to eat and rest while I conclude the meeting with the League. Then, after maintenance on the ship, we return."

"Well, that doesn't sound so bad. We'll only be away like around ten or twelve hours tops, right?"

"In Earth time, yes, but in Tyerra time we'll be away for near on four days."

"What! I don't want to spend four days cooped up in a meeting and on the ship. Why does it take so long?"

"Tyerra time runs slower than Earth time."

"Then you should've explained this in Tyerran time," Carla protested. "So now you're telling me that an Earth hour is around ten of your hours. So when you say we'll be at the meeting for a few hours, we could be there for days!"

"The meeting won't last that long; it's just the resting time. You'll sleep a lot longer on Tyerra than you do on Earth —it's the quality of the oxygen we breathe here plus your body getting used to the changes in a different atmosphere. Besides, we need to ensure all is checked on the ship for the return journey and that conditions are okay for travel."

Carla felt a sudden headache coming on. "I don't suppose you carry painkillers onboard. I forgot mine on Earth."

Commander smiled reassuringly. "Don't worry. You'll be fine. Just think, after the meeting you can relax and by the time you wake up we'll be on our way back."

This pacified Carla somewhat, but she did not like it. Her recently infused calmness began to dissipate. "Rhys told me there are around two hundred representatives in the League, each from a galaxy. Is there a representative for the Milky Way?" She thought changing the subject would bring things back to an even keel.

"Yes. The planet Hergon."

Carla regretted she'd brought it up now. "You mean the planet where the Prima guy is supposedly hiding?"

"Yes. But he's escaped and we're looking for him. It's a matter of time until we catch him. Prima was an evolved planet, but not as evolved as Tyerra. In any case, this fugitive managed to escape the destruction, but he can't run forever."

"Well, he seems to be making a good job of it so far!"

Commander ignored the sarcasm in her tone. "We'll catch him," he stated.

Carla changed the subject again. "I read somewhere there are like a hundred billion galaxies in the observable universe. This is an Earthly estimation of course, but with so many galaxies out there, how come there's such a low number of representatives in the League?"

"Good question. You must know many galaxies haven't made contact and some don't even have intelligent life to speak of. The reasons are many, in any case."

Carla finished her coffee and decided to remain silent. She wanted to clear her mind and relax before the big meeting.

"Thanks for the coffee," Commander said, reading her thoughts. "I'll leave you to relax and enjoy the rest of the trip. Come to me if you have any other questions." He then left the chair he had been sitting on and went over to join the rest of the crew.

Carla was grateful for the privacy. The beauty before her was amazing and though Commander had helped filter her emotions, she still felt like crying. She wasn't happy at having to spend so long away from Rhys. She had only expected to be away for a half day at most. Then, she reminded herself that this was a small price to pay if it meant saving Earth, and she felt her strength of spirit return.

At dawn the next morning, Rhys and Tom went for a walk after Rhys tuned in on the signal and found it had not changed. Something or someone was in the region of the Jamison Valley and they were purposely blocking detection at all costs. The fact Rhys could still pick up on the signal, albeit faintly, meant either the threat was small or the being blocking the signal was not as evolved as he.

After decades of tuning in on all sorts of living organisms, Rhys's experience in detection of others' signals was quite strong, especially after he had worked with Commander to develop his gift. Therefore, even though weak because it was being blocked, Rhys could tell several things about this signal—it was definitely extraterrestrial, it was hiding somewhere in the valley, and it represented a threat against Rhys himself and not the planet.

Picking up on the signal, however, did not mean Rhys could pinpoint its exact location, not when it was so faint. So the only way to find the individual behind it meant Rhys had to put himself at risk, especially as he had no weapons to speak of.

When he had come to Earth on his mission, he had come to mix with humans, observe, and gather information. Besides, the use of weapons was frowned upon on Tyerra as evolved beings had no need for them. The only weapons Tyerrans possessed were those of mass destruction, to use when a planet was voted for annihilation. This was a dichotomy between the peaceful and highly evolved races that belonged to the League of Galaxies and the destructive and sometimes unforgiving nature of its members when the fabric of consciousness was being threatened.

Rhys shook his head at the irony, admitting evolved races were not so different from others. Earthlings referred to the antithesis of everything as Ying and Yang. Without evil you couldn't have goodness; without war you couldn't have peace; without hate you couldn't have love; without suffering the consequences of life you couldn't develop and grow into a more evolved being. For once, Rhys thought with cynicism; all things being equal, there was very little difference between these humans he had come to understand and love and the other so-called evolved races in the cosmos.

Tom growled, bringing Rhys out of his thoughts. They had reached the path bordering the Jamison Valley from which bushwalkers had the choice of several tracks to descend into it. Rhys stopped and took a look around. It was a few minutes past six and the sky was lightening, the sun's first rays only just beginning to show themselves. In the cold of the valley, which was partially covered by low cloud, Rhys could not see anything out of place. The signal was around him, but he had difficulty in trying to track it to its source. Then, quite without warning, Tom leaped in Rhys's direction with a fierce look on his face and in the split second it took the dog to do this, Rhys realised the source he'd been looking for was just behind him and about to push him off the path and into the depths below.

As Rhys turned to face his foe, he saw a hooded figure dressed in black and struggling with Tom. The dog behaved like a wolf rather than the gentle setter that he was, and the figure under him could not fight him off. Before Rhys could act, Tom had his open jaw around the figure's neck and Rhys noticed the fear in the eyes of the being from Prima. In the shock of the attack, Prima man's blocking ability of his signal disappeared and Rhys scanned his entire mind within seconds of the attack.

Tom was ready to tear out the attacker's throat, but Rhys communicated to the dog to stand down. For once, Tom did not entirely obey and he drew blood by biting the enemy in the neck, breaking through the skin, but he did not go for the kill. He simply stayed as he was, keeping hold of the being by the throat.

Rhys knelt by Prima man and communicated with him via thought. "The smallest of moves and you die. I'll spare your life if you answer my questions."

The being responded in the affirmative, again via thought, his large grey eyes full of fear. Rhys told Tom to stay put as long as the intruder did not move and he then pulled off the captive's hood to reveal long black hair with a streak of bright blue running through the middle of his head. His face was not entirely like that of a human. Primans had very large eyes and tiny noses in an elongated face with thin lips, but they could pass for humans if they wore a hat or hood to partially cover their faces. Rhys sent his thoughts to his enemy. "Why are you trying to kill me?"

"You destroyed my planet," the Priman replied with anger. "I know who you are! I met you on Prima once. You had us all fooled that you were gathering information, but you came to judge us, and then you destroyed us."

Rhys sighed. "That's not true. I did report events on Prima, but I emphatically recommended for the planet to be spared. Unfortunately, the League did not agree with me. I even had a falling out with them because of this. So how can you blame me for your planet's destruction?"

"I know all of this already," the Priman responded, still full of anger. "But you didn't put up much of a fight, did you? And now look at what you've achieved for Earth, simply because you're with that woman. The League asked to meet her, too. In the past, they never asked for anyone to meet with them, did they? This is all your doing, and I blame you for it. So kill me if you must. I will never forgive you."

Rhys could only stare at the Priman in astonishment. His thinking was so twisted. The reason he had fought so much for Earth was due to the fact that he had failed with Prima. It had nothing to do with his love for Carla. "I made a choice to stay here irrespective of whether the League decides to destroy Earth or not. I don't agree the League should have the power to destroy other planets and I severed my connection with them as a result. Whatever happens to Earth has nothing to do with me anymore."

The Priman sneered. "You never severed anything! Commander's your father. Do you think he'll allow Earth to be destroyed if you remain living here?"

Rhys felt sudden anger course through him. "And do you really believe Commander can bend the rules and convince all members of the League to spare Earth just because of me? I doubt it. He's fair and just, and he'll call no favours on my behalf. I can assure you of that."

"I don't care what you say. I don't believe you."

"How did you get here?" Rhys changed the subject. Having read the Priman's mind, he knew, but he wanted to see if the guy told the truth.

"If you must know, there are a few of us on Hergon who think as I do, and they've agreed to help us."

Rhys could not believe what he heard and yet Prima man was telling the truth after all. Things were getting out of hand

and while the Hergons should know better, he couldn't really blame them. It seemed the League had just gone too far by setting itself up as judge and jury, as Carla put it. Rhys made a decision.

"If I let you go, will you promise to forget about your hate? You already know I tried to fight on behalf of Prima; I never wanted your planet to be destroyed. You still have a chance to make a life on Hergon. So put this behind you and get on with your life."

The Priman threw Rhys a defiant look. "I can't promise what I'm going to do or if my colleagues will agree. Perhaps, we will one day form our own League and mete out justice. So kill me if you must, but I won't stop fighting."

Rhys sighed. He had blocked his thoughts since he'd gone looking for the signal this morning, so he knew the Priman could not read Rhys' mind right at this very moment; otherwise, he would have known the minute Rhys let him go that he would report what had happened to Commander. So the Priman had a small window of opportunity to get away, which Rhys was giving him, because the League could not apprehend the Priman immediately, and Rhys could hardly show up at the nearest police station to hand in an alien.

"You take your fate into your hands," Rhys told the Priman. "This time, I'll let you go, but if you don't leave the planet right now the League will capture you. You have no business being on Earth in the first place. Go back to Hergon."

The Priman did not reply, but Rhys knew the minute he asked Tom to release him that he would go. There was nothing the Priman could do right now, but with a chilling thought Rhys was positive he hadn't seen the last of him.

Rhys gave the go ahead for Tom to release the captive and the Priman was on his feet immediately and running down one of the bushwalking tracks towards the valley floor.

20

Commander had just finished communicating with Rhys for the second time and gazed towards Carla thoughtfully. She seemed impervious to anything else other than the beauty of space. He didn't want to spoil the trip for her nor did he have any intention of relating to her what Rhys had just told him.

"Don't tell Carla just yet," Rhys had said. "I don't want her worrying."

Commander agreed. "So now we have a small band of renegades, not just a lone wolf. I'll have to report this to the League. Who knows how many of them are following this Priman. Did you get his name or where he's hiding out?"

"I caught a few things when he was frightened by the dog and his mind unblocked his thoughts. He's evolved to a certain level and was doing a good job of hiding his signal, but when he opened up I was able to get bits and pieces. He was surprised by the attack. I was, too. I never saw a friendly dog like Tom become so fierce."

"That dog loves you and will die for you. You know that, don't you? Anyway, he saved your life."

Rhys agreed. "I think the Prima guy's name is Tovo. He had a shuttle waiting for him in the valley, very close from where you departed last night. The shuttle's manned by Hergons. I honed in on about four of them. No Primans onboard, except Tovo. I believe there's a small band of these malcontents or so-called space terrorists on Hergon as well. Tovo's full of hate about what happened and he's been watching us, possibly with the help of someone in the League. He knows about Carla and about you being my father."

"When the Hergon delegation arrived for the last League meeting, there was a being that looked similar to how you describe this Tovo. I'm sure he somehow infiltrated the meeting, but he must have had help to filter his thoughts from us; otherwise, I would've tuned in on him at the time."

Rhys sighed. "This explains the surprise attack on me. I didn't even get him standing behind me when it happened." Rhys sighed again. "This is a mess. Anyway, they're gone now and I imagine they'll go back to Hergon to work out their next move."

"I'll speak to the Hergons after the meeting. Don't worry about Carla, either. She's fine and I'll keep her close to me. I'll see you soon." Commander shut off communications.

As if she knew she was being watched, Carla turned to meet Commander's gaze from across the control deck. Commander joined her and sat on one of the seats close to her.

"Was that Rhys you were communicating with?"

Commander was surprised. "How could you tell?"

Carla smiled. "You guys forget that although you communicate via thought you still gesticulate as humans do when talking on the telephone. Something about your body language told me you were chatting with Rhys."

Commander returned her smile. "Good tip for next time. I'll remember that."

"Is something wrong? How's Rhys?"

"Nothing's wrong and Rhys is fine. He just wanted to check in on us before we go through the wormhole." Commander hated to lie to Carla, but it was for a good reason.

"How much longer until we go through?"

"You mean the wormhole? About ten more minutes," Commander replied. "I think you'll enjoy the experience."

"Is there going to be a lot of shaking and stuff?" Carla looked a little uneasy.

"No. The ship is equipped to maintain conditions just as they are now. Besides, going through the actual wormhole will take but seconds. The space is warped to its full extent." Seeing

Carla's questioning eyes, he explained further. "It's like having a piece of paper with two holes, one at each end. You fold the piece and align the holes so that there's really no distance between them, and anything you put into the hole comes out at the other end immediately."

Carla shivered. "This is too weird, but I'm glad I get to experience it." She then regarded Commander thoughtfully. "By the way, I think I've seen you guys about twenty years ago, when I was a teenager."

"What do you mean?" Commander's curiosity was piqued.

"When we got off the shuttle to board this ship, I noticed the shuttle was orange in colour, and suddenly I experienced a strong sense of déjà vu. I remember years ago, I went outside one night to get something off the clothesline and as I looked up at the sky, I saw something I've never been able to explain. There were four bright orange triangular shapes suspended in the sky, high above me. Together, they formed a circular shape. Anyway, I watched on as they just floated there, but within seconds of my looking at them they broke apart and each triangle flew off in a different direction at such speed that they disappeared quite instantly. I always wondered whether I'd just seen a UFO. Since then, the memory never left my mind."

Commander nodded as if in recognition. "Sounds like us. We often send more than one shuttle when doing reconnaissance. What you saw was probably a recon squad, gathering information from afar. They usually travel in groups of four and tend to form in a circular shape as they come together to rest or visit with each other for meetings and such."

"Do we have time for another question?" Carla did not want to miss out on experiencing the wormhole entry.

"Sure."

"It's about the apocalyptic nightmares I used to get. They stopped since Rhys finished his report for the League, and he seemed to think somehow things he'd seen and reported on were filtering through to me. The thing is, these dreams felt so real."

"What Rhys told you is right. His mind is so evolved

that much of what he took in probably did filter into your subconscious, but by shutting off his thoughts to the report and his past experiences, he's been able to make your dreams stop. This is my point about you living on Tyerra. Imagine what all the forces of consciousness would do to your mind. Even Rhys had trouble when he went to Earth and picked up on all the suffering on your planet. On Tyerra, you would be affected by higher levels of consciousness that your mind would not be able to sustain for long."

Carla sighed. "And because of this, Rhys is willing to give up his life for me?" she brought up the topic that was uppermost in her mind.

"Not even I could protect your mind on Tyerra, Carla," Commander confessed. "I can do it for a short span of time, which is why right after the meeting I'm bringing you back to the ship. I'm sorry it has to be this way because I've grown very fond of you and consider you a daughter, but I don't want anything to hurt you. At the same time, if the League decides to destroy Earth, I stand to lose both a son and now a daughter." Commander then changed the subject abruptly. "I'll leave you now so you can enjoy the show."

Carla gave him a wan smile as her emotions started to get the better of her, but when they approached the wormhole she pushed all thoughts from her mind and concentrated on what was ahead.

She looked through the ship's window and started to spot the bent shapes of stars, planets, gaseous clouds, and actual space with its debris and various belts of asteroids. The shapes grew more and more warped and converged around blackness. Beyond this point, there was nothing to see. It was as if she had shut her eyes and total darkness descended upon her. Carla knew this was the wormhole and the only reason she knew this was because the shapes in space became so bent that they were grotesquely twisted to the point of no recognition. But at the blink of an eye, and quite without warning, the shapes began to change again and Carla started to recognise them. They were the shapes of stars, planets, asteroids and space debris, plus in the distance she espied a pink grey planet that stood out like a beacon. Her eyes teared up when she realised she was looking at Tyerra, Rhys's home. The planet looked as though it was far in the distance, but within minutes it grew exponentially and before Carla knew it, they had entered its atmosphere.

As the ship made its way down, Carla could only look on in awe at her surroundings. The first thing she noticed before they started to get closer to the planet was that Tyerra had a much bigger landmass than Earth, and the mass was like one giant continent rather than the different shapes of countries and islands one found on Earth. In fact, the landmass covered most of the planet. The colour of the mass took on a dusky pink; it looked like a muted shade of dark pink. Dotted through some parts of the landmass, where pale grey bodies of what looked to be giant lakes. The sky was the palest of greens mixed with pearl grey, and Carla looked for the source of natural light and located a giant sun-like star which seemed larger than Earth's sun.

When the ship flew closer, Carla was able to make the shapes of mountain ranges, but they didn't look like they were as tall as those on her planet. In fact, from what she could see, Tyerra seemed rather flat, although she did spot a large number of moon-like craters that told of an ancient planet life full of asteroid and volcanic activity.

When Carla started to make out more of the details below, she saw areas of densely wooded landscapes with trees and a diverse plant life. Most of these were located near the giant lakes and, like on Earth, the plant life was mainly green.

"So how do you like our planet?" Commander's voice startled her.

"It's so different. You don't have oceans, only these lake-type bodies, and the colours are beautiful although totally alien from anything I've ever seen."

"Tyerra is a very dry planet with a gigantic landmass, but we have adequate supplies of subterranean water. We don't have different nations as on Earth; we all live on the same landmass.

The climate is temperate and our race is only one, even though we do have different skin pigmentations, as you can see from my own."

"At least, you guys don't need to have passports to go from one place to another," Carla remarked, thinking how simple this was and how conducive to peace if there was only one race on the planet.

"Over here, you can pretty much drive around the entire planet rather than fly as there are no oceans to cross and we're all connected. Of course, Tyerra is larger than Earth, approximately four times larger, so we fly to travel from city to city. The equivalent of your Earth cars fly or go overland here. They're like mini-shuttles."

"You mean orange and triangular?"

"We have different shapes and colours in fact, but they're all powered by clean energy, mainly from Gazer, the star you see in the sky that looks like a large sun. Gazer is an older star than your sun, hence its slightly darker colour. We calculate that in about four billion years it'll expand into a red giant and engulf our planet."

As Commander spoke, Carla kept looking out the window and now she could see what seemed like cities, close to the large lakes and plant life. "What's the population here?"

"About half of what you have on Earth; four billion or thereabouts."

"And you have such a huge planet compared to ours. That's a lot of space."

"Tyerra has a lot more desert than on Earth, though. You can see the cities and plant life are located close to the lakes. In between, there is only desert."

Just then, they flew past what looked like a large city with gleaming buildings made of what could have been reinforced glass with chrome structures or something similar. "Is that where we're going?" Carla couldn't take her eyes off the metropolis down below and now she could make out little flying shuttles plus vehicles on the roads.

"Yes. This is our main city or you may call it our capital city. The name is Tyrr, a derivative after the planet's name," he replied. "Anyway, we'll be landing soon at the spaceport behind the city and a shuttle will be waiting for us so we can drive straight to our destination. So if you wish to change or put on your war paint, as you call it, this is your chance to do it."

Carla felt her anxiety flooding back. "You mean we're going straight there? But I need time to prepare myself!"

"Well, you'd better do it now. You have about twenty minutes until we land, and the shuttle will take us through the city so you can at least get that bit of sightseeing you were talking about earlier. You have plenty of time to get ready if you get a move on."

Carla could already see their ship moving past Tyrr and heading outwards, where she imagined the spaceport to be located. She jumped out of her chair and on impulse hugged Commander and planted a kiss on his cheek. "Thank you for looking after me and being my guide. I like you a lot better now." She winked at a surprised Commander and gathering her backpack made her way towards the bathroom.

The surface temperature on Tyerra was cool, but not as the cold winter in the mountains back home. Commander informed her that the temperature outside was a mild 23C (73F), so Carla changed into a pair of black jeans and long-sleeved T-shirt of the same colour plus she took a woollen jacket for good measure. On her feet, she wore the same boots she had on earlier, which looked similar to the ones worn in the army. These made for safe walking in the bush and anywhere else.

Carla tied back her hair in a short ponytail and left loose her fringe, which was a little long and tended to fall over her eyes. This reminded her of Rhys and his fringe of hair falling over those purple blue eyes she could never get used to. She quickly applied a smattering of powdered make-up, made up her eyes with dark brown eyeliner and mascara, and wore lipstick in a muted red colour, giving her lips an enhanced and elegant appearance. As she examined herself in front of the mirror, she decided she looked presentable and smart enough for any occasion, even an extraterrestrial one.

By the time she was ready, the ship landed and Carla said her goodbyes to the crew before Commander whisked her away into the waiting mini-shuttle. The vehicle was triangular in shape and yellow in colour. It was a two-seater with doors on either side that opened upwards, very much like a Lamborghini. Once closed, however, the door seals disappeared, just like on the ship and shuttle they had used to travel to Tyerra. The entire upper side of the vehicle was made of a see-through glass like material, while the underside was metal. Inside, the seats resembled car seats, only they were more comfortable and there were no seatbelts, nor was there a steering wheel but a dashboard with a screen that seemed to work via thought process.

"Ready?" Commander asked and Carla nodded with an excited look in her eyes. Now that she was finally on Tyerra she felt like pinching herself to make sure she wasn't dreaming.

The mini-shuttle moved without sound or vibration and Carla was positive Commander steered the vehicle via thought, like most everything else Tyerrans did. "I'll drive past the big lake and through the city so you can get an idea of what our home looks like. And just a bit of advice: when we get to the League meeting don't freak out. Not everyone looks like us."

Right now, they were hovering a few inches above what looked like a road leading away from the spaceport.

"You mean there'll be beings with the head of an animal or something like that?" Carla was not alarmed, simply curious.

"Something like that," Commander remarked.

The mini-shuttle trip lasted about twenty or so minutes and took them past a verdant jungle-like landscape, bordering the shores of the giant lake she had seen from the ship as they were coming in to land. Aside from the strange colour of the sky and the land, they could have been driving through any rainforest on Earth.

Carla only had time to catch a few glimpses of animals;

some looked like birds without wings, but they could still fly. Then, there were a few land animals that resembled large cats like tigers and leopards. Commander noted Carla's amazement at the creatures and explained, "They're not harmful to humans, like the wild felines on Earth. For starters, they're vegetarian. You'll also notice their colouring a lot more because Tyerra is a land of soft and pale colours, and the living beings and animals tend to take on a more colourful and flamboyant appearance."

"That explains Rhys's colouring. He's got three shades of hair roots."

"On Tyerra, we can pretty much design our babies and how they will look. This can change when our offspring grow up and get different ideas, though."

"Interesting concept. Does this include changing bodies so you never look wrinkled and old?" Carla asked hopefully.

"No. But our medical technology is much more advanced; we live long lives and keep our youthful looks much longer than Earthlings. Even someone like me, a middle-aged man, according to you, will go on looking as I do now for at least another two hundred of your Earth years."

"I don't suppose..." Carla started to say, but Commander read her mind.

"Forget it. We can't do anything with an Earthling."

"But Rhys told me we share the same DNA, that at some stage your ancestors were the same as Earthlings."

"That is true, but we have ethical reasons as to why we don't meddle with other beings' DNA."

The rest of the trip was completed in silence and Carla fell in love with the capital city, Tyrr. The rainforest gave way to more manicured landscapes and gardens, and the city sprung up among thousands of acres of greenery and exotic flowers Carla had never seen before. There seemed to be no suburbs, either, Carla noted. The buildings were spread out as there was plenty of space and none of them was a high rise. The tallest buildings were around three storeys high, but they were large and wide in terms of floor space. They all looked pretty much the same, however, mostly made of a glass like material to optimise the light and supported by chrome like metal structures. Everything was clean, shiny, and looked rather new.

The residential and business areas were interspersed with large parks and botanical gardens. Other areas were reserved for commerce and Carla observed stores of all kinds selling food, clothing, furnishings, home wares, and such, plus yet other buildings consisted of health clinics, hospitals, and so on.

The whole thing went by like a blur as Commander did not want to stop anywhere, so Carla had to take in as much as she could and cram it all in the recesses of her mind.

Families were out and about, strolling along wide promenades made of some kind of white stone; others walked more briskly, as if they had business to attend to. The mode of dress seemed pretty much unisex and not unlike the kind of gear Carla wore. But Tyerrans liked their colours, and she admired the variety of attires in every possible colour and combination; this included exotic hairstyles and skin tones.

Every now and then she uttered the word "Wow!" without realising it, and Commander threw a fatherly smile towards her. His filter on Carla's mind was full on so she wouldn't be overwhelmed by the higher consciousness energy around her and she could enjoy her trip instead.

A few minutes later, they stopped outside a grand looking building made of glass, chrome metal and white stone, with a chrome shield above its massive doorway. Carla saw engraved in the shield what looked like the shape of five galaxies intertwined together with a garland of smaller galaxy shapes around the centrepiece.

"I take it we're here," she commented.

"Yes, we are." Commander gave a mental direction for the mini-shuttle doors to open, and Carla's light mood dissolved into growing anxiety.

"Don't worry. You'll be fine," Commander reassured her as he helped her out of the shuttle. "Remember, I'm filtering for you. The anxiety will go away in a few moments."

Carla nodded, feeling a little unsure, and hoped she wouldn't stuff up the meeting. This was her one and only chance to speak on behalf of her planet, and suddenly it felt as if the weight of her world was literally resting on her shoulders.

21

They entered into a massive lobby paved with gleaming white stone floors and walls; the stone looked like marble. Carla had enough time to notice a few pieces of abstract sculptures made from some kind of charcoal grey metal she didn't recognise. Commander led her through to a huge set of double doors, also made of the same material as the sculptures, and shepherded her inside when the doors swung open of their own accord.

The interior of the meeting room looked similar to a university lecture hall, with a semi-circle seating arrangement of elevated rows of seats from front to back and looking down onto a raised platform structure with a lectern to one side and a long narrow table in the middle with five seats facing the audience.

Behind the platform hung a very large, flat LCD type of screen reflecting a beautiful photo of the Milky Way galaxy with an insert on the top right-hand corner of the planet Earth. Carla did not notice any microphones, but figured the room was equipped with some kind of advanced technology that would amplify their voices so they could be heard. She assumed all meetings in the League took place via thought process, except for this one. The room had no lighting that she could see, but plenty of natural light filtered in through the glass ceiling.

Commander led Carla to one of the chairs at the end of the long table where four male beings sat alongside. A quick glance revealed they were Homo sapiens and around Commander's age. They were dressed in sober colours, mostly black or dark grey, and their hairstyles were tame in comparison to Rhys's and those of the crew from the shuttle. Carla knew these men were the elders of the League.

She sat quietly, regarding the audience in front of her, and tried not to panic. At least, two hundred people looked back at her and while they all seemed humanoid in some way, many looked quite different from Commander and the beings sitting at her table. Carla espied a number of females in the audience, or at least she thought they were female beings, while others looked quite androgynous, and yet others were unmistakably male. Some of the beings were thin with elongated features, others looked more solid in build and leonine, with long manes of hair in a palette of colours, and a few others, Carla didn't even know how to describe.

Commander remained standing and gazed in her direction for a few seconds before he made his way to the lectern. At that moment, Carla felt a certain calm descend upon her and she knew Commander's filter was full on, protecting her from the vibes in the room.

Commander spoke in English and, as Carla had thought earlier, his voice was amplified around the large hall for all to hear clearly.

"Welcome, esteemed colleagues, to this special meeting of the League of Galaxies. At your request, I have brought our guest from Earth, Carla Fiori. For the benefit of our guest, today's meeting will be conducted in spoken English."

Carla was not sure what to expect at the introduction. Applause or thumping on the small tabletops around the amphitheatre would have felt the norm to her. Instead, the audience crossed their hands over their chests in a gesture that Carla interpreted as unity. She noted Commander returned the gesture and wondered whether she, too, should do so. She decided not to, even though her companions at the table also returned the gesture.

Commander went on speaking. "Carla," he addressed her directly, "you are sitting next to our League elders. They represent clusters of galaxies at this meeting and our colleagues in the audience represent their home galaxy. Everybody in this room is multi-lingual, although we tend to communicate via thought. Today, however, everything you say will be fully understood. So please relax and be yourself. Therefore, if you join me now, we can open the meeting."

Despite the filtering with which Commander was protecting her, Carla felt her mouth go dry at the prospect of standing in front of two hundred beings from different galaxies and for a moment, she did not trust her legs to carry her to the lectern. But as she stood and walked across the stage, she was relieved her legs worked after all, and she stepped up to the crystal lectern to stand next to Commander.

Commander gazed into her eyes and to her surprise she heard his voice inside her head. He obviously had the power to communicate privately with her via thought without the others in the room being aware of it. "I've blocked everyone out except for you, so they can't read my thoughts. Only you can hear me inside your head and can also reply to me via thought, and I'll be able to understand. This way, I can give you a helping hand and ensure you don't become overwhelmed. Now, speak to the audience and thank them for inviting you to this forum."

Carla took a moment to adjust to being talked to inside her head and then did as told. "Greetings to all in this forum. I thank you for inviting me here today and I feel honoured that you should do so."

Again, everyone crossed their hands over their chest and Commander told her to do the same. "This is a greeting of approval and unity," he explained.

Carla crossed her hands over her chest. Then, one of the elders at the table where she had been sitting earlier spoke. "On behalf of everyone here, I would like to welcome you, Carla Fiori. Although you are not the first Earthling we have met, you are the only Earthling ever to attend a League meeting."

"I am humbled to be here and I thank you for your kindness." Carla had no idea from where her words were coming with such confidence, but she was sure it had something to do with Commander prompting her.

The same elder addressed her again. "Carla Fiori, you know why you've been brought here and we would like to hear from you as to why you think your planet should be spared. As you know, Rhys Lewis submitted a report recommending that Earth should be spared. But as an Earthling, we would like to hear from you, too. We believe you put forth a compelling argument to Commander as to why we should not destroy your planet and we wish to know more about this."

Carla stole a questioning glance at Commander and he responded inside her head, "He means what you told me through the thumb communicator that day. Just keep it civil and don't be a smartarse."

Carla blushed for a moment as she remembered how she had abused the League about being high and mighty and how they set themselves up as judge and jury. She couldn't very well tell them this now. She had to win them over. She took a few more seconds to compose her thoughts and then spoke.

"One of the things Rhys Lewis wrote in his report is that the human psyche seems to be compartmentalised. He was right in that observation," she said. "To give you an example, a thief will have the criminal intent of stealing food from a market, but at the same time he has a family he loves very much and he would do anything to protect and provide for them. So the question is: does this make him a good or a bad person? On a larger scale, and a very delicate topic in my world at present, is the plight of the refugees from Muslim countries.

"In Western countries, where we live under a democracy, we do not agree with the ways of Islam or I should say those who commit atrocities in the name of Islam. Unfortunately, horrible acts of terrorism have plagued many nations on Earth and groups, meaning the terrorists, the fanatics, and the radicalized have given a bad name to the Islam religion.

"So now millions of others hate anyone who is Muslim. We often see hate crimes committed against Muslims. We tend to tar them all with the same brush and we retaliate against them with more atrocities like air raid bombings and other violent acts, and yet millions of humans are sympathetic to the plight of the refugees.

There is a mass exodus from countries like Syria, Iraq, and Africa, to name a few, and many Western nations have opened their arms and their hearts to these people by providing aid and refuge. This has been done despite the terrorist atrocities committed by evil groups such as al-Qaeda and ISIS, who have threatened retaliation if we help refugees.

"This is only a small example of how human nature works. We may fear or hate something, but when it comes to compassion we often bring this to the fore and try to do what's right."

Carla paused for a moment to take in the reaction from the audience. Everyone was quiet and listening—possibly a good sign, she thought.

"I need some water." She sent the thought to Commander and he left the lectern for a few moments returning with a tall glass of cool water.

"Excuse me," Carla said to the audience and drank thirstily before she continued with her speech. "There is a concept on Earth we call Ying and Yang, which is really cause and effect. For instance, we are told we should tolerate our enemies; otherwise, how can we learn about compassion? If someone hurts our feelings, we should learn from this and be kind to others so that we don't in turn hurt their feelings. When evil commits atrocities we learn we must stick together and give aid to those that are needier than ourselves.

"Countless times, whether during war or peacetime, strangers give their lives simply to save someone they don't necessarily know. Heroic acts occur every day on Earth. This leads me to believe that it is the true nature of humans to have deep love, even if sometimes they don't know it.

"In certain cases this doesn't mean the love they are capable of is good—it could be fanaticism about religion or misguided love. My point is, however, that all humans have the capacity to feel and act upon their love—and even those who commit evil acts will at some point in their lives show love and compassion. This may only be directed at their family, pets, or their nation, but there is a balance in the end. This is what I call a collective balance.

"Look at global warming as another example. We're treating Mother Nature like she's a garbage bin. We emit noxious substances into the atmosphere that change weather patterns and which bring drought when we need rain, and rain when we need sunshine for crops to grow and animals to thrive. We poison our water supply and the air we breathe, but there are many out there fighting to introduce innovative solutions to cut back on carbon emissions and save the planet." Again, Carla paused for a few moments and took a few sips of water.

"I could go on for hours giving you examples where good and evil interact with each other in order to create an effect and how all things balance out in the end, but I'm sure you know this already.

"My final and most important point in this: Earth alone cannot be blamed for the corroding effect on the fabric of consciousness. We are all united in the process of cause and effect." What Carla was about to state next made her feel anxious, but she still went ahead. "The reason I say this is because we are all united by a unique force in the cosmos—the energy I call 'love'.

"I believe that 'love' just is. It's the only thing that matters; it's in the lifeblood of every sentient being, even in animals and plants. So when one of these beings, or a group of them, commit an atrocity, the effect will be the same as the one you see when you throw a pebble in a pond. You get a ring-like ripple that grows from the epicentre and spreads wider and wider until it goes all the way to the shore and even beyond, having an effect on everything in its way."

Carla took a deep breath before she continued. "Therefore, I respectfully put to this audience the concept that past actions taken by the League itself have also had a hand in this ripple effect. Right or wrong, when a planet is destroyed or a life is taken, we change the collective fabric of our universe. It's not just 'you' or 'them'—it's all of us that contribute to it.

"We are all united in this energy called love. This is the energy that drives the cosmos. It's what makes our universe the way it is. So how can we point the finger at someone else and blame them for the effects on the collective? We need to focus on the whole rather than the individual. Instead of annihilation we should focus on aid to others and the elevation of consciousness through our actions.

"Many on Earth hate the terrorists and anyone who shares their dogma, but wiping them all out would make us just as evil as those who commit the atrocities. So why not give assistance to the victims of atrocities? This includes the refugees that are being persecuted by their own so-called Islamist countrymen. If those of us who give aid and refuge can work together to build a stronger foundation, then evil will no longer be able to have an effect. The ripples will calm and life will go on at a higher level of consciousness and hopefully onto a better life with lessons learned.

"There will always be those who do not agree with us. They will turn away and keep on committing evil acts. But it is my deepest belief that good will always overcome evil. So if we focus on this, we can certainly create a more positive and stronger collective of love and our levels of consciousness will be elevated one step at a time."

Carla paused one last time and took a look around the room, making eye contact with many in the audience, some of whom nodded in approval at her. This small gesture overwhelmed her with love and she felt tears roll down her face. She didn't bother to dry them, but she went on to conclude, "In closing, I humbly request those of you who are so much more evolved than the beings on my planet that you practise love and compassion, and work together with us, who have yet to elevate our own consciousness to a higher level—and this will contribute in minimising the ripple effect and turn it into a tide of positive energy for the good of the cosmos.

"If we can open our hearts on Earth to aid those whom we sometimes view as our enemies, then surely the beings in this room can work miracles if they practise compassion and work together. Thank you."

When Carla finished speaking she remained at the lectern and again glanced around the room. She was surprised when she observed tears on some faces, but what truly overwhelmed her was the wave of pure love she felt directed at her. Despite Commander's filtering system, her legs almost buckled from under her as she wept openly at the spiritual beauty of this experience.

Commander caught her just in time and taking hold of her elbow and forearm, he led her back to her chair. Carla sat down gratefully and wiped at her eyes with her hands. When her vision cleared, she noticed that everyone in the room had their hands crossed over their chest. Carla returned the gesture and wept again.

The next hour or two were a blur for Carla and she was only aware of beings throwing questions at her and somehow she managed to give a response. When she thought back on this later, she remembered very little of the Q&A session, except the many topics they covered—not only about problems on Earth, but the question of Prima's destruction came up, and some in the audience felt the League had been too rash. Others asked about Carla's relationship with Rhys, and whether she felt this influenced her in trying to save her planet. Carla responded something along the lines of her always having been a sensitive person, even before she met Rhys, and her opinions today had been made despite her involvement with him. The rest, she did not remember, except that certain beings came up to her and shook her hand the Earthly way, wishing her all the best on her return trip.

Commander then whisked her off and Carla closed her eyes for a moment in the mini-shuttle. A little later, she found herself being carried in his arms and into the ship where he deposited her on one of the beds.

When she tried to speak, Commander interrupted. "You need to sleep now. The pure air plus all the emotions got the better of you. I tried to filter as much as I could, but even I couldn't stem that last wave of love sent to you by the audience." Carla noted the pride in his voice and she smiled.

Commander brushed back her hair, took off her boots, and threw a blanket over her. "You did well, my girl, but I need to rush back to the meeting as they're waiting for me. Sleep now and when you're feeling up to it eat something. The crew's on the ship and the boys will keep an eye on you in case you need anything. I won't be too long, but I expect to find you still sleeping when I get back."

He was about to leave, but Carla reached for his hand and pulled him to sit on the bed for a moment. "Wait," she uttered. "I want to talk to Rhys. Can you help me do this?"

Commander gazed at her thoughtfully; then nodded. "I don't have a thumb communicator for audio here on the ship, so you realise I'll be inside your head, right? This means I'll know everything you and Rhys say to each other. It's the only way you can communicate with him."

Although Carla felt exhausted, her eyes lit up. "I don't care. I promise we won't say anything to embarrass you."

Commander laughed. "Do you think I'm green or something?"

"No," Carla quipped, "but I'm sure you don't want to get images of Rhys and I engaged in wild sex inside your head—that would make you a pervert."

Commander's jaw dropped and Carla grinned wickedly. "I was only joking—as if I'm going to allow you to see that!"

"You're a real handful sometimes," he chided in good humour and drew out his thumb communicator. It lit up and for a few moments he communicated with Rhys silently. Carla figured he related what had happened at the meeting, and then he turned to Carla. "Okay. Rhys knows I can hear everything, so off you go."

"Do I talk with my voice or think the conversation inside my head?" Carla felt so tired she craved for sleep, but she wanted to hear from Rhys.

"I'm here, my love," Rhys said inside her mind. "I know you're tired, and I wish I could be there to hold you while you sleep. You did well and I'm proud of you."

"Rhys, I miss you so much!" Carla returned via thought. "I can't wait to see you again. I know Commander told you everything that's happened, but I want to tell you later when I see you. I just wanted to hear your voice and make sure you and the little ones are okay."

"Tom and little Rhys are just fine. Like me, they miss you, but I told them you'll be home soon," Rhys responded. "You must do as Commander says and rest now. The whole voyage will have taken a lot out of you and I won't keep you awake any longer. I love you, Carla."

Carla felt tears run down her face. "I love you, too, Rhys. I'll see you soon."

The communication was shut off from Carla as Commander watched her fall asleep instantly. He now communicated directly with Rhys. "I'm going back to the meeting while Carla rests," he informed him. "I need to report the attempt on your life by Tovo, and the League will want to discuss what to do about him and his band of renegades."

"Well, they're nowhere near Earth now. I think Tovo took my advice and left, but I need you to send over a reconnaissance crew to stay here until this whole thing is resolved. I can't act alone and I have a bad feeling this isn't the last we've seen of them."

22

"Time to wake up." Carla heard Commander's voice while she was being gently shaken awake. She opened her eyes and met his emerald green gaze as he stood by her bed, holding a glass with a dark purple liquid in it. "Here, drink this," he instructed and handed her the drink.

Carla sat up, running fingers through her hair, and took the glass. "What is it?"

"It's a cocktail of super vitamins. They'll repair the stress in your body from the space travel and give you energy."

Carla sniffed the liquid and could not detect any smell so she drank the concoction in one go. When finished, she handed the glass back to Commander. "It tastes like wine," she remarked.

"Well, it isn't," Commander replied. "Our bodies don't tolerate alcohol."

Carla smiled. "Bully for you. On Earth, most people drink."

"Yet another reason you have a shorter lifespan."

"Hey!" Carla protested. "Not everyone's an alcoholic, you know. I barely touch the stuff. Anyway, how long have I been asleep?"

"About twenty four of your Earth hours."

Carla jumped out of bed. "Oh my god, I must stink badly! I need a shower and change of clothes." She went directly to her backpack and took out personal items and a change of clothing.

"When you're done," Commander told her, "join me for lunch. We still have some time to wait until we make our way back."

"What exactly are we waiting for?"

"The ship needs to be serviced. We never travel unless we

do a total overhaul, especially when we're going through warped space."

"Fair enough," Carla said, heading for the door. "I'll see you in a while."

Carla tried not to rush through her shower, but since Commander told her they'd be going home she couldn't wait; she ached to see Rhys.

When done, she dressed in the same outfit she'd worn when travelling from Earth, except she put on fresh underwear and wore a clean T-shirt under her pullover. She then looked around for a hairdryer and sighed. She had found the shower easily enough, although it had no regulating faucets, which meant she had to regulate the temperature of the water via thought. But the shower consisted of a small spout over a cubicle at one end of the bathroom, which made its function obvious. The hairdryer, on the other hand, presented a challenge. There was a vanity top of sorts and a mirror, but there were no drawers in which to keep personal items and no shelves, either.

Carla looked around and couldn't quite figure out where the hairdryer was hiding, until she espied a concave indentation the size of a person's head on the wall near the vanity. She stood close to it and thought of warm air. Sure enough, warm air was instantly directed at her wet hair, the dryer only emitting a low hum.

When done, Carla tied back her hair in a ponytail and applied some make-up. The last thing she wanted was to greet Rhys looking washed out. She was still a little sleepy, but the vitamins Commander had given her were helping and she felt the energy beginning to surge through her body.

After lunch with Commander and the crew, which consisted of strange looking but tasty vegetables on a kind of pie base, Carla went off to the kitchen to make coffee for the group. The crew went back to their various duties, taking their coffee with them and Carla and Commander stayed at the table, lingering over the fragrant aroma of their drink while they sipped it slowly, savouring its taste.

"Tell me something," Carla remarked, "how could Rhys's wife die in a volcano eruption, especially when I didn't see any in Tyrr?"

Commander replied, "Why don't you ask Rhys about Xaye?"

"I don't want to cause him any pain by bringing up sad memories."

Commander gave her a kindly look. "For an Earthling, you're okay, Carla Fiori. Although I'm not happy about Rhys staying on Earth, but I must admit that if he's set on living there I'm glad he's going to live with you. I've come to love you as my daughter," he confessed, "and if I could have you both live on Tyerra, I would."

Carla felt the pinprick of tears at what Commander said, but she kept her emotions at bay. "Well, thank you. I appreciate it and I'm honoured you see me as a daughter." Then, with a twinkle of humour in her eyes, she added, "But don't expect me to call you 'Dad'."

Commander laughed heartily. "You're a funny one, my dear."

Carla threw him a serious look. "And you're evading my question about Xaye."

"No, no. I was sidetracked, that's all. Your love for Rhys is so pure." He paused for a moment, looking thoughtful before he continued, "It's like what you said to the League about love and this being the energy that drives all things in the cosmos. It's exactly like the love you have for Rhys. I can feel it, and it moves me. In fact, I felt it on Earth when I first met you, and it moved me to tears then."

Carla nodded. She understood exactly what he meant.

"You know," Commander went on, "I've lived for a long time and saw so much in my lifetime. I've experienced the beautiful and the base; I've been involved in destruction of other planets, for which I'm not proud; I've seen wars and dealt with beings all over the universe, but during all this time, I never believed love could be so pure or genuine. This is why I never married. Then, I came across Rhys and recognised the special being he is, and I thought how lucky I was that I could at least have a son to follow in my footsteps and make this universe a better place." He paused momentarily, sipped his coffee, and went on, "When Rhys married Xaye, I didn't see that kind of purity in her even though she was a lovely girl, and they were happy."

At this, Carla experienced a tinge of jealousy, but she shook it off instantly. Why should she be jealous that Rhys had loved another? She, herself, had loved before, albeit the wrong man. But Carla believed in making mistakes and learning from them. This was what she had told the League, and this was what helped one grow emotionally.

Most people learned from their mistakes and thanks to her own bad relationships she learned to recognise the love she had for Rhys was love in its purest form. She asked nothing of him and even if he had voted to leave Earth, she would accept it. After all, she wanted him to save himself if Earth were to be destroyed. Rhys was her life, her soul, and her everything. Carla wanted him to be happy, no matter what. The fact he loved her just as completely was the biggest blessing she had ever known.

"But to answer your question," Commander's voice brought her out of her reverie. "Xaye was a volcanologist. She studied volcanoes from all over, even on other planets. Tyerra has a few active volcanoes and at the time she died, she and Rhys were living in another city, close to where the volcano was located." Commander regarded Carla with fondness in his eyes. He had tuned into her thoughts about her unconditional love for Rhys. The girl was the genuine thing. She had spoken the truth to the League and she lived the truth about love. "In any case," he went on, "Xaye had one fatal flaw in her personality."

Carla waited to hear more, curious about what Commander would reveal.

"She didn't know where reality finished and fanaticism began. She was totally obsessed with volcanoes to the point she didn't want to settle down in any one place and have children, which was something Rhys would have liked. Sometimes, I think she loved volcanoes more than her husband. Rhys was patient, though. After all, they were young and had plenty of time for a family afterwards, but the erupting volcano turned out to be Xaye's Achilles heel in the end.

"She wouldn't listen to the warnings from Rhys that they should get out. She wanted to wait a little more; she wanted to take more readings, and hopefully record all the data, even though the eruption was seconds away." He sighed, shaking his head. "Anyway, the whole thing backfired on her, but she almost got Rhys killed because of her obstinacy. Thankfully, Rhys managed to survive. He had to drag her away from her monitoring station, just as the volcano erupted, but she broke free of his hold and ran back, telling him she had to at least save some of her recording equipment. When she broke loose of him, he went to follow her, but the volcano exploded at that very instant and Xaye was engulfed in the eruption. Rhys managed to get away by a hair's breath."

Carla uttered, "But how could she put him in danger like that?"

"I don't know. She was obviously overcome by her determination to save her equipment or perhaps she miscalculated how much time she'd have before the explosion. The thing is, it would've been really difficult for me to forgive her if she'd gotten Rhys killed. I feel sorry for her, but she died doing what she loved best, and that was her choice. I'm just thankful she didn't get Rhys killed."

Carla pounced on this last statement exclaiming, "But without my wanting to, I'm doing the same thing!"

"What are you talking about?" Commander had been too busy reliving the story he was relating to tune into Carla's thoughts.

"Well," Carla explained, "if the League destroys Earth, Rhys will die, too—all because he won't leave and save himself."

"That's an interesting point you make," he replied. "But Rhys made this decision of his own accord; and like Xaye, he has the right to choose for himself."

Carla said, "Let's hope things work out then. I don't want you blaming me if Rhys gets killed because he stays on Earth."

"I would never blame you, my dear," Commander stated. "Rhys is a grown man and he makes his own decisions. Besides, it's not like you're forcing him to stay."

Carla nodded in silent agreement and finished the rest of her coffee. "Let's hope it doesn't come to this."

"The League will have their decision in a few days. I'll keep both of you posted." He then placed a hand on top of hers. "Know this, whatever happens, I'm happy you and Rhys found each other."

"Thank you," Carla replied feeling teary-eyed.

***

The return trip went without a hitch and though Carla marvelled at everything she saw all she could think of was Rhys.

When they finally arrived with the shuttle to the Jamison Valley, Commander informed her, "I'll walk you back to the town and then return to the shuttle."

"You're not coming in?" Carla wondered why he was in such a hurry to leave again.

"I have a few things to do—Rhys will fill you in on it. I'll be in touch in a few days."

Carla did not question him further. Despite the incredible journey she had been on, she was glad to be home.

It was evening when they arrived, and a moonless one. Luckily, they had clear skies and made the journey back up to the town quickly. Had it rained, it would have been a tough climb back to Katoomba.

Commander walked her right up to the top of her street and after a farewell hug from Carla, he disappeared into the night. Carla ran towards the cottage and threw herself into Rhys's arms when she saw him waiting for her on the doorstep.

"Oh Rhys!" she uttered in between kisses as he held her

tight. "I couldn't wait to get back."

Rhys responded with a deep kiss that turned her legs to jelly, but their bliss was short-lived as Tom barked excitedly and insinuated himself between the two of them. Carla knelt down and hugged the dog. "Hello, Tom. Did you behave yourself while I was away?"

Tom wagged his tail furiously and licked Carla's face.

"Okay, okay!" Carla laughed at his greeting. "So you missed me after all, and now I'm going to have to wash your slobber off my face."

They went inside and Rhys locked the front door behind him. Carla made her way straight to Rhys Junior, who was out of his blanket pouch and looking perky. "Oh, you look great, my little Rhys. Your ears are healing so well. How are you, my baby?"

Little Rhys hopped up to her for a pat and she crouched down. "He looks wonderful," Carla said to Rhys while she patted the kangaroo. It was then she noticed the look on Rhys's face. "What is it?" She felt her heart in her throat.

"Nothing to worry about," Rhys reassured her. "Only the wildlife people called and they found him a foster farm."

Carla stood up, looking dejected. "A foster farm?"

"Yes. He has a few months before he'll be ready to be released back into the wild, but they need to get him used to his natural habitat. The farm specialises in the rehabilitation of joeys who've lost their mothers. They'll teach little Rhys how to fend for himself."

Carla burst into tears. It was all too much, and without Commander's filtering system to help her along her emotions came to the fore, engulfing her to the point where she needed an escape. The imminent departure of Rhys Junior proved to be the proverbial straw that broke the camel's back.

Rhys went to take her back in his arms, but Carla pulled away. "I'm okay," she said, still sobbing. "I'll go and wash my face and get ready for bed. It's late."

Rhys looked unsure. "But…"

Carla reassured him by patting his arm. "Get them settled

for the night and I'll see you in a bit." She left the room, leaving Rhys with the animals.

In the bathroom, Carla sobbed until there were no more tears left in her. The cause was a multitude of things: the whole experience of the trip to Tyerra and the meeting with the League; the wait in regards to Earth's fate; her deep love for Rhys and the fact that they may die along with the planet.

The thought of all existing suffering and loss on Earth and other planets also overwhelmed her. She knew so much more now and it was as if her senses had undergone yet another change and her level of empathy had expanded to enclose the entire cosmos. She needed time to process all this, she admitted to herself while she prepared for bed.

The knowledge she had gained in the last few days exhausted her mentally and she felt the urgent need to earth herself with something that was real to her. She knew she had to reconnect with the basic human side of herself, and now she understood why Commander insisted she would not be able to cope if she stayed on Tyerra for long.

The fabric of consciousness was so powerful that only the highest of evolved beings could handle it. Carla, a mere human, had not reached that level. Perhaps, a day would come in future when Earthlings would achieve what the Tyerrans had, but she would not be around to see it.

At this thought, Carla felt small and insignificant compared to the likes of Rhys and Commander, who both had the ability to live for hundreds of years and be around long enough to see progress in their own lifetime. Instead, humans lived such a short life.

Then, another thing occurred to her, something worse than Rhys dying prematurely if Earth was destroyed—if life on Earth went on, Rhys would become like the average human in terms of lifespan because the air was different on Earth and their technology so backward. Not only this, but Rhys would no longer have access to the advanced medicine they had on Tyerra. Cutting his ties from his home planet meant all of this for him.

Commander had made it very clear, so Carla would have to live with the knowledge that even if Earth went on Rhys would age, just like herself, and live a much shorter life, and all because he loved her. This alone made her tears return and Carla stayed in the bathroom for much longer than she had intended, until after a while she heard a knock at the door.

"Carla, are you okay?" Rhys sounded concerned.

Carla splashed water on her face and made her voice sound normal. "Yes. I'm done. I'll be out in a tick." She dried her face and pulled herself together, making up her mind that she would need to discuss this with Rhys tomorrow. Tonight, however, she needed to reconnect with all things normal—her true human nature.

She came out of the bathroom and found Rhys standing on the other side of the door, regarding her worriedly. "Are you sure you're okay?" His heart ached for her. He knew something of what she was experiencing, especially from his early days when he had discovered he was an SSE, super sensitive empathic, and he hadn't known how to handle it until Commander trained him to filter through his emotions.

"I'll be fine," she smiled. "Bathroom's all yours."

Rhys looked at her retreating figure for a moment and then walked into the bathroom.

Carla noticed it was well past midnight when she climbed into bed. She did not feel tired physically, but on a mental level she felt absolutely spent. When Rhys joined her a few minutes later, he switched off the light and brought her close to him. They lay in the silence of the night around them.

"You'll feel better in the morning," he reassured her. "Right now, you need sleep."

Carla snuggled closer to him, the urgent desire to feel her base human instinct suddenly hitting her like a tidal wave. "I don't want sleep," she stated rather firmly. "I want you to fuck me."

"What?" Rhys exclaimed in shock.

She sat up in bed and took off her nightclothes, throwing

them on the floor. She then turned to him and pulled off his garments. Rhys allowed her to do this while his mind tuned into hers. All he sensed was a red hot desire that clouded everything else. Carla's thoughts were stored so deep inside her that even he could not get at them. In their place, he discovered a deep animalistic instinct that needed no words of expression, only satisfaction.

Carla straddled him and leaned forward with one hand at each of his wrists, trapping his arms above his head. She licked the perimeter of his lips and then penetrated his mouth with her tongue, assaulting his senses all at once. He grew hard, but managed to stem his desire for release. When Carla came up for air, she uttered, "I said, fuck me!"

Rhys's consciousness looked on, still in shock, from a higher place while his body took over and with his superior strength he freed his arms and threw Carla onto her back. He then climbed on top of her and his mouth attacked her body: tasting, kissing, biting, and with a wild hunger that stunned him, he first penetrated the wetness between her legs with his fingers and then he thrust his member deep inside her so forcefully that it brought a yelp of pain from her.

His higher consciousness suddenly slammed back into his body at full force and he paused abruptly. "I'm sorry! I've hurt you!" he uttered, about to withdraw from her, but Carla was beyond reasoning and in response she wrapped her legs around his waist to keep him inside her. Their coupling was frantic and intense, culminating in a number of simultaneous climaxes.

23

While Carla slept, Rhys lay awake in bed, a hand behind his head, the other resting on his chest. Although he tried to come to terms with the shock of their sexual union, he found it difficult to explain his own violent behaviour towards the person he loved.

As a Tyerran, he was not used to physical sex, even though he had learned very quickly to enjoy it. Lovemaking using both the spiritual and physical senses had transformed him to the point where he knew true love.

It wasn't like having an idea of what love was but, rather, he had experienced the exchange of souls between himself and Carla. He had become one being with her. It was something he couldn't explain logically, but a realisation of which he was in awe—an experience that reinforced their union with the rest of the cosmos.

The one thing Rhys had trouble coming to terms with at present was his own behaviour at what had occurred with Carla earlier. He understood her need for getting back to her basic human nature; after all, her experience travelling to Tyerra and subsequent meeting with the League had to have been surreal for a human who had never travelled in space. People used defence mechanisms to block shock and extraordinary experiences by using substances to help them cope or by adopting certain behavioural patterns. These usually came in the guise of alcohol, drugs, and comfort food, plus behaviours varied from person to person, be it aggression, anxiety, sex addiction, and so on.

Carla's reaction to her experience in this instance had

resulted in the kind of rough sex that Rhys considered tantamount to rape—but in their case, the sex had been fully consensual. What shocked him the most, however, was his own reaction to the events that played out between them. For a peace loving, highly evolved being, Rhys had always been against any form of violence. This was also the reason why he had pulled away from the League and their attitude towards annihilation. Therefore, it took him by surprise when he reacted to his intense lovemaking with Carla. The being he had become temporarily was aggressive and rough, and yet Rhys discovered enjoyment in the experience while at the same time his consciousness looked on in abhorrence.

Visions of rape and pillage around the planet flooded into his mind and he felt like screaming with the horror of it. His highly sensitive and empathetic self desperately needed to erase it, and he experienced a sudden moment that was tantamount to insanity. He was sure he would go over the edge, but reason soon came to the rescue, as did his filtering ability, and the moment passed.

All his life, he had had to filter out the gross, the ominous, the savage, the pain, and the suffering. He had managed to do this successfully; always knowing himself to be so evolved that nothing could touch him. And yet, with the part he had played during his sexual act with Carla, he'd allowed himself to tumble down to the level of someone less evolved. It wasn't so much the rough sex itself, but his own enjoyment of it that troubled him. He also knew that had Carla pushed for more roughness he would have gone even further.

This was the part that frightened him the most and he found it extremely humbling. He had never considered himself to be a proud man, but what he had done tonight debased everything he held in high esteem about his personality. To suddenly turn into some kind of carnal being brought him so low he felt ashamed of himself and his behaviour. He should have stopped the whole thing despite Carla's consent.

He couldn't blame her for what happened because she had

been in a position of having to deal with the surreal issues that affected her, so he should have known better and protected her. And now, he felt mortified at having hurt her instead. He knew while Carla had exulted in their union, at the same time she had endured physical pain from the frantic violence of their act. When it was over, she had tried to hide the soreness, bruises and bites that resulted from their encounter. Knowing her as he did now, Rhys knew she wasn't one for rough or violent sex. He sighed, again blaming himself for allowing the whole thing to happen. He should have stopped when he had the chance.

"What's wrong?" Carla spoke suddenly, turning towards him and laying her head on his chest.

Rhys cradled her close with one arm. "Are you okay?"

"Why shouldn't I be?" She sounded puzzled.

Rhys didn't feel comfortable bringing up the subject but knew he must confront it head on. "I hurt you physically tonight. I was really rough with you." He kissed the top of her head. "I've never been like this before."

Carla reached over with one arm and flipped on the bedside lamp so she could get a good look at his face. His eyes held a haunted look in them. "Rhys, don't be silly. I was the one that attacked you."

"But I didn't stop it," he replied. "I know I hurt you, Carla; you can't hide your bruises and bites, plus I've never used force on anyone I loved."

Carla smiled reassuringly. "I won't deny that I'm feeling somewhat tender at present, but it will go. Don't feel bad about what happened. If anything, it was my fault for using rough sex to bring me back down to earth. I really needed to try and erase a lot of what went on with the trip to Tyerra and what the League will decide. I was going to wait until morning to discuss it with you. But, Rhys, what we did is something I've never done with anyone else. I trust you one hundred per cent and I know you would never hurt me in a serious way."

Rhys shook his head. "I still should've known better."

"Well, you couldn't have stopped me," she reassured him.

"I must admit it's not in me to get rough, but it's something I needed to do. And I'm okay—really, I am."

Rhys gazed into her eyes and noted the candour in them, so he confessed, "What frightened me the most was the fact that I actually liked it. I was looking down on myself as we did it and I was shocked at my own behaviour, but I still liked 'fucking' you, and I couldn't stop myself."

"Wow! I don't think I ever inspired an out of body experience for a sexual partner before," Carla replied, trying to lighten the atmosphere.

Rhys looked troubled and did not respond so Carla kissed the tip of his nose and caressed the side of his face. "If it makes you feel any better, I don't *fuck,* I make love. This was simply an exception. That is all. Please, don't worry about it. And there's no reason why you shouldn't enjoy it. Plenty of people do this all the time and some go even further. We've only done it once, plus if you keep me from travelling into outer space, it won't happen like this again."

This time, she was rewarded with a smile. "I love you, and I would never do anything to hurt you."

"I love you, too." She kissed him softly on the lips. "What we have is so very special that nothing can destroy it, so let's leave it at that. We all have our demons to live with, right?"

He nodded in agreement. "And what's your demon?" Rhys sounded alert all of a sudden.

Carla sighed with resignation. "I was going to tell you tomorrow, but I may as well do it now. I came to the realisation that even if Earth does goes on, I'm responsible for trapping you into a short lifespan with the prospect of growing old and dying a lot sooner than you would've done on Tyerra. How do you think that makes me feel? It's a hell of a lot worse than some rough sex, right?"

The love in Rhys's eyes told her everything she needed to know, but Rhys vocalised it. "You're not responsible. I chose to stay with you and I'm fully aware of the consequences."

Carla felt happiness engulf her. His love was the only thing that mattered. "And 'ditto' to you. I chose to engage in some rough sex. You didn't do any damage and there's nothing wrong in you enjoying it. I wanted you to. Remember how we discussed last time the difference between fucking and making love?"

He nodded.

"Well, I did mention that fucking has its own dimensions and though I never experienced it with anyone else, I still felt I wanted to do it with you, but not for the sake of meaningless fucking, but because you ground me in essence as a person and at times I feel we're one whole person rather than two. I believe this is all part and parcel of truly loving someone."

"But you said fucking was just lust and that people often confused it with love," he argued.

"Yes, I did say that, but our love's real and we know this for a fact. So fucking is a sort of expression of our feelings and it may happen with us from time to time, but not in a meaningless or violent way. We are allowed to be aggressively lustful, you know."

In his mind, Rhys saw images of other sexual acts that they hadn't yet tried and he felt himself grow hard. Carla saw the flush on his face, reached under the covers and placed her hand on his erection. "Just know that emotions, good or bad, will affect our sexual life, but as long as we're both in agreement, no one gets hurt. And now, I'm going to sleep." She kissed his lips and flipped off the light. "Goodnight, my love."

***

Rhys was happy to see that over the next few days Carla readjusted after her journey to Tyerra, and things between them were back on a normal footing. Meanwhile, the foster farm made a time for them to drop off Rhys Junior and though Carla was engulfed with sadness she knew in her heart the little joey needed to learn how to fend for himself in the wild.

The night before they were due to take little Rhys to his new home, Carla and Rhys had a quiet dinner and Carla had an early night. She didn't want to show too much emotion about the impending parting from her furry baby and she thought having a cry away from Rhys would be best. She imagined Rhys knew what her intentions were, but these days she was past caring whether or not he read her mind. She trusted him implicitly and knew he would never take advantage of the situation.

"Tom's due for his evening walk," Carla said as she cleared the dinner things. "Why don't you take him out while I tidy up?"

Rhys chose not to tune into her mind, but he was glad she suggested he take out the dog for a walk. Commander had been in touch earlier to inform him the shuttles had arrived and were now in the valley, awaiting his instructions. Rhys wanted to go over and talk to the crew. He didn't want to take any chances should Tovo and his band of renegades decide to make for Earth again.

"Any news from the League?" Rhys had asked after Commander told him about the shuttles.

"Not as yet, but I believe it's looking good. They were moved by Carla. I guess they needed an Earthling to remind them of their own actions despite the fact they count themselves as being highly evolved."

"And she's right," Rhys affirmed. "We should never have been so high handed in the first place. Annihilating a planet because of their collective evil doesn't make us any better than they are."

"I agree. We, too, need to learn from our mistakes; and that's what Carla communicated so implicitly to the League. I like that girl. You're very lucky, my son."

Rhys momentarily basked in Commander's praise of Carla. "Well, she likes you, too," Rhys informed him. "She told me about her change of heart towards you."

Commander laughed. "She's a little spitfire, I keep telling you, but she gets under your skin somehow."

Don't I know it! Rhys thought to himself, but quickly blocked the thought lest Commander read what was on his mind.

"Keep what I said about the League to yourself for the time being; I don't want to raise Carla's hopes," Commander warned, giving no hint as to whether he had tuned in on Rhys's mind.

Rhys hoped not. Despite his talk with Carla about their night of rough passion, he still couldn't help but feel guilty for hurting her. "Any news on Tovo?" Rhys threw in quickly before he allowed his thoughts to reach across space to Commander.

"Not yet. I had discussions with the League and we believe a number of Hergons are helping him. Tovo, and any surviving Primans, are not as highly evolved and they wouldn't be able to keep their whereabouts from us so easily."

Rhys had a feeling of unease as Commander gave him this news, but he said nothing. They covered a few minor points and then shut off communication.

When Rhys took Tom for his walk that evening, he revised his conversation with Commander and the feeling of unease returned. He stopped before commencing his descent into the valley and in the quiet moonless night, he tuned into Tovo's whereabouts using his full powers of focus. Tom sat quietly by his master and waited, sensing Rhys needed time to reflect.

Rhys opened his mind while quickly filtering out anything not associated with Tovo, the Hergons or the immediate threat of danger. Nothing came to him except a feeling of dread that led to a bad headache. As far as he could tell, there was no threat near Earth at present. As Commander had said, Tovo must have someone helping him; otherwise, the League would have picked up something. The only thing Rhys was fairly confident about was that Earth was in no immediate danger at this point.

After catching up with the crew from the four shuttles, Rhys left strict orders that anything at all, no matter how small, should be reported to him immediately. The commanders of each ship assured him this would be the case and further reassured him they had brought enough ammunition with them should trouble arise. Rhys left them and made his way back out of the valley with Tom, hoping they wouldn't have to get into some kind of war against Tovo and his cronies.

It was past eleven when he returned to the cottage and after settling down little Rhys and Tom, Rhys got ready for bed and entered the bedroom quietly. Carla was asleep, but she kept tossing and turning. Despite his headache, which was quite strong by now, Rhys quickly scanned her dream but did not discover anything of serious concern. Carla was simply distressed at the thought of letting go of the joey, but she consoled herself with the knowledge that little Rhys would be happy to be back in his natural habitat before long.

Rhys slipped into bed without disturbing her, but the minute he lay down on his side with his back to her, Carla turned to him in her sleep and spooned him. She settled quickly after this and slept soundly.

When the morning sun filtered into their room the following day, Carla sat up in bed and stretched. Rhys was already awake and she noticed the dark circles under his eyes.

"Are you okay?" She automatically put a hand to his forehead to test his temperature. He felt cool.

Rhys ran a hand over his face and hair. "Just a headache."

"So extraterrestrials get them, too," she stated. "Are you allowed to take painkillers? I never asked you about that. I don't even know whether you can have Earth medicine."

Rhys smiled weakly. "Yes, I can take painkillers and any of your Earth medicines. But what I need right now is a really strong coffee and a nice hot shower. That should fix it."

"Well, coffee's coming right up." Carla hopped out of bed and started for the door. Then she paused, turned around, came back to him and kissed his lips lingeringly. "Good morning." The look of love in her eyes was more than evident.

"Good morning," Rhys replied, already beginning to feel better.

After breakfast, they both got ready and Rhys was back to his normal self by the time he showered and dressed. Carla was a little quiet and Rhys knew she was preparing herself for their trip to the foster farm for little Rhys.

On the way, Carla did not speak. Rhys drove past Katoomba and in the direction of Mount Victoria, where the farm was located. The trip would only take them twenty or so minutes and the only one in the car that seemed animated was Tom. Although he had tolerated the kangaroo's presence, he wanted Rhys and Carla to himself. Rhys briefly smiled at the dog as he picked this up from Tom's mind, but he was careful not to let Carla see his mild amusement as she would get upset at letting go of little Rhys all over again.

When they arrived at the farm Carla was relieved to see the owners, a middle-aged couple, were welcoming of little Rhys and quite experienced at what they did. Jenny, the wife, reassured Carla the joey would be just fine. "Mick and I've been doing this for years, love." Jenny smiled as Carla tried to keep back her tears.

"Best thing's to walk away," Mick advised. "Feel free to give us a call any time you wish to check on him or even visit. The little fellow will be here for a few months yet before we release him into the wild."

Carla and Rhys thanked the couple and without looking back, Carla made her way to the car, tears running down her face. She got in and hugged Tom while she waited for Rhys, who seemed to be exchanging a few words with Jenny and Mick. Then they shook hands and Rhys made his way to the car while Carla wiped away her tears with a tissue.

Back on the road, Rhys turned to her and ran a hand over her hair. "Okay?"

Carla nodded, not trusting herself to speak.

"Hey, why don't we go back to Merry Beach for a while?" Rhys suggested. "I think we need to unwind after all that's happened. The weather's getting warmer and we could use some sunshine and the sound of the ocean."

Carla nodded again and uttered, "Yes, that's a great idea. I don't have any projects on at present and I could do with a break, but not for too long, I don't want to use up all my savings."

Rhys laughed. "Don't worry about that. We have plenty."

She regarded him with curiosity. "What are you laughing for? We have to pay the bills, you know. Besides, how did you ever manage to travel and live around the world while you were doing your report for the League? It never occurred to me to ask."

Rhys explained, "Tyerrans are always prepared when travelling to other worlds, I'll have you know. I brought a whole lot of gold with me and exchanged it for currency."

"Oh," Carla replied. "So how much is a lot?" She couldn't help but ask. After all, she needed to know what kind of a budget they had to live on.

Rhys laughed again. "Let's just say we don't need to worry for many years to come."

24

Commander was waiting for them when they arrived at the cabin Carla had rented for a month. It was dusk by the time they reached Merry Beach and Commander was out on the veranda enjoying the view of the ocean as the sun went down.

"I guess it's silly to ask how you knew we'd be coming down here." Carla greeted him with a hug.

Commander returned the hug and then surprised Rhys by hugging him, too. "Let's just say I had a feeling you'd be around."

Tom came bounding out of the car to sniff at Commander's feet. "He's still not too sure of you," Carla said of the dog. "Last time he saw you, you came to take me away from him."

Commander patted Tom on the head and the dog became instantly friendly. "I don't see him protesting about my presence now," he chuckled.

The group went into the cabin, with Rhys and Commander bringing in the food supplies and other gear Carla had packed for their stay. Meantime, Carla opened the windows to air the place and she fed Tom. "Will you join us for dinner?" she asked Commander.

"Yes, why not?" he replied jovially. "I have good news for you."

Rhys and Carla glanced at each other and then turned their gaze on Commander.

"The League agreed to spare us?" Carla blurted out.

Before Commander could even nod she threw herself at him and hugged him again, this time raining kisses all over his face. "Oh, thank you, thank you, thank you!" She didn't notice

Commander's blush when she turned to Rhys and flew into his arms. "Oh, Rhys!" Her voice cracked a little, tears stinging the back of her eyes. "We can be together now. It's going to be all right!"

As he held her in his arms, Rhys addressed Commander over Carla's shoulder. He spoke aloud, "I don't know what to say. Is it possible the League actually decided to listen to someone other than themselves?"

Commander nodded. "I think Carla's meeting with them helped a lot; it drove home the big mistake they made with Prima."

Carla turned from Rhys, but remained in the circle of his embrace. "Surely, they didn't change their minds entirely because of what I said. Being from superior civilisations I'd expect they've known all along they made a mistake about Prima."

Commander smiled. "You're very perceptive and absolutely right. The League always knew deep inside that what they did to Prima was wrong, but it took Rhys's work on Earth to illustrate this, and you to drive home the point."

Carla and Rhys smiled, and Rhys remarked to Commander, "Well, let's just say it was a team effort. If it weren't for you, Carla would've never had the chance to speak to them. I certainly couldn't have done it on my own."

Commander nodded. "I daresay I agree." He then addressed Carla, "So how about that celebratory dinner for our team effort?"

"If you don't mind waiting a while, I'll make pizza. I know how much you like it," she replied and was rewarded with a nod of approval from Commander, who had told her on the ship that one of the things he loved most aside from coffee was Carla's pizza.

Carla disengaged herself from Rhys and made her way to the grocery supplies they had brought with them. "Luckily, I purchased some ready-made pizza bases, so it won't take too long to prepare."

The men nodded and while Carla got busy Rhys made coffee and he and Commander stepped out on the veranda, communicating via thought.

"Any news on Tovo?" Rhys asked. "I've been getting a bad feeling about him lately."

"Well, he's not near Earth at present and the Hergon leader is cooperating with the League to locate him. The last thing we need now is to deal with space terrorists."

"I might get a couple of the shuttles to move over here while the other two remain in the Jamison Valley," Rhys responded. "If anything should happen, I may have to make a quick move to catch him."

"You should've let your dog rip out his throat in the first place," Commander remarked.

Rhys looked at him with surprise. "Are you serious?"

"He was ready enough to kill you, wasn't he?" Commander argued.

Rhys nodded thoughtfully. "Perhaps, I was wrong to let him go, but I didn't want to take a life unnecessarily."

"Does Carla yet know about the attempt he made on your life?"

"No. She's been somewhat unsettled since she returned from the trip. I guess she's trying to process the whole thing in her mind. This is why I suggested we come here for a while. She needs a change of scenery."

The two men remained silent for a moment, each thinking their own thoughts in private while watching dusk turn into night. A short time later, Carla called them in to dinner and the three of them celebrated their success and talked late into the night about the future. Carla made more coffee and when they finished drinking it Commander announced he must go back to Tyerra.

"So soon?" Carla uttered. "You could stay on for a few days with us if you wish."

"Thank you, my dear, but the League is expecting me. I only came to deliver the good news in person and to give you both my blessing. I know now you two were always destined to be together."

Carla became teary-eyed at his words and didn't trust herself to speak, but Rhys said, "This means a lot to us and we thank you for your blessing."

Commander nodded and took his leave of them. Carla watched him walk off in the direction of the bushland behind the caravan park, and then she turned to Rhys. "We'll still see him, right?"

"Of course," he replied. "There's nothing to stop him from keeping in touch with us."

"So why did he look so strange when he left?"

"It's because once my choice was made to stay here there's no going back. This is a rule they have; I can never return to Tyerra. Earth is my home for good now."

Carla moved close to him and into his embrace. "Oh Rhys, I feel so bad about this. It's like I'm robbing you of everything—a long life, being with your father and the people you know. I..."

Rhys silenced her with a long and passionate kiss that left her in no doubt about the choice he had made. When they drew apart, he put a hand on either side of her face and gazed lovingly into her eyes. "Listen to me," he said softly, but firmly, "I don't ever want to hear this kind of talk again, okay? I made my choice freely and our love is more important than anything else."

Carla went to respond, but Rhys spoke on. "Commander knows exactly how I feel about this and he approves. You heard his blessing tonight, and he loves you like a daughter, Carla. Don't forget that. Besides, he can visit us any time he wishes."

Carla drew away and nodded. "I know. I'm sorry for carrying on like this. I should be jumping for joy that Earth will live on and that you and I will be together until we die. It's just... Well, I can't help thinking I'm robbing you of the long life you could've had."

"You're not robbing me of anything. Remember what happened to Xaye and how young she was when she died? No one knows when it's their turn to go," Rhys stated. "So enough of this talk and let's take Tom for a walk."

Upon hearing his name, Tom jumped down from his resting place on the sofa and the three of them headed for the beach. Rhys grabbed hold of Carla's hand while Tom ran ahead happily.

It was well past midnight by the time they went to bed, both of them tired from the day's travelling, the excitement of Commander's news, and their own emotions running high. They fell asleep almost immediately their heads touched their pillows. Tom settled at the foot of the bed and snored softly.

Rhys later woke up with a strong headache and sat up in bed, feeling dazed. He took a peek at the clock on the bedside table, which displayed 3.11am. A strong feeling of dread descended upon him and he debated whether he should communicate with the crew on the shuttle at Merry Beach, which had arrived at his request prior to him going to bed. He also intended to check with the Jamison Valley crew. He was sure either crew would have contacted him if they'd picked up anything; he had left them with strict instructions to do so.

Despite this and his strong headache, Rhys focused on Tovo, but nothing came up. He then slipped out of bed quietly, making sure not to disturb Carla or Tom, and headed for the kitchen. This time, he needed painkillers to clear his head. He took a couple of tablets and made strong coffee. When he was done, he took his drink out on the veranda where he sat in the darkness.

The sky was clear and the millions of stars twinkling in the heavens reflected their light upon the ocean waves. The moon was only a sliver, lending a little more light to the view before him. The sound of the waves as they rolled in rhythmically had a calming effect on him and after he finished his coffee he closed his eyes and shut off his thoughts for a while, clearing his head and at the same time getting rid of the headache. Even his feeling of dread lifted and Rhys enjoyed the sounds of nature around him in peace.

He stayed like this for quite a while until a faint signal

intruded into his mental idyll. His eyes flew open and he followed the signal with full alert. It took him a while to hone in as the signal was rather weak, but when he had a pinpoint on it he was able to identify it immediately. It was Tovo after all.

The hate Tovo had projected at the time when he'd tried to assault him in the mountains now came back to hit him full on. Rhys sat up in his chair and looked around him. The beach was deserted and he could not pick up anything coming from the bushland, either. He then filtered through the hate and tried to find a location for Tovo to no avail.

Rhys stood, pacing the veranda in deep thought. Someone was purposely blocking their location; this much was evident. The reason he had picked up on the weak signal in the first place was because Tovo's hate was much stronger than anything else. This worried Rhys and he immediately closed his mind in case his location was discovered. First, however, he would have to make quick contact with the shuttles. He did this without the thumb communicator as being on the same planet didn't necessitate the use of the device. Both crews came back to him immediately, advising all was clear and no signals had been detected.

Rhys walked back inside the cabin and went directly to the thumb communicator. He had Commander at the other end immediately.

"What is it?" Commander said, although he sensed the urgency in Rhys's mind.

"It's Tovo," Rhys replied. "I can't communicate for long because he's probably trying to locate me. His hate's so strong and overwhelming it's getting through despite the block on his signal. I still can't pick up on a location, though, but I wanted to alert you, and if anything should happen I want you to come for Carla."

"What do you think is going to happen?" Commander sounded concerned.

"I'm not sure. But if I have to give chase I may not have time to warn her. So I need you if it comes to that, or if anything should happen to me."

"Have you told her yet?" Commander asked, already knowing the answer.

"No," Rhys confirmed his thoughts. "But I'll tell her straight away because in the morning I'm going to have to go with the shuttles for reconnaissance. I can't just sit here doing nothing."

"Very well," Commander responded. "I'll keep an eye on Carla, but you must tell her."

"I will. I promise," Rhys reassured him before he shut off the thumb communicator.

"What is it?" Carla spoke from the darkness of the bedroom. "Are you okay?"

Tom came into the lounge area to ensure all was safe. The dog was able to report to Rhys that for now there was no danger. He had also picked up on the signal and confessed he still wanted to rip out Tovo's throat. Rhys thanked Tom for being such a great being and asked him to stay on guard. Tom planted himself by the sliding doors that led to the front veranda and assured his master nothing would get past him.

Rhys joined Carla in the bedroom. "I had a headache," he said, "but it's gone now. I took some painkillers."

Carla flipped on the bedside lamp, took one look at the concern in his eyes, and exclaimed, "You've been keeping something from me, Rhys! I feel it."

Rhys thought how far she had developed since they'd been together, plus her trip to Tyerra would have had an effect, too. She was a quick learner and he wouldn't be surprised if one day she may even read other people's minds. But this was not the time to muse about her potential capabilities. Rhys reclined on the bed, his head resting on a pillow. "I'm sorry, but something happened while you were on Tyerra and I didn't want to burden you with more problems."

Carla knelt on the bed, facing him. "What is it?"

Rhys went on to tell her about Tovo and the attempt on his life. As he related the whole story, bringing her up to date with the fact he had shuttles at both locations and the League was looking for Tovo and his little group, Rhys watched the play of emotions across Carla's face. She went from astonishment to fear and then anger.

"How could you keep this from me?" she berated him. "How could you let me think everything was okay?" Carla wanted to shake him for being secretive even though at the same time she understood he had done it in order not to add to her worries. Despite this, she had the right to know what was happening. Fear ran through her in a wave of panic that she tried to control. Her anger dissolved instantly and all she thought about was Rhys's own safety. "I'm sorry," she said, trying to keep calm. "Of course, I can see why you didn't want to tell me. But Rhys, this guy's out of control. He means to kill you."

Rhys tried to reassure her. "We're doing all we can. I've already arranged to go out with the shuttles at first light and Commander is on alert, too. We'll find Tovo one way or another."

Carla reached out and rested a hand on each of his shoulders. "I'm coming with you."

Rhys gently disengaged from her. "No. It could be dangerous. You need to stay here and look after Tom."

"But..."

"No buts," he interrupted. "Carla, I know what I'm doing. Besides, Commander will keep an eye on you."

"I'm not concerned about myself," Carla stated passionately. "It's you I'm worried about."

But Rhys was adamant. "Please, don't make this more difficult. You need to trust me, okay?"

Carla remained silent. The fear inside her flashed all sorts of horrible scenarios into her mind. If anything should happen to Rhys she would rather be with him than without him. Dying with him was the better alternative than to live a life alone, without the love she had found with this man.

Rhys read her thoughts and embraced her, bringing her body close against his. "Please, trust me on this," he implored her again.

Carla buried her face against his neck. His skin felt cool and soft, and she wanted to stay there forever. "I don't want to be without you." Her voice was muffled, but Rhys understood because he kept reading her mind.

"You won't have to," he reassured her. "I'll be back before you know it. Besides, Tom needs to be looked after."

"He could come with us." Was the still muffled reply.

Rhys smiled at her persistence, but his mind was made up. He gently drew her from him so he could look into her eyes. "If anything happens, Commander will come for you. I can't have you with me and focus on catching Tovo at the same time. I'd be too worried about your safety."

Carla's eyes held a pleading look. "So you admit you could die!"

"No," Rhys uttered. "Look, you have to trust me when I say I'll be fine, but if I focus on your safety, I won't be able to have full focus on Tovo. This is all I'm saying."

Carla sighed. She knew when she was beaten. She had to be strong for Rhys and remain on Earth. Now she could relate to how women the world over felt when their men went off to war. She nodded resignedly and put her head on his shoulder.

"Okay," she said in a soft voice, tears rolling down her face. She did not bother to dry them. She simply stared ahead at nothing in particular as she engraved in her mind the feel of his arms around her.

25

It was dawn when Rhys left the cabin in search of his crew. Carla was in a deep sleep and he decided not to disturb her. He found it difficult enough to focus on what was ahead and waking her now would only make it almost impossible to part from her. Instead, he left her a note on the kitchen table and made his exit quietly.

As soon as Rhys shut the door behind him, Carla's eyes opened. She had pretended to be sleeping and because Rhys seemed preoccupied with other things he had obviously not picked up on the fact that she was awake. Carla headed for the kitchen to make coffee and found Rhys's note.

"It's better this way," it read. "We're only parting for a short time. Take good care and wait until you hear from either me or Commander. I'll try to be with you as soon as possible. I love you. Rhys."

Carla put down the note, holding back tears. She did not understand why she felt like crying when Rhys would only be away for a few days at most. Still, something lurked at the back of her mind that not everything seemed as it was. She couldn't quite put her finger on it, either. All she felt, however, was a sense of dread and danger. Carla sent a silent prayer to the universe, hoping Rhys would return to her safely.

Tom came bounding into the kitchen to be let out for his morning toilet run and Carla was grateful for the distraction. She opened the sliding door for him and set about getting his breakfast ready while the coffee was on the stove. Later, when both of them had eaten, Carla showered and donned a pair of khaki cargo pants and a black sweater over a long sleeved T-shirt. Although spring was on its way, it was still quite cool by the ocean.

Carla slipped on hiking boots, tied back her hair, and filled a small backpack with bottled water, a flask of coffee, kibble for Tom and a sandwich for herself. She planned a long walk high up on the cliffs in order to expend her energy and ensure a good night's sleep. She knew that unless she did this she would only toss and turn with worry over Rhys.

Just as she set off with Tom, Rhys was sipping his own coffee with both the Merry Beach crews in one of the shuttles. All personnel were present, while at the same time Rhys maintained communication with the two crews in the Jamison Valley.

"I had confirmation from Commander on my way here," Rhys announced via thought. "Tovo's been tracked leaving Hergon in a large ship with two shuttles onboard. The League reported they'll be in warp drive within an hour. That gives us about ninety minutes to meet outside Earth's atmosphere and hopefully intercept his ship. It'll take them a few minutes to change from the main ship and into the shuttles."

"So what's the plan?" asked the commander of one of the shuttles.

"We intercept Tovo with our two shuttles while the Jamison Valley crews go straight for the big ship. Commander is sending reinforcements from Tyerra to help destroy it. We can only hope they arrive in time."

"Tovo will be on the lookout for us," one of the other commanders remarked.

Rhys nodded. "That's right, but Commander informed me the League will do what it can to scramble their tracking signals. If this works, Tovo's people won't see us coming until we're literally on top of them."

Rhys hoped this would be the case. If they could pull it off, then they would have the element of surprise and they'd be able to wipe out Tovo and his crew.

The meeting lasted for a few minutes longer with the crew from each shuttle clarifying points on their course of action, and with Rhys growing more anxious by the moment when a strong sense of dread descended upon him to the point where it took all his control to shut it off with his mind.

He jumped out of the chair he had been occupying and uttered aloud, "We have to go. Right now!"

The crew did not question his sudden vocal command and each of the crewmembers went to their post in their respective shuttles; within minutes they were airborne.

Rhys paced up and down on the command deck of the shuttle in which he travelled and he checked and rechecked their ammunition, making sure they had enough missiles for what was to come. The Jamison Valley shuttles reported they were fully stocked with their missiles and that if need be they could easily take on Tovo's shuttles plus his ship.

Rhys did not feel so confident. They had four shuttles against Tovo's two, but there was the matter of the main ship. Commander had not been able to tell him how big Tovo's ship was or how much ammunition it carried. The only reassurance Rhys had to go on was the fact that the League had sent reinforcements of their own.

When they were about to leave Earth's atmosphere, Rhys glanced down towards Merry Beach. The day was clear and he could see the beach and ocean in great detail. Somewhere down there was Carla, waiting for him. He felt a wave of love wash over him at the thought of her, but then something else caught his attention.

From the corner of his eye he observed what looked like a faint ripple line in the ocean below. Rhys focused on it and at first saw nothing unusual; it was merely some sort of current. He was about to turn away and dismiss it when suddenly a horrible thought entered his mind. Once again, he looked out the window and with a sinking feeling in his stomach he recognised what he was looking at.

Before he could give the command to abort the mission and return to Earth, the shuttle's commander cried out, "They know we're here! They just shot a missile at us but missed.

Instead, they hit Earth."

But Rhys knew Tovo's shuttle had not missed. Tovo had meant for the missile to go to Earth. This was where he thought Rhys would be. Rhys took out his thumb communicator and waited breathlessly until Commander acknowledged at the other end.

"You have to go and find Carla, right now!" Rhys could barely think straight, but he tried to focus on what he was saying.

"What happened?" Commander's tone was full of concern.

"The bastard just hit Earth with another of his missiles," Rhys replied while hope died inside him. "It hurtled straight into the ocean, sparking off a huge tsunami... and... and..." And Rhys could say no more.

Commander finished the sentence for him. "And Carla's right in its path. I'm on my way."

And before Rhys could gather his thoughts, his own shuttle was shaken violently by a massive explosion.

***

The day sparkled crystal clear as Carla and Tom made it to their usual ledge on the cliff. They had gone for a long walk prior to ending their jaunt and Carla had cut through bushland to reach the beach that lay next to Merry Beach, which was named Pretty Beach.

This beach joined the long expanse of yet another beach, Pebbly Beach, and access to Pretty Beach was limited to a winding track through bushland if one was driving or, as Carla had done, one could simply cut across on foot. Both these beaches were usually the domain of fishermen and those who knew the local area. The beaches were much more private than Merry Beach and unless visitors knew their way around, they did not venture out this way. Carla loved the solitude of the place. It was almost as if this was her own secret domain, one which she had not even had time to share with Rhys as yet.

The sun was now fully out, the fishermen had gone by this time, and Carla and Tom had both beaches to themselves. Tom ran up and down the two beaches, close to the surf, while Carla sat on the sand and tried not to think about Rhys and the potential danger of his mission. She sat for almost an hour and then took out her flask and poured herself some coffee. She couldn't relax, no matter how incredibly beautiful the view in front of her.

As she sipped on the coffee, she watched Tom amusing himself close to the shore, fetching sticks and hurling them in the air or picking up clumps of drying seaweed and dropping them close to the shore so the water would wash them back in. Carla sighed, knowing she'd have to bathe the dog once they got back or he would stink out the cabin.

As if Tom knew she was thinking about him, he suddenly stopped his antics and came running over to her, whining softly.

"What is it, boy?" Carla asked, checking his body in case he was hurt in any way, but she realised it wasn't that kind of a whine. Perhaps, he'd simply had enough. This thought was confirmed as Tom started to make his way up the incline that led back to the bush track. Carla shrugged, packed her bag, and followed him.

They left the beach and when they came to the forked path that led to Merry Beach or to the cliffs above, Tom took the cliff path and Carla had no option but to follow. It was a long way up the incline, but this would only add to her exercise for the day and she could look forward to a restful sleep that night.

When they finally reached their ledge, Tom sat next to Carla, but instead of relaxing as he usually did, he seemed on the alert.

"What's wrong, Tom? Carla looked directly at the dog. Something was not right with him and her stomach filled with butterflies as she experienced a strong sense of déjà vu.

A feeling of dread suddenly hit her and she stood on the ledge looking out to sea and trying to work out what it was

Tom was gazing at. The dog started to whine again, as he had done at Pretty Beach, but this time he made a strange shuffling gesture with his front paws, as if he were moving away from the cliff's edge. He then made eye contact with his mistress and took a few more steps back, but when Carla did not follow suit he returned to her side to do it all over again. This went on for a few moments while Carla looked on in fascination, trying to work out what he was trying to tell her. Then, a growing feeling of horror dawned on her and she instantly knew what it was.

She was reliving her nightmare, and Tom's behaviour confirmed the terrible reality of it. She quickly looked around her, but only noted the tranquil day. The sun was out, the sky a bright blue, the waters their usual azure colour, and the birds... Carla's heart jolted as a wave of panic rushed through her leaving her legs feeling weak and rubbery. Where had the birds gone?

Carla noticed the tide ebb beyond its usual stretch of beach, leaving exposed the sandy bank that led to a deeper indentation on the ocean floor. A variety of fish flapped around violently while a myriad of marine life lay marooned on the wet ground. Seeing this spectacle, people on the beach approached and children rushed to the creatures that were stranded to the elements of sun and wind.

Tom did his whining and shuffling routine yet again, but Carla's gaze was frozen on the people as they collected clams, while others picked up the flapping fish to take them closer to the water's edge. The kids ran around with their brightly coloured sand pails, gathering sponges and starfish, shells and other molluscs.

Carla then looked out to sea, where in the distance she noticed a long wave starting to roll towards the shore. The wave did not look big, but the moment she saw it Carla started to yell at the people down by the beach while she waved her arms frantically, trying to attract their attention to the oncoming tsunami. Unfortunately, no one heard her.

Carla wanted to yell louder, but her vocal cords could no longer produce any sound as she had screamed herself hoarse. The wall of water moved rapidly and grew larger as it approached the shore. Carla watched, horrified, as the monstrous mass of water suddenly became the size of a large mountain and crashed down on the people at the beach, sweeping them to their deaths.

Tom barked wildly and this time he bit down on Carla's trouser leg, pulling with all his might. Carla's mind had enough time to register the second wave coming in, just behind the one that had swept away everything below. The wall of grey green water was massive, but she did not wait to see how high it was. Instead, she took off after Tom, who was now running farther up the cliff through the bush. Carla left the track and followed the dog without looking behind her.

Only when they reached the very top of the cliff did she turn around, just as the second wave crashed against the rock wall and fully engulfed the ledge where they had been standing only moments earlier.

***

Rhys's shuttle shook so hard that the crewmembers hit the floor while pieces of equipment and other objects flew across the deck like projectiles.

"Ship's on automatic!" Someone yelled via thought amid the noise from the explosion and the violent vibrations of the shuttle. "Protection shields are up." As soon as this was said, the shuttle's motion steadied and everything returned to normal.

While the crew went through an equipment check and made contact with their companion shuttle, Rhys got Commander on the thumb communicator.

"We just entered Earth's atmosphere. Not there yet," Commander reported before Rhys had a chance to say anything.

"Keep me posted," Rhys replied. "Tovo's fired at us, but we're okay. What's happening at the other end with Tovo's big ship?"

"Still waiting to hear on that, but it seems we got a good

hit on it. I'll let you know..." And the rest of his sentence was lost when another huge explosion shook the shuttle and the communicator flew out of Rhys's hand as he hit the floor again.

The shuttle shook severely as a barrage of missiles from Tovo hit it, but this time Rhys and both his shuttles were ready and no damage ensued with the protection shields on. The small ships still shook, but they could not be destroyed. Rhys and the crewmembers of both shuttles returned fire and were astonished when one of Tovo's shuttles exploded into a million pieces.

"What was that?" This time, Rhys spoke vocally and the crewmembers followed suit.

"He didn't have his protection shield on. How can that be?" a crewmember remarked.

They looked at one another, but this was no time for speculation. Tovo's remaining shuttle was still around. Rhys had no way of telling which shuttle Tovo was on, but the fact he could feel his energy meant that Tovo was still alive.

"He's out there," Rhys uttered and then went to retrieve the thumb communicator. He thought he knew what had happened. "You still there?" he said via thought to Commander.

"Yes. You okay? I enjoyed seeing in my mind that shuttle you guys destroyed," Commander observed. "What a wonderful thing it is when signals get scrambled." He chuckled at this.

"I thought that's what happened," Rhys replied. "I guess this means the League was successful with the signal scrambling and they destroyed Tovo's big ship."

"Yes," Commander returned. "Tovo's on his own now and you still have two shuttles plus the other two from the Jamison Valley, which are on their way to you. So go get that bastard!"

But Rhys was not thinking about Tovo now. "What about Carla?" He asked as his heart contracted with fear for her.

"I'm at the beach now," Commander reported. "There's devastation everywhere."

Rhys observed the destruction through Commander's mind, but said nothing. He simply tried to control the overwhelming grief at what he saw—bodies scattered on the ground as the surf washed them back in after the tsunami hit; the sand on the beach eroded almost to the rock face; the caravan park and cabins erased as if they had never existed.

The place was desolate and deathly quiet, but the ocean waves went on rolling in and out as if nothing had happened. The eerie atmosphere shook Rhys to the core and he waited for Commander to continue.

"I don't want you to worry, my son," Commander assured him. "I feel her energy and I'm sure she's alive. I'll come back to you when I have more news."

Rhys watched the thumb communicator screen go black and then closed his eyes, conjuring up the image of Carla's face. He sent her his love across the distance between them and hoped this would be enough to sustain her.

26

Carla sat on the clifftop, dumbfounded, with Tom sitting next to her, his body lending heat to hers, which felt icy cold. The fact she was still alive was thanks to her dog warning her plus her recognition of the nightmare she'd had some time ago. Although her dreams had been distorted to a certain extent, it turned out they also carried with them a prophetic underline. In this case, her dream had saved her life.

Below her, the waters calmed down after the second tsunami and the beach would have looked normal had it not been for the total devastation the killer waves had left behind. Carla watched with detached and horrified fascination as hundreds of people descended upon the beach, mostly in shock, while others arrived in desperation, searching for loved ones.

Ambulance, police, and other rescue personnel worked tirelessly among the crowd while helicopters circled the scene from above looking in vain for survivors and water patrol boats skimmed the waters in the hope they could rescue anyone caught up in the strong currents.

Carla observed the group below starting to remove bodies and treat survivors for shock and injury while rangers helped with wildlife. The whole hive of activity in the aftermath of the disaster made Carla want to scream with rage at Tovo. She knew he had been the cause of the disaster and, just like the bushfire in the mountains, this was the result of one of Tovo's powerful missiles.

For a moment, Carla felt panic flood her body and mind at the thought that Rhys may have been killed. She took a deep breath and forced herself to stay calm and rational. Rhys had left at the crack of dawn to meet with his crew, and Carla was sure they had departed from Earth well before the tsunami struck.

The one thing she didn't know for sure was whether Tovo had shot down Rhys's shuttle. Carla suspected the missile Tovo sent to Merry Beach had been aimed at Rhys. This meant Tovo did not know that Rhys was out in space looking for him. By the same token, the missile could have been a near miss on the shuttle and instead it had hurtled down to Earth, but this was too much of a coincidence. Tovo must have thought Rhys was still at Merry Beach. Even so, there was a slim possibility the missile that caused the tsunami could have been accidental.

Carla took a deep breath in order to maintain control over her emotions and she pulled out her mobile from her backpack. She scrolled through the latest news and read about the tsunami hitting Merry Beach and neighbouring beaches. Other than this, no other disasters were reported. The world went on as normal. This did not prove whether Tovo's missile had been deliberate or an accidental hit, but it did lend more strength to Carla's belief that Tovo was behind this latest disaster. She also had to believe Rhys was alive and well, and hopefully crushing Tovo with the help of the League.

Tears rolled down her face and she didn't try to control them. She cried for the waste below, the innocent victims of a renegade who had it in for Rhys and the League. The repercussions of evil the League had believed responsible for the breakdown of the fabric of consciousness was now showing itself on Earth. This was not evil caused by Earthlings, but evil resulting from other beings—beings that were supposedly more evolved than humans.

Carla shook her head in frustration. While she sympathised with Tovo because the League had destroyed his planet, she could not forgive him for his fixation on Rhys—the only being who had tried to stop the League from annihilating Prima. But Tovo's thirst for revenge did not entirely focus on punishing the League for the destruction of his planet. His revenge was born out of envy and jealousy because the League had granted Earth the right to go on existing. This was the reason why Tovo had lashed out, not only at Rhys, but at Carla herself.

How Tovo must hate her, knowing she had attended a meeting with the League to plead on behalf of her planet. It was obvious Tovo had spies and if he knew about the League giving Earth a chance at survival, he definitely knew about Carla getting involved in trying to save her planet. By now, he surely would have heard Earth was in the clear.

The worst part for Tovo must have been that Rhys had fallen in love with her and had decided to live on Earth, which in Tovo's twisted mind would have translated to favouritism given to Rhys by both the League and Commander. After all, Commander, being Rhys's father, had a lot of influence with the League, and this would have made Tovo think he had been involved in convincing the League to allow Earth to survive. And yet, nothing could be further from the truth. While Commander had made it possible for her to meet with the League, he had had no influence over its members. They voted democratically to spare Earth; but somehow, Tovo would not see it this way.

Carla shivered as once again she thought of Rhys. Where was he? How could she communicate with him? There was no way of getting in touch with Rhys or even Commander. She needed the thumb communicator, but Rhys had taken it with him. Not only this, but Carla would need to arrange to get back to the cottage in the mountains. Everything she had brought with her to Merry Beach has been swept away in the tsunami, including Rhys's car.

An image of Rhys's face popped into her mind and she thought she would break down and cry again in desperation, but she must contain her emotions in check. Rhys was super intelligent plus he had his crew and weapons. His chances of survival were high. She almost laughed at the irony, however, of Rhys thinking she'd be safe on Earth while he was gone. Even he hadn't seen this one coming.

Tom suddenly nudged Carla with his head and she looked

around her in dismay, thinking some other disaster was about to unfold, but the dog seemed calm. Carla wished she could communicate with him as Rhys could. "What is it, boy?"

Tom took hold of her wrist with his mouth and pulled gently.

"You want me to get up?" Carla stood immediately, hoping in her heart that Rhys was coming to fetch her. She looked around the clifftop again, but saw nothing. "I don't understand," she said to Tom. "What are you trying to tell me?"

Tom's butterscotch eyes gazed at her and then at somewhere beyond the cliff. Before Carla could respond, the dog took off and disappeared into dense bushland. Carla followed immediately, anxiety mounting within her. She reached an overgrown path and stopped, trying to get her bearings. She had never been to this part of the cliff and it would be easy to get lost in here. The forest that spread inland was huge and in parts impenetrable.

"Tom!" Carla called out. "Tom!" Then, she stopped and listened. She heard the faint sound of barking ahead of her as she took in the density of the forest. She knew it would be foolhardy to go in there. Not only could she get lost, but the place was probably crawling with spiders and snakes. Even so, she must find out where Tom had got to. "Stay where you are, Tom," she called out to him. "I'm coming."

Carla crossed the overgrown path and stepped into the cool shadow of the forest. Tom barked a few more times to give her a sense of direction, and right now it seemed all Carla had to do was follow her nose. She did this, and each time she thought she was getting closer to the barking, she noticed the barking grew fainter because Tom had moved on. She stopped momentarily, feeling spooked, but then continued to follow the sound of Tom's barking once again. The barking seemed to come from a north-west direction, whereas before she had been heading west.

Carla walked on, watching out for snakes and creepy crawlies, when she suddenly jumped in fright as a kangaroo crossed her path. The bush seemed to be more alive than ever, especially since the tsunami would have pushed the wildlife to move to safer ground.

Carla came across koalas, peacefully asleep in tall gum trees, wallabies and kangaroos hopping in and out of her way, a few snakes slithering away at the sound of her footsteps, and she even espied an echidna burrowing itself into the forest floor so that all Carla could see were its needle-sharp spikes.

The forest became colder as the density of the bush blocked out the sun and Carla began to feel tired after trekking for almost an hour. Every few minutes she heard Tom's bark guiding her, but she could not understand why the dog didn't come to her so he could show her the direction he wanted her to take. Finally, when she reached a point where she thought she would collapse from fatigue, Tom startled her by jumping out from behind a clump of dense bushes.

Carla fell to her knees and hugged the dog, chiding him. "I hope you've got a good excuse for this, dragging me in here. I think we're completely lost."

"No, you're not," a voice replied from the direction Tom had appeared.

Carla breathed with relief when she saw the figure of Commander materialise out of the trees, extending a hand in order to help her to her feet.

"Oh, thank god!" She uttered as she fell towards him in a storm of weeping.

Commander picked her up in his arms and carried her beyond the trees from where he had appeared. Carla wept uncontrollably, no longer caring what anyone thought of her, while Commander strode in silence with Tom beside him. They walked thus for a further twenty minutes before they reached a small clearing in the forest where to Carla's delight was an orange shuttle waiting for them.

Carla quickly dried her eyes when she noticed the same crew she had met when she travelled to Tyerra. The boys wore an expression of concern when they saw Commander carrying her, but Carla managed to produce a smile of greeting as she took in their young, handsome faces. She still didn't know their names, but she knew them by their distinctive appearance—the pilot with the platinum blond hair and amber eyes; the crewmember with bright orange hair and tawny skin; and the other one, who was light-skinned and sported a long mane of metal grey hair that reached down to his waist.

"Put me down," she whispered to Commander. "I can walk from here."

Commander did as she asked, but kept a light hold on her arm in case she should trip. The boys smiled a welcome and when they were assured by Commander that Carla was slightly dehydrated and in need of rest, they immediately scrambled inside the shuttle to get her something to drink while one of them prepared a room for her.

"Rhys... Have you heard from Rhys?" Carla asked Commander when he led her into the small room where a narrow bed was waiting and the crewmember with the metal grey mane placed a large glass of green liquid in her hand.

Carla espied Tom out on the main deck being fed by the boys and getting quite a bit of attention. Commander shut the door to the room and sat on a chair while she slumped on the bed, making every effort not to lie back just yet.

"What is this?" Carla screwed her nose as she took a whiff of the green liquid in the glass.

"Drink up; all of it," Commander directed. "It'll pick you up and help with the shock."

Carla took a few sips and decided it tasted like mint so she finished the drink thirstily, her water having run out long ago. "You didn't tell me about Rhys," she said when she finished the drink. "Is he okay?"

Commander nodded and now she collapsed back on the bed with the relief of it.

"I want you to rest until your body's had a chance to recover." Commander threw a blanket over her.

"But..."

"I'll tell you all you want to know later, but first you get some sleep, you hear?"

Carla nodded. She was bursting with questions and wanted to talk to Rhys, but she thought it prudent to follow Commander's wishes. She trusted him and knew he wouldn't lie to her if something awful had happened.

"I know you want to speak with him," Commander said in response to her thoughts. "He asked me to pick you up. He saw the tsunami from the shuttle and knew Tovo had sent the missile, thinking he was still at Merry Beach. But that's all you need to know right now. I'm going to tell Rhys you're okay so he can focus on destroying Tovo. And don't worry; he'll be safe." With this said, Commander left Carla alone, closing the door behind him.

Commander tried to contact Rhys, but could not get through. He then tried the crew from the different shuttles, but again no response. At this point, he wasn't worried. He knew Rhys and the crew were engaged in battle. Still, with Tovo's main ship having been destroyed, Commander thought by now Tovo would be dead and Rhys and the crew on their way back to Earth. He decided to give it more time before he tried to contact Rhys again.

When a couple of hours elapsed, Commander tried once more. No response. This time, he began to worry. He scanned with his mind but felt nothing, which only made him worry all the more. He then contacted one of the senior members of the League.

"Tovo's ship has definitely been destroyed," the League member informed him. "As you know, we managed to scramble their signal for a while and we were able to approach without detection."

"So why haven't we heard anything by now?" Commander tried to keep the concern out of his mind.

"We lost contact with them after Rhys and his crew destroyed one of Tovo's shuttles. Since then, everything's gone quiet. Not even a faint signal."

Commander's worst fear reared its ugly head, but he refused to let it control him. He thanked his colleague and shut off communication, all the while wondering what to tell Carla.

***

There was a ceasefire for a while after they had destroyed one of Tovo's shuttles and the crew communicated excitedly among themselves, filled with the exhilaration of being in a real battle. They were trained for war, but had seen no action during their lifetime, especially as they were part of an evolved civilisation. But being young made them feel invincible, as with most young people in any part of the universe, and seeing some action was a bonus in their estimation.

While this went on, Rhys sipped coffee and waited to hear from Commander. Surely, by now he had made contact with Carla. He checked the news broadcasts from Earth to get more information on the devastation caused by the tsunami, but this did not tell him whether Carla was alive.

Meanwhile, Tovo's shuttle was nowhere to be seen and the Jamison Valley shuttles had arrived. They were ready for action, but their target had vanished. Something about this bothered Rhys, and he scanned for Tovo to no avail.

When they had destroyed Tovo's other shuttle, Rhys had still picked up on his signal, but now there was just a blank; not even a peep as to what was happening out there.

Rhys finished his coffee and joined the other crewmembers. "Any signals?" he asked the commander of the shuttle.

"No. Nothing. It's like Tovo never existed."

"That's what worries me," Rhys replied. "Keep trying to locate him."

The commander nodded and turned to the control panel. No sooner had Rhys stepped away from the deck with the intention of trying to contact Commander again that a huge explosion shook the ship and everything went black.

***

"What do you mean you can't make contact?" Carla felt icy cold fear grip at her heart. "You said everything was okay!"

Carla had slept until early evening and as soon as she awoke she tidied up her appearance, washing away the dust on her face and brushing her tangled hair before she joined Commander and the crew at the control deck. She was hungry and ready for some strong coffee, but when she saw the look on Commander's face she instantly knew something was not right and her appetite left her.

Commander, seeing the query in her eyes, told her straight out that he couldn't get in touch with Rhys, and she stood in front of him, fear written all over her face, demanding to know what was going on.

"I don't know," Commander replied. "I even contacted Tyerra and though they confirmed destruction of Tovo's big ship they haven't heard from Rhys, either."

Carla was glad Commander reached out at that moment and took hold of her arm, just as her knees buckled from under her. The blond pilot rushed over and helped her to a chair while Commander went in search of coffee.

"It's okay," said the pilot, trying to comfort her. "Rhys is indestructible."

Carla smiled sadly for her lost youth. If only she could think like these young boys. The pilot was so fresh faced he could have been her son. "Thank you," she said softly. "You guys never told me your names."

The pilot blushed and introduced himself as Vehn. Then, he pointed to the orange haired youth. "That's Ty." Ty smiled shyly at her. "And that's Zeer." This was the guy with the long mane of metal grey hair. Zeer winked at Carla.

She smiled back at the boys and thought under any other circumstances she would be having fun with them, but the way things stood at present she could not share their exuberant faith that Rhys was indestructible.

When Commander came back with the coffee, the boys went back to their duties.

"I'm taking you back to the cottage," Commander said.

Carla glanced at Tom, who was snoozing happily on a mat the boys had provided for him. She wondered whether the dog knew where his master was. If he did, he gave no sign of it. Carla turned back to Commander and nodded. "Okay."

Commander gave the order to the crew via thought and before Carla knew what was happening, they were on their way.

27

Commander walked with Carla and Tom all the way to the cottage and stayed for a while to ensure Carla was okay. "We'll keep trying to contact Rhys," he said. "Meanwhile, I'm going to leave you with a thumb communicator in case you need to contact me." He handed her a device similar to the one Rhys carried with him. "This one operates with voice so we can have a two-way conversation."

Carla took it from him, grateful that at least she could maintain contact. Commander scanned her emotions and patted her arm. "Don't despair, Carla," he tried to reassure her while keeping his own concern hidden from her. "We'll have news of him soon."

"I hope so," Carla replied in a tone that threatened tears.

"I have to go now, but feel free to contact me any time, you hear?"

Carla nodded and saw him to the door, watching after him as he waved and walked off into the darkness. She felt tired despite the long sleep she'd had on the shuttle and after feeding Tom she went to bed, not bothering to eat anything.

She slept right through the night and the following morning she was woken by a wet nose making contact with her face. She opened her eyes and gently put Tom from her. "Give me a minute and I'll take you for your walk," she told the dog and dragged herself out of bed.

There was nothing wrong with her except grief and all Carla wanted to do was curl up under the blankets and keep sleeping, but Tom would never allow that. He had to be walked and fed and Carla had to eat something to keep up her strength.

She told herself not to give up hope. It was early days and Rhys could be anywhere in outer space chasing after Tovo. But for Commander not to be able to pick up on any signal was a serious worry. He was extremely powerful and probably the only one to be able to pick up on Rhys. The fact that even he could not make contact was not a good sign. She tried not to dwell on this and forced herself to go through the motions of her daily routine. She took Tom for a short walk in the morning sun and then returned to the cottage and fed him. She managed to eat a small portion of scrambled eggs on toast and drank really strong coffee, which helped. She then went on to clean up the cottage, do the laundry, and go down to the shops for groceries—but all the while her mind kept returning to Rhys.

The thought that he may be dead was something she tried not to entertain, but she had little success with this and plunged into despair instead, which in turn threw her into a sense of emptiness that was hard to bear. The only thing that kept her going was the fact that she had to look after Tom. So for the next couple of days, Carla operated on automatic. She walked Tom, fed him, forced food into her own person, slept for hours on end to shut out the reality of the situation, and then she did the same thing all over again the following day.

By day three, she could not stand it anymore and she contacted Commander on the thumb communicator. She knew he would be busy somewhere out in space, leading a search party for Rhys and the crew. She also knew if there had been any news he would have contacted her by now. Despite this, she figured unless she talked to someone associated with Rhys she'd go mad, and so she contacted Commander.

"How are you holding up?" Commander asked, knowing the answer before she replied to his question.

Carla did not bother to respond. She knew Commander had scanned her emotions. "I don't suppose you have any news?" she uttered instead.

"We're in the area where we last heard from Rhys and the crew," Commander informed her. "We haven't heard anything, but we found evidence of a battle. We picked up some debris from Tovo's destroyed shuttle."

"How do you know it's not Rhys's shuttle?" Carla asked with her heart in her mouth.

"It's different from the shuttles we use," Commander reassured her. "There's no evidence of any material from our shuttles, so I can only assume they're still out there somewhere. Right now, we're following the course they would have taken in pursuit of Tovo's other shuttle. It could very well be that Rhys shut off all contact so Tovo can't pick up on his signal."

Carla experienced a momentary ray of hope. "Is this something Rhys would do?"

"It's hard to know. It all depends on what happened," Commander replied.

Carla sighed resignedly. She was not going to learn anything else and she didn't want to take up any more of Commander's time. "I'll let you go then. Just keep me posted."

"You know I will," Commander returned. "Don't lose hope, my dear. You have to stay strong."

"Okay." Carla shut off the communicator, feeling despondent. She didn't want Commander to hear her weeping.

Once again, she went to bed early hoping to obliterate her despair in deep sleep. She tossed and turned for the better part of an hour and eventually dropped off, only to be awakened by the sound of a sharp yelp from Tom.

She sat up, flipping on the bedside lamp, and the sight before her froze her to the spot. Tom lay on the floor, not far from the bed; a trickle of blood flowing from his nose. Carla wanted to scream, but nothing came from her throat as she took in the being standing by the foot of the bed, staring at her with large grey eyes that had black horizontal slits for pupils.

This is not a Tyerran, her brain shouted inside her head. He looked human despite the eyes, a very small nose, and an elongated face. He sported long black hair with a bright blue streak down the middle and his skin was the colour of death—a dun, off-white hue. Even before he spoke Carla knew she was in the presence of Tovo.

With overwhelming rage coursing through her, Carla's voice returned with a blood-curdling shriek and she jumped out of bed and went at him with full force. The element of surprise knocked Tovo off his feet, but he soon gained the upper hand and pinned Carla to the floor with the weight of his body while he held her arms above her head with his hands.

"I knew you'd be a beauty, and now that Rhys won't need you anymore, I'm going to sample the goods myself," he said in a hoarse tone, using perfect English.

Carla spat in his face and this earned her a slap so hard that she bit her lip open and blood flowed down her chin and into her mouth. "You bastard!" she yelled. "I'm going to kill you!"

Tovo gave her a smug look. "How? Your dog's dead, and so is lover boy."

At his words, Carla felt like she'd been kicked in the stomach. If Tovo was telling the truth, that both Tom and Rhys were dead, then she had nothing to lose. "Try me," she taunted him as fury spread through her body in a hot rush of adrenaline.

Tovo laughed, revealing pointy teeth that resembled those of a vampire. "It'll be a real pleasure to 'try you'. That is, before I kill you, bitch!" He slapped her again, this time even harder, while he kept hold of both her wrists with one hand.

Carla thought she was going to black out from the pain, but she'd be damned if she was going to let him win. She didn't care if she died, but hell would freeze over before she'd let him enjoy her suffering. Her intuition told her to keep him talking as long as she could while she waited for that brief moment when he might not be holding her so tightly.

"How did you kill them?"

Tovo laughed again, enjoying her discomfort and distress. He smelled her fear and it excited him. "Your stupid dog almost killed me once before, so I zapped him with a stun gun this time. As for lover boy, let's just say he's been sucked into a vacuum along with all his crew. They thought there was only my shuttle left, but we had a whole army waiting. We just let him and his precious League believe that we were acting alone."

While Tovo crowed with more laughter, Carla turned her head so he wouldn't see the tears escaping her eyes. Again, if what he said was true, then this was indeed the end for her. She didn't want to go on living without Rhys.

From the corner of her eye and through the blur of tears, she suddenly noticed one of Tom's paws moving slowly, as if flexing, and his beautiful butterscotch eyes opened and Carla's heart wanted to sing. Tom was alive! She didn't know how badly injured he was, but he was still with her.

Before she had a chance to do anything, however, Tovo stood abruptly, dragging her up with him. He then threw her on the bed. Carla was wearing a short black shift for nightclothes and as she landed roughly on the mattress the shift ended up around her waist, revealing black panties.

Tovo licked his lips with a pointy tongue, and Carla thought she was going to vomit. But before she could move, Tovo covered her body with his and she was trapped under him again. He bit at her neck a couple of times, drawing blood, and though it hurt, Carla did not cry out. She simply prayed for Tom to recover enough strength so he could jump the bastard and give her a chance to escape.

Tovo went to kiss her, but she turned her face away and uttered, "I don't believe you killed Rhys. He's too good for the likes of you. You're lying!"

This stopped Tovo momentarily and one of his hands, which was about to rip off her panties, rested on her thigh instead. Carla felt her skin crawl at his touch, but she didn't show any emotion when she turned her eyes to his.

"You're just a pathetic Earthling," Tovo yelled at her, spittle from his mouth flecking her face. "We pushed him towards a black hole, until it was too late for his shuttles to retreat. They got swallowed up, never to be seen again."

Carla turned her face away from him, but only to check on Tom. He was attempting to stand up while he snarled in a very low growl towards Tovo. Carla had to keep Tovo's attention on her lest he realise the dog was still alive.

"Well, we'll see about that, won't we?" she returned defiantly.

This had the effect of enraging Tovo and his obviously massive ego. "Unlike the lilly-livered Tyerrans, on Prima we still practise physical sex," he informed her with relish and a leering look in his alien eyes. "I'm going to fuck you so hard you'll beg me to kill you."

His savage tone as he yelled this into her face frightened Carla into shock and she had no doubt he meant every word of what he said. She lost her nerve all of a sudden and struggled in order to get away from him, but Tovo was far too strong for her. With his free hand he punched her near her temple and Carla almost blacked out, but instead felt disoriented for a short while.

When she recovered her focus, she found her panties gone and Tovo trying to enter her. She felt so sickened that in a last attempt at freedom she summoned up all her strength and with her forehead she hit him as hard as she could on the nose. Although small, his nose seemed to feel the pain intensely and Tovo screamed wildly and slapped her hard in return.

Carla bit her lip once more and fresh blood flowed down her chin while her jaw ached from the punch he'd given her earlier; nonetheless, she made an attempt to escape her foe, but Tovo grabbed her body roughly, turned her face down on the bed, and climbed on top of her again. "You're going to die screaming, bitch!"

Tovo had her arms pinioned between his knees as he sat astride her. Carla knew exactly what his intention was and she closed her eyes, wishing herself dead before he sodomised her. If she had a weapon right there and then, she would have taken her own life.

"Goodbye, my love," Carla said to Rhys inside her mind as she felt Tovo's first attempt to enter her. She wept silently and prayed for death to take her, when she heard a loud growl and next thing she knew she was free.

She jumped off the bed and turned in time to see Tom's teeth sink into Tovo's throat as the dog managed to pin him to the floor. Tovo fought the dog violently, and unfortunately Tom's strength seemed to fail him.

Carla grabbed the bedside lamp closest to her and turned it upside down to wield the brass stand as a weapon just as Tovo knocked Tom off him and sent the dog flying across the room to land with a loud thump against one of the walls.

Carla took the opportunity and struck at Tovo's head, but he was too quick for her and moved out of the way before she could smash his skull. With a sinking heart, Carla knew she was as good as dead.

Tovo pushed her on her back against the floor and jumped astride her. His obvious rage was such that his horizontal pupils turned into huge black circles. "You wasted my time, bitch, so it seems I'll have to forgo the pleasure of fucking you and simply kill you instead." His hands then wrapped themselves around Carla's neck and he squeezed until her oxygen supply was cut off.

Carla did not have the strength to fight him and her fading awareness dissolved into a black void, studded here and there with stars. The last image in her mind was of Rhys's face. When death was upon her, she relaxed and let go of everything. She only thought of Rhys and how if there was an afterlife she'd soon be reunited with him. The void enveloped her as she started to slip away. Rhys's face disappeared, the stars were gone, and the only thing left was the silent welcoming of the darkness around her.

Then a white point of light appeared as if escaping from a tunnel and Carla floated towards it. She looked for Rhys and saw him standing in the distance. She couldn't wait until she reached him. She floated closer, but she became confused at what she saw. On the bedroom floor of the cottage, Rhys knelt behind Tovo with his enemy's neck held in the vice- like grip of his arms. Carla watched in detached fascination as Rhys squeezed the last breath out of his enemy before she heard his neck snap and Tovo's limp body fell to the floor with his evil eyes open, looking into nothing.

Rhys rushed to Carla's side and lifted her body onto the bed. He checked her vital signs and the rest of her body to make sure she was okay. Carla was alive. No broken bones, no serious wounds; only a split lip and an aching jaw.

The image of Rhys suddenly came into her sight in full 3D and Carla took a deep breath at the beauty of his face and the love in his eyes. She wasn't sure whether she was dead or alive, but she soon found out when Rhys went to kiss her mouth, and her lip stung where it had split.

Rhys disappeared for a moment and upon his return he gathered her in his arms and helped her sit up on the bed. He made her drink a few sips of water from the glass he had brought with him from the kitchen.

This was all the proof Carla needed to know that she was not dead or dreaming. She was alive and Rhys had returned and killed Tovo. Then, Tom suddenly jumped on the bed to join them and nuzzled his way in between their bodies. Carla burst into tears of relief and happiness, and she couldn't stop crying as Rhys cradled her to him, caressing her hair and whispering loving words.

"You're going to be okay, my love," Rhys said in a soft comforting tone. "We won. Tovo's no more."

Carla did not reply, nor did she ask for explanations. She simply held tight onto Rhys and gave thanks to the universe for bringing back her love.

EPILOGUE

Carla and Tom made a speedy recovery thanks to Commander, who smuggled in some Tyerran medicine. While it was frowned upon for use outside his planet, this time Commander decided he would break the rules as a big thank you to Rhys that Tovo had been exterminated and the threat of an intergalactic war avoided.

As soon as Rhys killed Tovo and made sure Carla and Tom were alive, he contacted Commander to bring a crew so they could take Tovo's remains back to Tyerra for disposal. This was done in record time and Commander administered the Tyerran medicine himself to both Carla and Tom.

Commander stayed on for a few days and during this time Rhys explained what had happened and why neither Commander nor anyone else could contact him. It turned out Tovo had much stronger support by way of the League's own representative for Hergon. Therefore, with this kind of help and technology behind him, Tovo managed to scramble all signals long enough to amass an army to fight not only Rhys and his crew, but to mount an attack on Tyerra and destroy the League of Galaxies.

Tovo almost succeeded in pushing Rhys and his team into a black hole so they couldn't warn anyone about what was happening and others would believe they went to their deaths by accident. But Rhys and his crew proved to be better pilots and once they recovered from the initial shock of being attacked, they responded with missiles of their own while weaving in and out of danger as they shot down as many shuttles as possible. In the midst of all this, Rhys decided not to try to reach Commander, who was on Earth looking for Carla. Rhys, knowing Tovo had his eye on killing Carla, did not risk any communication with his father in case Tovo tuned in.

The League soon discovered the Hergon representative had been behind the entire thing and they arrested him while reinforcements left Tyerra and joined Rhys and his crew, where a full scale war took place between the shuttles and ships. Only Tovo had escaped in order to destroy Carla when he picked up on her signal while she communicated with Commander via the thumb communicator. Meanwhile, the allied forces of the League cleaned out the enemy while Rhys raced back to Earth just in time to intervene when Tovo almost killed Carla.

It was later discovered by the League that Hergon and Prima had been in negotiations to break away from the League of Galaxies long before Prima had been annihilated. At this point, Hergon had taken it upon itself to give sanctuary to any Primans willing to overthrow the League.

"If they got away with it," Rhys recounted over dinner one night, "Tyerra would have been destroyed as revenge for what happened to Prima."

"But why this hate for you, personally?" Carla asked, touching Rhys's hand as if she still couldn't believe all danger had disappeared and he was alive and well.

Rhys shrugged. "Tovo was envious in a way. He hated the fact that I fought so much for Earth to be spared, and he put this down to my love for you and because Commander is my father. He truly thought this was the reason why Earth got off so lightly."

Commander remarked, "But being your father, wouldn't I have also listened to you when you spoke in favour of Prima?"

"You would think," Rhys replied, squeezing Carla's hand

reassuringly. "But Tovo believed Carla was the tipping factor. After all, he came for her in the end. All this time, I thought he set off the tsunami to get back at me, but I realised later it was Carla he was really after. He already knew I was on my way to find him with my crew."

Carla shivered. "And he had worse plans for you—pushing you into a black hole and sparking off a full scale war with the members of the League, starting with the destruction of Tyerra."

Commander shook his head. "Let this be a lesson to us all, especially the League," he confessed. "Carla was right to say that we set ourselves up as judge and jury. We had no right to do this in the first place."

Carla agreed. "I'm sure the League did this for the greater good, but as I said in the past: it's a Ying and Yang thing. You can't have goodness unless you have evil. Goodness is always reinforced wherever evil lurks. Evil, whether we like it or not, unites us in good deeds. We learn patience, tolerance, and even forgiveness from evil—and these qualities make us better beings. This is the true nature of things, both here on Earth and in the whole universe."

Commander left when he was convinced Carla and Tom were back to normal health. He'd taken a shine to the dog for his heroic efforts in trying to save his mistress and promised to babysit him if Rhys and Carla ever wanted to get away from time to time. "Right now the League has a lot to discuss moving forward so I'm needed on Tyerra, but I'll be by to visit frequently," Commander said in parting as he hugged Carla and Rhys and gave Tom a fond pat on the head.

Rhys and Carla spent a few days recovering physically and emotionally from their harrowing experience at the hands of Tovo. They loafed about the cottage, making homemade meals and going for long walks with Tom. They sat in the sunshine, chatting about pleasant things and laughing a lot, and at night they made tender love and slept in each other's arms in the knowledge that they would be together until the end of their lives.

As time passed, they managed to put behind them the horrific events they experienced and they came to terms with the loss of the many innocent lives in the disasters caused by Tovo. More importantly, they learned to forgive themselves, too. After all, in their own way they were a part of the fabric of consciousness, and they were fully aware that for every evil act there was a causal effect. But of more importance was a greater lesson to learn: the fabric of consciousness was love, and love had a way to heal itself and go on—for love was the energy that fuelled the universe, and the universe was love.

THE END